Lauren straddled Adam's lap, setting the plate of food on the table

She'd dreamed of this. The dream still clung as she faced him, his eyes brimming with hot interest.

She *hadn't* been mistaken. He wanted her. He *was* her secret admirer.

Lauren squeezed off a bite of egg. Cupping one hand to catch the sauce, she held it to his lips.

His gaze never left hers as he chewed slowly. "Eggs Benedict has never tasted this good."

Spatters of sauce dotted her hand, but before she could wipe them, he brought her hand to his lips. "Allow me." With deft strokes, he licked the drips.

Her heart quickened with every stroke of his tongue, filling her with desire. "You have a bit..." She leaned forward to skim her lips along the corner of his mouth. She flicked her tongue to capture the sauce.

He angled his head and pressed his mouth to hers. Time stood still as he opened to her. Her breasts pressed against his chest. She shifted on his lap, stirring that part of him that had filled her dream with pleasure. Heat spiraled through her. He skimmed his hands up her sides, as his tongue stroked hers with an intensity that sparked a hunger she had never known.

Adam pulled back slightly. "Lauren, I really want you."

Blaze™

Dear Reader,

It's a thrill for me to be able to share my stories with you. I love the latitude Blaze gives writers and readers in exploring the hotter side of romance. Thanks to all of you who have helped to grow this line. I hope it'll be with us for a very long time.

I brainstorm using a technique I've stolen from Orville Redenbacher. I gather together all my ideas, then sift through them until I'm left with only the biggest kernels. The premise of a headstrong workaholic seducing her laid-back best friend when she mistakes him for her secret admirer was one such kernel. Add in an erotic cookbook and we have Blaze magic.

When Lauren Bryant lets friends and family—and perhaps her own secret desires—convince her that her best friend, Adam Morely, is the man behind the anonymous romantic gifts she's receiving, she decides to take their relationship to the next level. Adam, on the hunt for a serious relationship for the first time in his life, finds her too tempting to resist. Once he tastes Lauren's forbidden fruit, he embarks on a mission to steer her toward hearth and home, a place she hasn't visited since their days of playing house together.

I hope you enjoy their journey toward compromise. It was certainly a pleasure to write.

Happy reading,

Dorie Graham

P.S.—Don't forget to check out www.tryblaze.com!

Books by Dorie Graham

HARLEQUIN BLAZE
39—THE LAST VIRGIN

TEMPTING ADAM

Dorie Graham

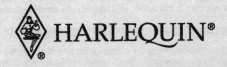

HARLEQUIN®

TORONTO • NEW YORK • LONDON
AMSTERDAM • PARIS • SYDNEY • HAMBURG
STOCKHOLM • ATHENS • TOKYO • MILAN • MADRID
PRAGUE • WARSAW • BUDAPEST • AUCKLAND

To my girls,
Jessie, Lauren and Lindsey,
for loving me and sacrificing their "special times,"
even though they might not have understood
their mother's strange obsession.
I love you.

ISBN 0-373-79062-7

TEMPTING ADAM

Visit us at www.eHarlequin.com

Printed in U.S.A.

1

"I NEED A WIFE."

Lauren Bryant tore her attention from the advertising contract she'd been studying. Putting aside her worries over her company's solvency, she focused on Adam Morely, her best friend. She smiled, drawing comfort from his familiar presence.

Then his words registered. She cocked her head. "Excuse me?"

He dropped neatly into the chair facing her desk. Long hours outdoors had burnished his dark hair and etched premature crow's-feet beside his gray eyes. An earnest light glittered in those eyes. "I said, I need a wife."

Trying to shake off the inexplicable sense of panic that swept over her, she quipped, "Don't we all?"

"I'm serious. Taxes are killing me. It just doesn't pay to be single. Besides..." He shrugged. "I need...more out of life."

"More?" She set down her pen and raised her eyebrows in disbelief.

Exasperating man.

"This from the guy who has it all—a successful business, a gorgeous new home and a different woman for every day of the week?" she said.

He straightened, a deep groove forming between his eyebrows. "You're exaggerating."

"Okay, a different woman for every month. Same thing."

"Exactly."

She continued to stare, anger filling her. How dare he not be satisfied? She'd give anything for half his success.

"They're all the same. One relationship after the other. Meaningless. Empty."

"So, you're tired of mindless sex."

"I'd like a relationship that carries a little weight. Like what you and I have, only with the sex thrown in."

"I see."

For some ridiculous reason his words triggered outrage in her. Not that she'd ever thought of him in a sexual manner. From the time Adam's family had moved in next door to hers some twenty years ago, the two of them had shared an uncommon bond. With his parents' constant absences, she and Adam had grown up together, conquering their quiet neighborhood in Roswell, Georgia, a suburb of metro-Atlanta.

He drew a quick breath. "Not that there's anything wrong with what we have. It's special, no doubt, but, well…it isn't like we get naked together."

"True."

With an effort, she reined in her irrational emotions. Why was she getting upset? They had a great relationship. It was comfortable, convenient. But, no, they'd definitely never been naked together, not unless she counted that time when they were very young.

"You don't have to get married to have a meaningful relationship," she said.

"But if I find the right woman, I'll want to hang on to her."

"Sure." Her stomach tightened.

Needing a distraction, she glanced down at the contract. "Look, I'm going to have to break our lunch date. I have to get this deal finalized, then we're meeting with the Bennett Bagel people.''

She allowed herself the smallest glimmer of hope. ''They're thinking maybe some local TV exposure will help the opening of their new sandwich shops. I've already scoped this new actor who spreads mayo like it's foreplay.''

His gaze narrowed on her. ''Only you could make hawking bagels a sensual experience.''

''Food is always sensual. Besides, you know it's not me. Entice Advertising does it. Elliot's the one with all that creative talent. We'd go belly-up without him.''

Adam nodded toward a vase on her desk filled with a rainbow bouquet of condoms. *''Need spice, think Entice.''*

''That's it.''

She quirked her mouth to one side. Her partner's preference for other men hadn't hindered their fledgling agency in earning a reputation for using sex better than anyone else to sell their odd range of clients and products to the general population. In fact, Elliot came up with all the provocative campaigns, while Lauren spent her energies rounding up clients, keeping the books straight and feeling a little like an impostor for not being the sexy siren others assumed her to be.

''So, can I take a rain check on lunch?'' she asked.

''Sure, I just thought you might have some quick advice.''

''Quick advice?''

She rose, then moved around to lean stiffly against the desk. Did they really have to pursue this strange new idea of his? He couldn't have thought this through.

''This is another case of your impulsiveness, isn't it?'' she asked.

He pursed his lips. ''I am *not* impulsive.''

''Oh? Who was it who hopped a flight to Hawaii for just

the weekend last month? Who bought that huge house? Who got a tattoo on his—''

''You promised not to ever mention that—''

''All on the spur of the moment? Who was that? Oh, yes, it was you.''

''Okay, so maybe I have an impulsive moment from time to time.''

She stared at him.

''And maybe I hadn't thought about having a wife before I said that, but I still mean it. I *do* need a wife. Sometimes, when you know something, you just know it.''

That funny feeling churned again in her stomach. It swirled around inside her, sending unexplainable anxiety racing through her. With an effort, she curved her mouth into a grin. ''Let me get this straight. You want my advice on how you should go about finding a candidate for a wife?''

''Yes.''

''A wife? You're serious?'' Her grin stiffened. To her dismay, the anxiety swelled. Nervous laughter spilled from her.

After a moment, she straightened. ''I'm sorry.''

She bit her lip and swiped at her eyes. She'd been under way too much pressure lately. That was it. She was displacing her worry over her business's finances. It did *not* bother her that Adam wanted a wife.

''Look, given my track record, I can understand your amusement, but you help me with this, and I'll do something for you…I'll owe you big time.''

''And I'll collect.''

After drawing a calming breath, she faced him. ''But didn't we have this conversation when you were ready to buy your car, then your house, then all the furniture to go in it?''

"What's wrong with that? I value your opinion. And in return you got those hydrangeas, a fine lesson in negotiating price—"

"Ha! Who do you think negotiates all the deals around here?"

"And that new fountain in your backyard."

"Hey, *if* I do this, it's going to cost a lot more than that fountain."

"Fine."

"I'll have to think about it. But don't expect me to come cheap for this kind of thing."

"An eye for an eye."

"Right. Not that *I'm* looking for a relationship. I don't have the time."

"No, you don't." He regarded her a moment.

She steeled herself. He'd been very vocal of late in criticizing her work ethic, but he continued, "So, where do we start?"

"Well, this isn't like those other times."

"It's not so different. You know my tastes."

"Yes, Adam, but don't you see what you're doing?"

The muscles of his shoulders rippled in a half shrug.

"This is not another acquisition of personal property." She spread her arms in appeal. "It isn't like you can shop for a serious relationship at the mall."

"Well, of course I'm not looking to *buy* a wife."

"Good." She cocked her head as another thought occurred to her. "What will all your women friends say?"

"You'll *all* have to get used to the idea. I've made up my mind."

He settled back in his chair, the look of resolve she knew all too well settling over his features. "On the serious relationship anyway. I'm not going to jump into marriage, though that's the ultimate goal."

Drawing up straight, she shoved aside her nervousness. Of course she'd help him. *He'd* never let her down before. Hadn't he rushed over last week when she'd been up late working and found a half-live mole her housemate's cat had dragged in? He'd disposed of the poor creature without uttering a single complaint, even though she'd wakened him from a sound sleep.

Adam was a great guy. *The best.* He deserved whatever happiness he could grab. "Okay, then my advice is to go about this with one thing in mind."

"What?"

"Romance her."

His eyebrows arched.

"When you find the right woman, woo her."

He folded his arms across his chest.

"Roses, Godiva chocolate, perfume—"

"Diamonds, chartered vacations?"

"Yes. You've got the idea."

"Right. You want me to buy a wife."

This was what she got for offering her advice? "No. That's not what I'm saying."

A quick rap sounded on the door. Elliot Star leaned around the doorjamb. He swept a hand over his graying curls. "Oh, hello, Adam."

Adam shifted, not quite meeting the man's admiring gaze. "Elliot."

Lauren could never have gone into business without Elliot's help. After one too many prima donna fits over his need for artistic license, he'd been fired from one of Atlanta's premier ad agencies. Ever ready to champion a new cause, Lauren had left that same agency, plotting with him to try it on their own. The man was a genius. Giving him free creative reign had put Entice Advertising on the map in just under two years.

Elliot sighed and shifted his gaze to Lauren. "Those proofs are back. You ready to talk bagels?"

"Sure." She gave Adam's shoulder a quick squeeze. "Sorry about lunch. I'll make it up somehow."

"Yeah? How about tonight? I've got a taste for that Cajun meat loaf you make so well."

Surprise welled up inside her. "You want me to *cook?*"

"It isn't like you don't know how. You're one of the best cooks in Georgia."

"Now *you're* exaggerating."

Adam simply raised his chin and leveled his gaze on her.

"But I haven't cooked—"

"Since you started this agency. It's way past time. I postponed a meeting and traveled across town just for you to blow me off."

His mouth curved into the smile she'd never been able to resist. "Besides, I'll bring the ice cream."

She glanced sideways at Elliot, who shrugged. Throwing her hands in the air, she gave in. "Okay, but it'd better be chocolate."

"You've got it."

With a slow nod Adam rose to his full height. Lauren let her gaze travel over all six foot three of him. His career in landscaping had left him sculpted and tanned. Even though he now spent most of his time supervising his own independent contracting company, he never turned his back on physical labor.

And it showed. Adam would have no trouble finding a wife.

Her heart thumped dully as she scooped a file from her desk. She didn't want to think about Adam with a wife right now. "Great. We'll finish this discussion then."

"Can't wait."

She paused at the door, throwing one last glance at him.

He emanated quiet strength and power. It was what people noticed most about him, though he seemed unaware of it.

Sunlight slanted through the office window, highlighting the angular planes of his face. She shivered. She knew no other face better than his, yet somehow it seemed she'd never really seen him before. Like when viewing a hologram, where a slight shift brought a new picture into view, her perspective of him altered in that moment. With his eyes shining and his wide lips curved in that playful tilt, she could almost see what all the women who had chased him must have seen.

"Well, goodbye," she said, hoping he missed the funny catch in her voice.

He nodded as he turned his attention to the ringing cell phone he extracted from a holder on his belt.

Drawing a deep breath, she hurried after Elliot. Her pulse thudded and a thought she hardly let herself acknowledge whispered through her consciousness.

What would it be like to get naked together?

THE SUN SLIPPED below the horizon, casting long shadows across the porch as Lauren headed up the steps to her town house—a quaint brick-front featuring a small but private backyard. Balancing her mail, keys and bulging briefcase, she kneed open the door.

The scent of roses enveloped her as she dropped her load on an antique bench in the entry. She turned, inhaling the heavenly aroma, then stopped. A tall vase stood on the table gracing the opposite wall of the tiny foyer. Roses with delicate white petals crowded the vase, spilling over the sides.

An envy-filled sigh escaped her. Kamira Davies, her housemate, always dated the most considerate men. She'd received more flowers in the six months since she'd moved in than Lauren had received in her entire life.

"Lauren?"

Kamira emerged from the kitchen, her dark waves captured in a loose braid. Her green, almond-shaped eyes glittered with amusement as she wiped her hands on a dish towel. Nala, her silver tabby, glanced up from her spot by the window. "Beautiful, aren't they?" Kamira asked, scratching the cat behind the ears.

"Gorgeous." Lauren tore her gaze from the blooms. "Things are going well with Greg, then?"

"They're okay, but these aren't from Greg."

"You're seeing someone else?" Lauren asked, surprised.

"No. No. They're not for me. They're yours."

"Mine?"

"That's what the card says." Kamira plucked a small envelope from beside the vase, and handed it to Lauren.

Frowning, Lauren scanned her name on the front, then read the neat writing on the enclosed card.

> I send you a cream-white rosebud
> With a flush upon its petal tips;
> For the love that is purest and sweetest
> Has a kiss of desire on the lips.
> —John Boyle O'Reilly (1844–1890)

She glanced up at her friend. "Love that is purest and sweetest?"

"I've never heard anything so romantic."

"It doesn't say who they're from."

"You don't know?"

"Who do I know who would have the class to do such a thing? Besides Elliot, who obviously didn't send them. It can't be Todd. I haven't heard from him in months, and roses, not to mention any pure, sweet love, were never his style."

Her two-year relationship with software guru Todd Jeffries had ended some nine weeks ago, when he'd left the country to share his expertise with a company in Japan. He hadn't understood why she wouldn't chuck her job to go with him.

She turned to Kamira. "Are you sure they delivered them to the right address?"

"Definitely. Sure you aren't keeping secrets?"

"I have no life. You know that."

"Ah…then there's only one thing it could be."

"What's that?"

Kamira squeezed her arm. "You, dear, have a secret admirer."

SHE'S KEEPING SECRETS. Adam frowned later that evening as Lauren pulled her meat loaf from the oven, a mysterious smile curving her lips. She'd never kept anything from him before. What could it be? Steam rose around them, filling the kitchen with the spicy scent.

Beside her, he inhaled deeply, his worry easing with the distraction. If she ever realized how easily she could control him with the promise of her home cooking, he'd be in big trouble.

"Ah, I knew you still had it in you." His gaze fell hungrily on the delicacy. "It's a rare treat. You've been holding out on me."

With a shake of her head, she set the pan on the stove. "You know I've been busy." She cast him a sideways glance. "And I'm not getting into another argument about my long work hours. I'm doing something productive and worthwhile with my life. Nights like this will have to remain rare treats."

"I can help you round up more business. Then you could hire an assistant to help out."

"I appreciate the few clients you've referred. And I'll certainly follow up on every lead you send my way, but you know how I feel about you trying to fix all my problems."

"It doesn't hurt you to accept a little help now and then."

"And I have and I thank you. But I'm a big girl. This is my agency and it's my responsibility to generate the business. You can't do everything for me."

Adam popped the top on a beer he'd pulled from the refrigerator. He handed the drink to her, before grabbing another for himself. He let the conversation drop. They'd discussed her work habits too many times already. Not that he'd quit doing what he could to round up clients for her. He ran into so many people while playing tennis and golf, that it wasn't an effort to scrape up a referral or two. He just didn't have to tell her what he was doing.

He took a sip and let his thoughts drift. Funny how the moment he'd said he needed a wife, he'd known it was true. Yes, this was what he wanted. A home-cooked meal and someone to share it with. Sipping wine at the local bistro just didn't cut it anymore.

Not that Lauren spent her evenings casually sipping wine, unless she was courting a new client. Then there was nothing casual about it. The woman spent way too much time with her nose to the grindstone. Maybe she'd eventually come to realize that work did *not* make the world go round.

He saluted her with his can, too relaxed to argue with her. Maybe she would enjoy this off night enough to begin wanting a personal life for herself again. "It doesn't get better than this."

She raised her beer in return. "Another big account or two would help." After taking a long swallow, she continued, "But I have to admit spending time in the kitchen wasn't so bad."

His gaze traveled over Kamira's mini jungle of plants that

softened the white cabinets and the tan and white–striped walls. Lauren stood framed by the stove and the assortment of pots and pans brimming with the side dishes she'd taken such pleasure in creating, even though she rarely indulged in her old pastime anymore. Her face radiated contentment.

Again, that mysterious smile flickered across her lips.

Was it the mere act of cooking that had brought on that glow, or was she really hiding something?

"So, how's everything going?" he asked.

"Great. Finalized that deal with the car wash."

"I didn't mean with work."

A soft pink flushed her cheeks. "What makes you ask?"

"I don't know. There's something…different about you tonight." When was the last time he'd seen her blush? He shifted, trying to pinpoint exactly what *was* different about her.

She busied herself with transferring food into serving dishes. "Did you notice the roses on your way in?"

He glanced through the kitchen's archway toward the foyer. A bunch of white roses filled a vase on a table near the door. "So, who sent you roses?"

Her eyes brightened and her lips curved into a smile. "Don't know. Kamira thinks I have a secret admirer."

"Ah, this wouldn't have anything to do with that talk we had earlier?" He couldn't keep the slight annoyance from his voice as he helped her move the dishes to the drop-leaf table.

"No. You think I'd anonymously send myself flowers, just to prove a point to you?"

He laughed, perplexed. "Of course not." Why *was* he annoyed? "It's just a strange coincidence, don't you think?"

"I'm as surprised as you are."

"And you have no idea who sent them?"

"No, but I have to admit it's very flattering. Which brings us back to our earlier conversation. Romancing the woman of your choice is definitely the way to go."

She cocked her head. "I hadn't thought about it in exactly these terms, but the whole secret-admirer thing does add a nice touch."

He made a deliberate effort to relax his jaw. So Lauren had a secret admirer. She'd had a fair number of men in her life, and that had never bothered him before. Wasn't this what he'd been pestering her about over the past months—encouraging her to find a life outside of work?

She was a phenomenal woman, a flower among thorns. With her golden beauty and welcoming way, she was bound to draw masculine attention. Her allure lay not only in the deep green of her eyes and the generous swell of her hips and breasts—though those were enticement enough—but also in the patience and love she extended to all lucky enough to fall into her life.

Adam had always considered himself fortunate in that respect. Though his parents had never seen their way to spending more than a two-week span in his presence, Lauren had remained steadfast by his side for well over twenty years.

"You need to be careful, though," he said. "He could be anyone."

"Don't go getting all protective on me, Adam. Whoever sent those roses is the sensitive type. I can't imagine he'd be dangerous."

"At least he's not ostentatious in his gift giving. I hate gift buying for its pure material value."

She turned toward him, her hands planted on her hips. "I never meant it that way."

Waving his hand in a gesture of peace, he continued, "In

this case, the value is on the thought, since the sender remains anonymous.''

''Well, it does build a sense of expectation, which is kind of nice. Of course, we could be making a mountain out of a molehill. This could be an isolated incident.''

Adam appraised her a moment. In the soft light of the kitchen, with her cheeks flushed and her eyes glowing, Lauren was one hell of an attractive woman—a desirable woman.

As he'd done so many times in the past, he stifled the thought. Somehow it just seemed wrong to think of her in that way. She was like a sister to him. She'd surely be horrified to know he harbored a fantasy—or two—about her.

''Somehow, I don't think so,'' he said. ''And eventually, he's going to make himself known. Otherwise, what's the point?''

A sound of exasperation escaped her. ''The point is the anticipation, the thrill, the *romance.*''

That irrational annoyance rose again in him. ''The point is, this guy wants to get you in bed.''

''That's not fair. You don't even know him—''

''He's a guy. What else is there to know?''

''Well, you're a guy.''

''And you think I've never thought of you in that way?''

Her eyes widened. Silence hung over them. Adam gritted his teeth. Why had he blurted *that* out?

The front door slammed a moment before Kamira breezed into the kitchen, her cat at her heels. ''You didn't tell me you were making your meat loaf.''

''We're just getting started.'' He pulled out a chair for her.

Lauren retrieved another plate from the cabinet. *And you think I've never thought of you in that way?* Adam's words rang through her mind. Well, he *was* a guy. She should have expected this…but somehow, it was so…surprising.

She set the plate before Kamira, then sat beside her, purposely avoiding looking at Adam as he took his place on her other side. The weight of his gaze bored down on her.

"I thought you were at the clinic," she said to Kamira, a nurse at the women's center.

Kamira heaped large portions of the meal onto her plate. "Mmm. I just dropped off the tile samples. I'll be happy when this new section is ready. I swear, there's a baby boom going on. We need the space for all our new patients."

"The women's center is expanding?" Adam asked. He hadn't made a move toward any of the dishes.

"Didn't Lauren tell you? She's been volunteering down there. She helped knock down the wall between our offices and the empty space next door. Boy, can she swing a sledgehammer."

"Patterson, the building's owner," Lauren added for Adam's benefit, though she still refused to look at him, "wanted to give me the first swing, but I had this fear the roof would tumble down on us, so he went first."

"Ha, but we all got into it after a while." Kamira smiled.

Keeping her attention on the bowl of whipped potatoes, Lauren bobbed her head. "Very cathartic. I got all my aggression out."

Kamira's eyes rounded. "I'll tell you who else looked good swinging a hammer. Patterson's son. If that boy was five years older, I'd drop Greg in a heartbeat."

"Mark?" Lauren chuckled, then stopped. She'd filled half her plate with potatoes. "I think he's Rusty's age."

She smiled, thinking of her younger brother. He'd taken off to work the oil rigs in Texas after graduating from the University of Georgia last year. It'd been harder to let him go than she'd thought, having felt responsible for him for so long.

"Of course, he dropped me a line a while back that he was dating an older woman. Mark's young, but you'd better be careful. You just never know," she said.

"He's a very mature twenty-two, and is well read in all the classics." The one dimple in Kamira's left cheek flashed as she grinned. "He'd be a great cause—so much to teach that young, open mind. But Greg's safe. I'm no cradle robber."

"I've got a cause for you." Heat filled Lauren's cheeks as she glanced at Adam, then back at Kamira. "Help me find Adam a new lady friend."

Maybe Kamira would take over the task for her. Somehow, playing matchmaker for him held little appeal.

"What?" Straightening, Kamira turned to Adam. "Since when are you having trouble finding women?"

"Since he wants to get serious with one," Lauren answered for him.

Kamira's mouth spread slowly into a wide smile. "Adam, you're wanting to settle down?"

"If I find the right woman."

"Wow. That's so sweet."

Lauren picked at her potatoes. "He wants a new best friend he can have sex with."

The words tumbled out, surprising her. The heat in her cheeks intensified. She glanced at Adam.

He blinked, then his mouth quirked to one side. "Friendship and mutual respect like we have are vital to any relationship."

"And where did you read that?" Eyebrows raised, Kamira nodded toward his empty plate. "What's wrong? Not hungry?"

"Starved, actually." With great relish, he piled food on his plate, then consumed several bites.

Lauren pursed her lips and poked again at her potatoes. How could he drop such a bomb, then stuff his face as if nothing had happened?

Because nothing *had* happened. Evidently, any sexual thoughts he'd had of her hadn't been strong enough for him to act on.

A feeling of foreboding stole over her. He'd always been there for her, with his brawn when she needed it, and with his broad shoulders during times of crisis, like when her father had died thirteen years ago. Would he still be there if he found a wife?

A small sigh rose in her chest. She was losing her best friend. Once he found a woman to give him all Lauren did and more, he would no longer need his old buddy. She'd be superfluous.

Adam reached across the table and squeezed her fingertips. "We're as good as family. It isn't like you'll be getting rid of me." As usual, he'd read her mind.

"No. Of course not. And if you do marry it'll be like gaining a sister for me," she said through stiff lips.

"Right." Apparently satisfied, he picked up his fork and again dug into his meal.

Kamira sat back in her chair, her expression puzzled. She turned to Adam. "Tell me, do you have a plan for finding this woman?"

"I thought I'd just open myself to the possibility and see what happened."

A speculative light glimmered in her eyes. "Hmm, I see. That's good, being open."

"I told him when he found the right woman he should romance her."

Kamira beamed. ''Excellent idea. What do you think, Adam? Are you up for the romantic approach?''

His shoulders shifted. ''Could be. Real romance should be more than just blatant gift giving, though.''

''Blatant gift giving?'' Kamira asked.

''I want a woman who'll want me for who I am, not what I can give her. It isn't my style to make a big display over buying gifts for a woman.''

Lauren rose to carry her dishes to the sink. ''I only meant you should try to make her feel special. Gifts are just a part of that.''

With measured movements, Adam followed her to scrape the spare remains of his meal into the disposal. ''Okay, I can see that.''

''So, have we got ice cream for dessert?'' Kamira left the table to pillage the freezer. ''Death by Chocolate, my fave. Why don't I dish some up, and we'll eat it on the deck.''

''Just a little for me,'' Lauren said.

''Adam...'' Kamira ushered him toward the sliding door that led to the deck. ''Can you light the citronella torch? We'll be right out.''

''Sure. Make mine two scoops?''

''You've got it.'' With a smile, she slid the door shut behind him. Then she turned to Lauren, her eyes shining.

''You know the mosquitoes don't seem to notice that torch, Kamira. What are you up to?'' Bending low, Lauren rummaged through a drawer for the ice-cream scooper.

''When did you and Adam have this conversation?''

''About his settling down?''

''About his wanting to have a serious sexual relationship involving friendship and mutual respect.''

''Around lunchtime.''

''And you suggested he woo the woman of his choice?''

"I hardly think his tactic of wham, bam, thank you ma'am will work toward establishing anything long-term."

"Don't you find it interesting that he's opening himself to the possibility, but that he isn't actively searching for this woman?"

Lauren shrugged. "He's not going to find her in his usual haunts. Do you see a woman like that patronizing Charlie's Corner Bar?"

"Of course not. But what about the fact that you received those roses anonymously *after* your conversation?"

"What does that have to do with Adam? There's still the chance Todd sent them."

And you think I've never thought of you in that way?

"Todd, the man you're no longer seeing? The man who gave you a new calculator for your two-year anniversary?"

"Point taken, but I still don't see how Adam figures." Blood rushed through Lauren's ears.

And you think I've never thought of you in that way?

Kamira glanced out the window to where he'd anchored the torch into its stand. "I've always had a feeling about you two. I just think it's odd—the timing, the fact that he's against what he calls blatant gift giving. Seems he would be the anonymous type."

Lauren's breath caught. "Tell me you're not suggesting what I think you are."

"Don't you see? It makes sense. He isn't looking for a woman, because he's already found one. *You.*"

2

"ARE YOU NUTS?" Lauren stared at her housemate.

"Don't you see? It all adds up."

"I hardly think a couple of random coincidences add up to anything."

Kamira took the forgotten scooper from Lauren's hand, then dished up the ice cream. "Let's ask him."

"No!"

"Why not?"

"Do you know how insane that sounds? He'll have us locked up."

After handing Lauren one of the bowls, Kamira carried the other two toward the sliding glass door. "What are you afraid of?"

"I'm not afraid. I just don't see any point in pursuing this line of thought. Okay?"

With a heavy sigh, Kamira nodded. "Think about it, though."

Lauren opened the door, shaking her head. The torch glowed and night insects chirped and whirred around them. Above, stars glittered in the darkening sky. Adam sat at the patio table that dominated one end of the deck.

She perched on a chair beside him. "It's nice out here."

Thanking Kamira, he took the bowl, then savored a bite of ice cream. "It's these simple things that make life worthwhile—a hearty meal, pleasant environment and good friends."

"Yes, good *friends*." Lauren cocked her head at Kamira, sending her a smug I-told-you-so grin.

"He sounds like a commercial," Kamira laughed.

Adam grinned. "Lauren's cooking makes me want to endorse the good times."

Reaching over, he clasped Lauren's hand. "*You* are a remarkable cook. I hope the woman I marry knows her way around the kitchen."

Lauren's grin faltered as the warmth of his hand enveloped hers. She wiggled her fingers in an effort to free herself from his grip, but he didn't seem to notice. Instead, he carried her hand to his lips for a quick kiss.

"Now that you've gotten rid of Jeffries, maybe you should find a real man." He released her.

Kamira leaned forward. "You could *both* be open to a serious relationship."

Lauren stared at her, speechless. How could she say such a thing?

"Right." Adam swatted away a mosquito. "We learned to swim, ride bikes and drive together. Why not learn about love together?"

He dropped his hand to Lauren's knee. "You've worked so hard, Lauren. You deserve a little happiness."

Her gaze swept from his hand to Kamira, who waved her spoon enthusiastically. "She sure does."

Heat crept up Lauren's neck and along her knee beneath his hand. He gave her leg a squeeze, then busied himself again with his dessert. What was wrong with her? He'd touched her a million times in the past and she'd never thought twice about it. Kamira's wild speculations had her reading more into his friendly gestures than was there.

Of course Adam wasn't her secret admirer.

"So, Adam…" Kamira licked a drip of chocolate off her spoon. "Tell us what kind of woman you're looking for.

Maybe we can help. I see a lot of women in the course of the day.''

He pushed his bowl away, then sat back, gazing into the distance. ''I think for a substantial relationship, I want a substantial woman. Substantial in spirit and body, too. Not a big woman, necessarily, but one with a little more meat on her bones.''

Lauren raised her eyebrows. ''You mean you're done with all those ultrathin model types?''

He grinned. ''Well, I wouldn't object, as long as she didn't mind getting pregnant.''

His head bobbed as he continued to stare into the night, as though the woman of his dreams might materialize if he looked hard enough. ''I'll want some kids along the way.''

''Hold on,'' Lauren blurted. ''I thought you were going to wait awhile before jumping into marriage. Now you're talking *babies?*''

The thought sent a wave of shock through her. Adam with a wife was one thing, but with a baby? She couldn't quite bend her mind around the idea.

''C'mon, you know I like kids.''

''No, I don't. When have I ever seen you with kids? I can't even picture it.''

He cocked his head and laughed. Though she'd heard that laugh countless times before, for some reason it wrapped around her and sent gooseflesh skittering up her arms.

''Come to think of it, I guess you haven't.'' He shrugged. ''I liked us when we were kids. Don't ask why, I just know I want kids, a bunch of them.''

''A bunch?'' Lauren blinked at him. To think she'd thought she'd known him all these years.

''Well, we'll start with a couple, then see.''

Frowning, she turned to Kamira, but her housemate grinned broadly. ''I can see Adam as a dad.''

Lauren gaped at her, then rounded on him. "What do you know about caring for kids? They're lots of work. You've got to feed them, and play with them, and…and feed them."

"I'll read up on it. Hopefully my wife will know a little about all that."

"Read up on it? They don't come with manuals, you know." She folded her arms. "You can't just decide all of a sudden that you want a wife and kids."

"Why not? I told you I wanted more in life. And that's what I want…eventually, anyway," he said.

His smile faded and he shifted in his seat. "She'll have to be the stay-at-home kind of mom, though. None of that palming the kids off on the neighbors."

Lauren stared at him a moment, a mixture of surprise and compassion swirling through her. "Adam, your parents didn't palm you off on us."

"Sure they did."

She straightened. His parents *had* traveled a lot. He'd probably spent more time at her house growing up than at his own, but she'd never known this had bothered him. Having Adam around had always been a way of life.

Needing to soothe him, she touched his arm. "Good thing for me they did, then. Who else would I have whomped all those times in Crazy Eights?"

"*I* was the Crazy Eights champ. Your memory's flawed." The corners of his mouth lifted in an easy grin.

"Well, maybe…" She again had that feeling of a shifting hologram. Adam the Dependable morphed into Adam the Sexy.

An unprecedented wave of desire rippled through her. She swallowed. As with his laugh, it was as if she'd never before experienced the charm of that grin. Sure he'd used it to cajole her into giving him his way hundreds of times before, but never had the mere curve of his mouth sent her pulse speeding.

Damn Kamira and her imagination. Damn this new Adam. His pupils dilated and he tilted his head. Did he feel it, too?

Lauren blinked, hoping the old Adam would slide back into view, but the new Adam remained, exuding sensuality. How had she not noticed before?

"I'll get that." Kamira stood, bowls in hand, her gaze intent on Lauren.

The wall phone in the kitchen pealed. By the look on her housemate's face it wasn't the first ring. "No. I'll get it. I'm sure it's Elliot. I'm supposed to have that marketing plan done."

Without a backward glance she hurried inside.

ADAM PULLED INTO his driveway. His house loomed above him, dark against the blackness of the night. Why had he bought the monstrosity?

His footsteps rapped against the hardwood floor as he entered. He flicked on a light and the great room he'd once so admired stretched before him, still and devoid of life. He dropped into a leather chair set by the tiled fireplace.

"Honey, I'm home." The words echoed through the structure.

He leaned back his head and closed his eyes. The silence pressed in all around him. He used to think he wanted peace and quiet.

He'd have stayed longer at Lauren's, but she had her usual work she'd brought home. Besides, she'd seemed tense tonight. He could have sworn she'd breathed a sigh of relief when he'd hugged her goodbye. Sure, she'd come clean on the secret-admirer thing, but something else was bothering her.

She *was* keeping secrets.

Dinner had been enjoyable, as usual, in spite of his slip of the tongue. But something had changed when she'd come out on the deck. She had acted even more uncomfortable, or distressed somehow.

Moments from the evening drifted through his mind. Had he imagined it, or had she… Words escaped him. His stomach tightened. If he didn't know better, he'd say she had reacted to his touch earlier. They'd danced together, even wrestled each other, but never before had there been…what? A feeling? An awareness?

And you think I've never thought of you in that way?

Was that what had rattled her? Surely she knew he'd never act on such passing instincts. Lauren was like a sister to him. Yet, the possibility tugged at the corner of his mind. Something new, something different had shone in her eyes when he had smiled at her earlier. The moment swept over him, her gaze soft, dreamy, the first rings of the phone going unheeded.

Could it be she wasn't upset by his admission, that instead, she was *intrigued?*

"You're losing it, Morely. *Losing* it."

Even if Lauren was suddenly thinking of him in other than brotherly terms, she certainly wasn't supporting his plans to settle down. She had sounded decidedly disappointed in his new scheme.

Couldn't she understand he needed the warmth and energy that filled her house, made it a home? He missed all the evenings he'd spent with her there, playing poker, finishing some project she'd half started, knowing he'd pitch in to help, or just talking till the wee hours.

But that had been before she'd started the agency.

His gaze took in the oversize couch and matching chairs in warm plaids she'd helped him choose. She had a nice touch, had even managed to bring some of her essence into these rooms, though not enough to capture the same homey feeling of her town house. Furniture alone would not make this house a home.

People—warm bodies would help. A wife and kids really weren't a bad idea. He hadn't actually thought much about having either, until today. Actually, he'd told Lauren he needed a wife more to get her attention, but the idea had sounded right even as he'd said it. The patter of little feet, the smells of dinner cooking and the warm greeting of a wife, happy to see him after a long day's work, held an intoxicating appeal when faced with the emptiness of his house.

He drew a deep breath. He had to face facts. Without Lauren, he didn't have much of a life. Though she'd been too busy to notice, it'd been months since he'd taken a woman on a date. He couldn't work up the stomach for it. Lauren was right. Meaningless sex wasn't all it used to be.

He had to make something more of his life.

Exhaling, he rose. He plodded to the sprawling master bedroom. It was a shame she was so wrapped up in her work that she couldn't see that she, too, was missing out. Having her life revolve around her agency might sustain her at the moment, but once she got her business on an even keel and learned to work smart, not hard, she'd realize what he'd just begun to know over the past year.

Work did *not* make the world go round.

As a contractual landscaper, he'd found more work over the years than he could handle on his own. With a full crew at his disposal, he spent much of his time meeting with landscape architects, implementing construction plans on site and inspecting projects. Sure, his work fulfilled him to an extent, but it wasn't enough.

He stripped down to his Skivvies, then stretched out on

his king-size bed, made up in the green and maroon linens Lauren had handpicked for him. At least she'd squeezed time into her schedule to help him shop. He couldn't have done it on his own.

She'd been invaluable in choosing this house, too. Perhaps it wasn't such a monstrosity, after all. Not only did it offer the flexibility needed to accommodate his plans, its market value had already increased by a tidy sum. She knew how to pick them. Now, all he had to do was get her to turn her energies toward finding him a wife. No one knew him better than she did. If anyone could find the right woman for him, Lauren was the one.

Unless, of course, she had thoughts of filling the position herself.

LAUREN TURNED from her computer as Elliot breezed into her office the next morning. With a grand gesture, he deposited a thick stack of flyers on her desk. "For Bennett's mass mailing."

Stifling a yawn, she glanced over the stack. "Too bad we couldn't afford to have them folded."

"You need a hand?"

"No." She waved him on. "Go appease that atrocious director. He's called twice and wants nothing to do with me. If Bennett wasn't so adamant about using him on the commercials, I'd tell him to take a hike."

"Ah, but if Mr. Bennett wishes to pay for a special caterer to stroke said director's ego, where's the harm?"

A dry laugh worked its way up her throat. "You know the money comes out of our pocket first, Elliot." She cocked her head. "We're cutting it close on this one."

He waved a dismissive hand. "You know I can't clutter my brain with those worries. Aren't we in the black?"

"Yes, we're in the black. Just not as much as I'd like to see us, but we'll survive."

She sighed. Lately, their funds seemed to be going out faster than they'd been coming in, but with the two small jobs she'd picked up that morning, they'd survive until Bennett paid them. Thank goodness Bennett's bend toward extravagance blended with Elliot's elaborate campaign ideas. As long as she could keep them afloat in the interim, the Bennett account offered the hope of a tidy profit.

Elliot helped himself to coffee, while she stirred creamer into hers. "We picked up two new clients this morning, and Nancy with Magic Cleaners called to say she thought the ad was simply decadent. She's cutting us a check today."

"Good. That's great." He gestured toward the door. "I'm going to get on that caterer."

Steam curled from her mug moments later as she sat, stretching in a wide yawn. She'd hardly slept last night. It was Adam's fault. What made him think he qualified as husband material, not to mention *father* material? He'd never had a relationship that had lasted more than a few months. What was he thinking?

After a fortifying gulp of caffeine, she grabbed her phone and punched in his number. She drummed her fingers, waiting for him to answer.

"Top of the morning. Adam Morely here."

"What're you so chipper about?"

"Lauren, could you hold a sec? Let me finish this other call."

"Sure."

A short pause followed.

"Entice Advertising, they're at 500 Sun View—"

"Adam? You've still got me. Who are you giving my address to?"

"Damn. Hold on."

Curiosity filled her as silence hummed across the line. Who was he talking to? *A florist?* No. She shook her head. She couldn't let Kamira's wild imaginings get to her.

"Lauren?"

A slight shiver ran through her at the sound of his voice. She shook it off. "What was that about?"

"Um…it was nothing."

She straightened. "Come on, Adam, you were giving out my address."

"Oh…yeah, well, I wasn't going to say anything in case it didn't work out."

Her heart thudded. "What didn't work out?"

"Just a referral."

"Referral?" A twinge of disappointment pierced her. "Oh."

"I met this guy who has a carpet-cleaning service. He needs help getting the word out, so I gave him your name. No big deal. Just this one referral."

She drew a deep breath. "Great. Thanks. As long as you're not out trying to round up business for us when you should be working on your own stuff."

"No, ma'am. I take care of my business, too, while I'm soaking up the sun."

"Okay, like I said before, we'll take all the business we can get then."

"Sure. Hey, do yourself a favor and get outside today. It's incredible out. The sun is shining, the breeze is light. Perfect for a walk on the greens."

She stiffened. "Don't tell me I'm sitting here with three hundred or so flyers to fold and you're playing golf."

"I'm networking, love."

"Adam, watch this," a feminine voice called in the background.

"Who's that?" Lauren asked.

"Gloria. She's practicing her swing." He whistled softly. "That's a beauty."

Irritation grated through Lauren. What on earth had she been worried about? Adam hadn't changed. "The swing, or the girl?"

"Both, actually."

"I knew you couldn't be serious about all that settling-down talk."

"I *am* serious."

"Shall we?" the woman called to him.

"Lauren, I'll call you later. We're getting ready to tee off. Maybe we can get together again for dinner tonight. I've got to go."

"Wait—"

He hung up. She stared at the phone a moment, then blew out a breath. What was she upset about? He was the same old Adam. All was right in the world.

Relief flowed over her. She had just been imagining the glimmer of awareness between them last night. She should have known not to let her housemate's crazy ideas get to her.

Lauren turned back to her computer and frowned. So why was she suddenly feeling…jealous?

"ELLIOT, CAN YOU SEE Adam with a wife and kids?"

Lauren leaned in the doorway of her partner's office. She couldn't get her mind off Adam's comments. Why did the thought of him as a family man send trepidation racing through her?

Elliot peered up at her over his half-rim glasses. No doubt, she was interrupting a brainstorming session. A red feather boa taken from a rack of lingerie in the corner draped his shoulders.

"Adam? You mean *your* Adam?" he asked.

"He isn't my—never mind. Dumb question." She turned to leave.

"What's bothering you, doll?"

She pivoted back toward him, her arms wrapped tightly around her stomach. "Nothing. I'm fine."

Elliot pursed his lips. "Adam wants to settle down, and you're afraid you're going to lose your best friend."

With a sigh, she sank against the door frame. "Oh, God, it's so stupid. I really do want him to be happy. I just feel so…disturbed."

"Let me guess. He wants you to help him find this wife."

She gave him a wry smile.

"And she's supposed to be some upstanding citizen willing to sacrifice all for her husband and little bambinos."

A small grin tugged at her lips. "That's amazing. Do you read palms, too?"

"No, doll, I just see the obvious."

"Obvious?" She stared at him. "How can it be obvious? I've known the man all my life, but never saw *this* coming."

Elliot shrugged. "You don't see the two of you together."

She stared at him, eyebrows raised.

"I suspected this all along."

"Suspected what?"

The desk chair creaked as he shifted back. He smoothed his hand down the row of red feathers. "C'mon, Lauren, surely you have some inkling?"

Exasperation rose in her. "Of what?"

"Seems to me you're an upstanding citizen willing to sacrifice all for your cause."

She stared at him in disbelief.

"First Kamira, now you. I am *not* in the market for a husband. And kids are out of the question!" She sliced her hand through the air to emphasize her point.

Elliot laughed. "For now, at least, but were you to put your mind to it…"

"My mind is on this agency. I don't have time for anything else. You of all people know that."

A loud buzzing announced a visitor's arrival in their exterior office. Lauren turned as the mail carrier entered. She moved beside him as he set a stack of mail and a package on the desk they'd use for a receptionist, if they ever acquired one.

"Hey, Frank," she greeted the heavyset man. "We thought you'd forgotten us."

"Oh, no, ma'am. Got a late start. Had to run the missus downtown."

"What have you got for us today?"

He pulled on his bushy eyebrow. "Usual junk, that package, but at least no bills."

Her gaze fell on the parcel. "What's this?"

His shoulders shifted in a shrug. "Beats me. No return address." He heaved his mailbag more securely on his shoulder and backed toward the door. "You have a good one."

She nodded, her attention on the mystery package. She turned it over in her hands. It bore a printed label, addressed to her. As Frank had said, the sender hadn't included a return address.

Whatever it was, it had a solid feel to it. Anticipation stole over her. Was it another gift from a secret admirer?

"What's that?" Elliot's voice sounded beside her.

She started, then chastised herself for being jumpy. "Don't know."

He reached around her to scoop up the mail from the desk. "So, open it."

For just a split second, she hesitated. Then, with a sigh, she tore at the tape binding the box. She held her breath as she removed the lid. A rectangular gift lay inside, adorned in floral wrap and tied in a satin bow. She lifted it out, then peered inside the empty container. "No card."

"Here." Elliot stooped to pick up a folded sheet of paper that had fallen to the floor. He handed it to her.

She opened it, then silently read the typed words.

> Let me lie,
> let me die on thy snow-covered bosom,
> I would eat of thy flesh as a delicate fruit,
> I am drunk of its smell, and the scent
> of thy tresses
> Is a flame that devours.
> —George Moore (1852–1933)

"What's it say?" Elliot peered over her shoulder.

She clutched the note to her chest, while heat bloomed in her cheeks. "It's private."

He nodded toward the package in her hand. "You going to open that, or should I leave first?"

Her gaze fell to the present. "It feels like a book." She hesitated a moment, then tore away the paper.

She drew a deep breath as she turned what was indeed a book over in her hands. Rose petals covered the front. Nestled among them stood a pair of wineglasses, candlesticks and a serving dish filled with heart-shaped pastries.

"*The Lovers' Cookbook: Essential Ingredients to Sensual Evenings,*" Elliot read over her shoulder. "Now, who did you say that was from?"

"I...don't know."

The phone pealed. She started.

Elliot grabbed the handset. "Entice Advertising, Elliot Star here."

Again, his gray eyebrows rose as he glanced at Lauren.

"Sure, Adam, she's right here. We've just been opening the mail."

She snatched the phone from him with unsteady hands. Had Adam sent the cookbook? Did he truly harbor such a romantic heart? "Hello?"

"Hey, sunshine. I'm getting ready to cut out of here. Are we on for dinner? I thought I'd push my luck and see if I could convince you to cook up another of your decadent dinners."

3

THE CLOCK STRUCK eleven that evening as Lauren tossed the last flyer onto the stack heaped at one end of her sofa. Her stomach rumbled. Not only had she turned down Adam's dinner proposition in favor of working some overtime, she'd skipped the meal entirely.

After staying late at the office, she'd brought home the file on one of their new clients to complete her marketing analysis. Then she'd gone on to ready Bennett's flyers for the morning mail. She'd meant to keep her mind too busy to jump to conclusions about her latest gift.

The plan had failed miserably.

Was Adam her secret admirer? Goose bumps prickled up her arms. She eyed the rose-covered corner of the cookbook peering from beneath the avalanche of flyers. With a shake of her head, she slid the book free.

The phone on the end table rang. Who was calling at this hour? Her heart skipped a beat as she picked up the handset. "Hello?"

"Hi, sweetie," Delores Bryant's voice greeted her.

"Hi, Mom. What's up?"

"Oh, I don't know. Not much. Just wanted to say hello, see how you were doing."

Lauren sighed. Her mother's voice held a note of strain. "Come on. Claire giving you a hard time about paying the bills again?" Delores had some trouble getting her housemate to cover her share of the costs.

"No, when she postdated her check for the electric bill then went out and bought a new stereo, I stood up to her like you suggested."

"Good for you."

"She returned the stereo and wrote me a new check."

"Great. So what's the problem?"

"We've got a new district manager." She managed a children's clothing store in a local mall.

"Oh? What happened to old Bernie?"

"He got transferred."

"So, you don't like the new guy?"

"He just rubs me the wrong way. He doesn't like the way we do anything. So we've got to redo everything—the way we place orders, the way we handle customers, the way we count down the drawer."

"Don't you have company policies on all those things?"

"He's not changing the policies, just the way we follow each procedure, the nitpicky stuff. He's got his own procedures within the procedures. He's making everyone crazy."

"Well, at least you don't have to deal with him on a daily basis, right?"

"I don't know. Now that the North Point store is picking up so much business, he's talking about setting up his office here, letting this be his home base. He thinks we have the most potential and wants to help us 'come into our own.'"

"Well, I'm sure you'll win him over."

"I'm not so sure I want to. Anyway, enough about me. Why are you home on a Friday night?"

"Mom, don't start. Besides, I could ask you the same question."

"Let me guess. You brought work home over the weekend."

Lauren drew a deep breath. "It'd be really nice if you, at

least, would support my decision to make something of myself."

"Honey, I do. I wish Entice Advertising great success. You know that. I just don't want you forgetting there's more to life."

"Believe me, between you and Adam, I'm not likely to forget."

"So, how's my number-two son?"

Lauren paused, considering keeping silent about Adam's new direction in life. "He's been acting...different lately."

"Really? How so?"

She frowned. "He's talking about settling down."

A short silence hummed across the line, then Delores said excitedly, "Oh, this is wonderful! It's about time. I was wondering when he'd come around. He's always kept his word and I knew he wouldn't let us down this time. What have you two planned?"

"I don't know what he was supposed to keep his word on, but the plan is for us to find him a wife, pretty much the same way we found his house and furniture."

"What do you mean, find him a wife?"

"Well, a serious relationship, anyway. He's prepared to wait awhile before jumping into marriage."

"He wants *you* to help him find a woman?"

Lauren's gaze fell to the cookbook. "You know how he values my opinion. He likes consulting with me on most of his major decisions. Even when some of those are spur-of-the-moment."

"Yes, dear, that's why I always thought... Goodness, I can't believe I've been wrong all along. Tell me, has your relationship changed since he decided all this?"

"Changed?" Lauren closed her eyes and dropped her head back against the sofa. *She'd* certainly changed. Seemed suddenly she got all hot and bothered whenever Adam was around.

"Has he indicated in any way that he might like to share this new experience with…well, with you?"

Lauren opened her mouth to protest, but Adam's words echoed through her mind. *And you think I've never thought of you in that way?*

She sat forward. Was it possible Kamira, Elliot, and now her mother were right? "Mom, why do you ask?"

"You remember shortly before your father died. I had stayed the night at the hospital and Adam brought you and Rusty by that morning. You had that bunch of azalea blossoms and Rusty went with you to put them in water."

"The vase I'd brought was leaking, so I had to track down a new one."

"That's right. While you were gone, your dad had one of his lucid moments and grasped Adam's hand. He really recognized him for the first time in a long time. Dad was so happy about that. He told Adam how he'd always loved him like a son. I think we were all teary at that point. Anyway, that's when Adam made that promise."

The old ache of losing her father thudded dully in Lauren's chest. "What promise?"

"He promised to look after you and care for you. He promised you'd never want for anything."

Tenderness welled up inside her. Adam had been all of sixteen at the time. She swallowed past a lump in her throat.

"That's incredibly sweet," she said. "I wish I'd known that, but he *has* looked after me. We've always looked after each other. That's what *friends* do."

"I don't know. Something about the way he said it…I took it to mean he intended for your relationship to one day grow into something more. Your father thought so, too. One of the last things he said was that he was sorry he'd miss seeing Adam become an official member of the family. You know, Rusty has always looked up to him, too. I think we've all felt that way.''

"Oh, Mom...I know how much you all love Adam. I can't imagine how my life would have been without him. I just think that maybe you were jumping to conclusions about this.''

"But you think it may be possible?'' Hope colored her mother's voice.

It also stirred in Lauren's heart. Could it be she *wanted* Adam to want her that way? "I'm not sure. Maybe...''

"Has he said anything that might insinuate he's interested? Maybe he isn't sure how to go about it with you.''

"It...it's possible he's been trying to tell me, but I've been afraid to listen.''

Lauren smoothed her hand across the cookbook. Her throat tightened. Surely, he didn't mean for *her* to fill the role of wife and mother? If only he'd accept there was more than one kind of wife.

"Well, listen up, darling girl! You've got to give him a chance. I've always hoped the two of you would get together. I just never said anything because I wasn't sure how you'd take it.''

"I'll tell you what. I'll start paying closer attention. If it looks like Adam's interested, I'll keep myself open to the possibility.''

"You do that, dear. I know you won't be sorry.''

Lauren's stomach gave a loud rumble. "I'll talk to you soon, Mom.''

"Keep me posted, and tell Adam he should give an old woman a call every now and then.''

After hanging up, Lauren headed toward the kitchen, cookbook in hand. Was it possible? Could Adam be interested in taking their friendship to the next level? She stood for a long moment, staring at the heart-shaped pastries on the cover before opening the cookbook.

The book presented two kinds of recipes. The first were for the actual food, which contained an abundance of sauces and creams. The other recipes, which incorporated the first, displayed titles like "Sunday Morning Bubble Bath," or "Moonlit Picnic for Two," included explicit instructions on how best to serve each meal. Body parts tended to replace dishes, and fingers silverware.

Colored photographs showing couples "dishing up" the meals accompanied a number of the entries. Warmth filled her. Had Adam sent the book? Was this the level he wanted to take her to? She closed her eyes and imagined the two of them replacing one of the pictured couples.

With a lazy motion, Adam drizzled a honey glaze over her breasts, while she offered him a morsel of chicken. He accepted the bite from her fingertips, then bent to lick the glaze from her nipples.

Her body tensed, as sensual heat filled her. Her nipples tightened and her sex pulsed. If they became lovers, would they remain friends? Could she make love with him, risk losing his friendship forever?

A kaleidoscope of memories danced over her: a twelve-year-old Adam helping her set up her very first business, a dog-walking service; Adam standing and cheering wildly when she placed fifth in a local teen pageant; and finally, Adam holding her and keeping the world at bay after her father had died and she thought she'd break into a million pieces. He'd kept her together through it all.

Her heart swelled as realization dawned. All she had to do was convince him that he could be every bit as happy without overcomplicating his life. She could lose him to another woman, or risk losing his friendship, but if she gathered her courage she stood to gain so much more.

She *was* ready for the next step. She stood motionless as the possibility shimmered before her. Then she straightened, drawing her shoulders back and lifting her chin.

"There's just one thing to do, then."

She hugged the book to her front. The future stretched ahead of her, her path crystal clear. Since Adam seemed bent on remaining anonymous, she'd have to let *him* know of *her* interest.

She'd seduce her best friend.

ADAM'S STOMACH RUMBLED the following morning as he peered hopefully into his refrigerator. He peeled back the cover of a plastic container. "Hmm, what have we here?"

A fine covering of green coated the remains of some forgotten meal. Wrinkling his nose, he dumped the entire container into the trash.

Too bad he hadn't talked Lauren into dinner last night. He'd settled for Chinese takeout, which had done the trick, but hadn't stuck to his ribs the way one of her hearty meals would have. His stomach continued its protest as he scavenged his pantry to no avail.

He shoved an old can of anchovies back onto a shelf and straightened. There was only one thing to do. He'd go out for breakfast, and he'd drag Lauren along with him. Frustrating woman had probably skipped dinner last night.

Shaking his head, he grabbed his car keys. She worked way too hard. If he didn't intervene, she'd probably waste away to nothing.

A scant fifteen minutes later, he pulled into her driveway. The maple tree in front scattered its golden leaves as he strode up her walk. He inhaled the early-morning air, crisp with the promise of fall. Bypassing the front door, he headed through a little gate to the backyard. The fountain he'd installed bubbled quietly at the center of a small flower garden. The curtains in Lauren's bedroom window remained drawn.

"Stayed up late working, sleepyhead?" he murmured to himself as he searched the ground for a couple of pebbles.

With a practiced aim, he tossed the pebbles at her upstairs window. After the fifth throw, the curtains moved, then the window slid upward and she peered blearily down at him. "I'm sleeping."

The sun caught her tousled hair, turning it a dazzling gold. She looked warm and rumpled and utterly attractive. A soft breeze rustled the thin fabric of her oversize T-shirt, skimming it across the swells of her breasts. He stood rooted in place, those generous curves holding him entranced, until he tore his gaze away.

"You worked late into the night, didn't you?" He forced a note of accusation into his voice.

She spread her arms in a long, languorous stretch, again drawing his gaze to her breasts as they thrust forward in a most enticing way. The open neckline shifted, teasing him with a glimpse of her creamy shoulder.

His throat tightened. In spite of his long history of taming his libido around her, Lauren's womanly nature proved impossible to ignore this morning. He couldn't take his gaze from the clear outline of her erect nipples.

"Quit nagging." She gathered the cotton shirt in her hand, pulling it up to reveal the soft curve of her belly. She rubbed it, running small circles around her navel. "Hmm…my stomach's empty. If I don't eat right now, I think I'll drop. Let's make breakfast, then you can tell me why you rousted me from my bed."

Her bed. He stood speechless. Didn't she realize her words, not to mention that little gesture, set his mind on a track he made a habit of avoiding? As her hand made another pass, he imagined his tongue following in its wake.

That he was having this fantasy about Lauren made it all the more intense. Forbidden.

What would it be like to make love to a woman he actually cared about? Not that he hadn't cared for any of his previous partners, but he'd never felt the depth of attachment he felt for Lauren with any of them.

The idea invoked a strange warmth in his chest.

"Well, if we're not going to eat, then I'm going back to sleep." Her lower lip rounded in the sexiest pout he'd ever had the honor of witnessing.

"Uh, no. Breakfast, I mean, that's why I came—I'm here…to take you to breakfast."

"I don't feel like going out." She motioned him toward the back door. "I'll meet you in the kitchen. We'll see what we can cook up."

Was he imagining that challenge in her gaze? His mind raced with the possibilities. She *had* been intrigued by the idea of them being more than friends. He hadn't imagined the awareness in her eyes the other night.

He stood dazed, staring at the assortment of potted plants gathered by her back door. Then dropping to one knee, he lifted half a dozen of them before finding her door key.

Seconds later, he stood in her kitchen. His gaze fell on the table where they'd eaten so recently. It suddenly seemed small, intimate. Her footsteps padded down the carpeted stairs. His pulse raced.

He turned to face her as she entered, still wearing the oversize T-shirt. Rather than conceal her, its loose fit accented her curves with every movement. His gaze traveled below the hemline, down the tantalizing length of her legs. Apparently, she wasn't wearing much else.

He'd seen her in various states of undress before, but he'd never reacted like this, not even when they'd gone swimming at their hideout by the lake and she'd worn that skimpy bikini of hers. What was different now?

She moved toward him, a smile playing across her lips. Her gaze drifted over him, sending his hormones tripping. *She* was different. He hadn't been imagining it the other night. One thing he'd become very adept at over the years was reading the signals. As she closed in on him this morning, she was throwing out all kinds of signals.

Open-armed, she stood before him. "I need a hug. You're right. I stayed up too late."

She slid into his embrace, as she had done throughout the years, but her arms slipped tighter around his neck and she lingered long enough to imprint her body on his. A bolt of lust pierced him. Then she breezed away as though nothing unusual had passed between them.

He exhaled as she moved to the refrigerator. Maybe he was imagining it all. Without taking his gaze from her, he settled at the table. He'd follow her lead. What he'd do if she took him down the same path as his wayward mind he wasn't sure, but the temptation of her forbidden fruit might prove more than he could resist.

"How about eggs Benedict?" She glanced back at him as she bent low over the bottom shelf of the refrigerator. The T-shirt rode up the back of her legs. Satiny, cream-colored panties teased him, hinting at the treasure guarded by her thighs.

A small groan escaped him.

Her eyebrows furrowed. She rubbed one hand over her hip, further exposing the sight of her covered mons for his view. "No? Maybe French toast, then?"

Somehow, he managed to move his gaze to her face. "*Whatever* you want, Lauren."

The glow in her eyes intensified. "Eggs Benedict, then. I have a taste for something familiar but new."

His throat constricted, so he nodded his agreement, then closed his eyes as she finished rummaging through the fridge. He drew deep breaths and tried to relax the tightening in his groin. This was Lauren, familiar, yes, but definitely new and exciting this morning.

Once he had his libido under control, he stirred himself to make coffee. Perhaps the task would busy his mind. She stood at the counter, whisking sauce in a bowl, and he leaned around her to reach the filters she kept in an overhead cabinet. He took advantage of the moment, fumbling with the filters, while he inhaled her warm scent. She smelled clean and earthy, without the trace of perfumes or soap.

"Excuse me," he said as he pulled a filter from the stack and bumped against her.

"No problem." Her gaze traveled over him again, and that same intriguing smile played at her lips.

Once he got the coffee brewing he took his seat, trying to relax as she prepared their meal, her gaze drifting to him on occasion. She hummed softly to herself, and he savored the sight of her hips' gentle sway. Mouthwatering scents filled the air as the coffee gurgled and Canadian bacon sizzled on the stove.

"Taste." She scooped sauce from a ladle with her finger, then held it to his lips.

He met her gaze, his throat tightening. By the glint in her eyes, they were definitely charting new territory here. His rational side reeled from surprise, but his adventurous side refused to quell its curiosity.

He drew her finger into his mouth, laving the sauce from her skin. She withdrew her finger, then dipped it again into the ladle.

This time, she took it into her own mouth, closing her eyes as she slowly withdrew it. "Mmm, it's hollandaise, with a twist. I put a secret something in it, something I got from my new recipe book.''

''It's decadent.''

Her eyes sparkled. ''According to the recipe, the real secret is in how you eat the meal.''

With deft movements, she spooned the sauce over one plate, covering the layers of English muffin, Canadian bacon and eggs. Her teeth worried her bottom lip as she returned with the dish to his side, but her eyes remained bright. ''You see, in this particular cookbook, they recommend sharing.''

''I like to share.''

Blood rushed through his ears. Was this really happening? She stood so close that he couldn't resist the urge to slide his hand along the back of her thigh.

Her eyes widened slightly, and her breath stirred her lovely bosom, but she made no attempt to pull away. ''Well, then, it says we should start like this.''

Lauren drew a deep breath. Excitement flowed through her. Balancing the plate, she straddled his lap. She'd dreamed of this last night. The dream still clung to her as she faced this flesh-and-blood Adam, his eyes brimming with interest.

She hadn't been mistaken. He wanted her. Adam *was* her secret admirer.

''This is all rather sudden, but so far I heartily approve of this new cookbook.''

''Of course you do.'' She gave him a pointed look.

''Silverware seems to be an option,'' she murmured, pinching off a bite of the eggs. After setting the plate aside, she faced him again. Cupping her other hand to catch the dripping sauce, she held the morsel to his lips.

His gaze never left hers as he took the bite, then chewed slowly. ''Eggs Benedict has never tasted this good.''

Lifting her hand to her own mouth, he urged, ''Taste.''

She drew her fingers into her mouth, savoring the creamy taste and the shiver of awareness passing between them. Spatters of the sauce dotted her other hand, as well. "I forgot napkins."

Before she could move away he took her hand, bringing it to his lips. "Allow me." With deft strokes, he licked the drips of hollandaise from her palm.

Her heart quickened with each stroke of his tongue, filling her with confidence. "And you have a bit of sauce..."

Every nerve in her body stood alert as she leaned forward to skim her lips along the corner of his mouth. She flicked her tongue over the dab of hollandaise.

He angled his head. For one heart-rending moment, their breaths mingled, expectation hovering over them. Then he pressed his mouth to hers. Time stood still as he opened to her. The tang of the sauce melted from his tongue to hers.

Her breasts pressed against his chest. She shifted on his lap, stirring that part of him that had filled her dream with pleasure. Heat spiraled through her. He skimmed his hands up her sides as his tongue stroked hers with an intensity that sparked a hunger she had never known.

She broke the kiss, pulling back to gaze at him as she drew deep breaths. His pupils had dilated and his eyes glowed with sexual hunger. His lips beckoned, lush and inviting.

With a small groan, she leaned back into him, mating her mouth once more to his. She shifted again, giving him better access as his hands slid up over her rib cage. Desire burned in her as his thumbs traced the lower swells of her breasts, then found their taut buds. He teased them until she squirmed against him, pressing her cleft to his hardness.

She drew back, her breasts heaving. Then her gaze fell on the clock mounted on the wall behind him. Alarm raced up her spine. "Oh my God."

He cupped her bottom and pressed her closer. "I know. Why haven't we done this before? It's incredible."

All that work on those flyers, and she was already behind schedule. "Yes, no, I mean…it's eleven-thirty. I have to go."

"Go?"

Her gaze swerved back to him. "The post office closes in half an hour. I should have mailed those flyers yesterday."

"Flyers?"

"I've got to get dressed. I'm so sorry."

She pressed a quick peck to his cheek, scrambled off of him, then dashed toward the stairs. If she skipped her shower, she might make it in time.

"Wait!" His chair scraped the floor as he bolted after her.

A wave of guilt stopped her on the bottom stair. She pivoted to face him. "Adam—"

"Do I have an overactive imagination, or did we just get hot and heavy in there?" He wrapped his arms around her and pulled her close.

Her traitorous body melted against him. "Um, yes, we got hot and heavy in there."

His eyes rounded in disbelief. "And…you're leaving?"

Frustration billowed inside her. "I have to."

"No, you don't."

"I do. We've planned this whole campaign to tie in with the TV ads. Timing is everything. They should have gone out yesterday."

"Okay. I'll drive you. We'll pop those in the mail, then come back here and…pick up where we left off."

She cupped his cheek. "I wish we could, but I promised Kamira I'd help at the clinic today. She's probably leaving Greg's now to come get me."

His eyebrows drew together. "You're not running away because you regret that we—"

"No." She traced her finger along his lower lip. "No. I had hoped we would…you know."

He tipped up her chin. "Are you sure?"

She nodded and he ran his lips lightly across hers. "Then we will. Tonight."

"Yes." Her heart thudded. "Tonight."

"I'll see what I can rustle up at the grocery store, then I'll pick you up from the clinic."

Anticipation thrummed in her veins. "Yes."

"Now, go take care of all your distractions. Tonight you're all mine."

"Yes." She gasped. "Ohmygosh, I have to hurry." She turned, then fled up the stairs.

"Oh, and Lauren," Adam called. "Don't forget that cookbook."

4

THE TRAFFIC LIGHT turned yellow and Kamira gunned the car through the intersection. She turned to Lauren. "You're so quiet. Sure you're up to this?"

Lauren nodded absently. "I'm just tired. I didn't sleep well."

Truth was, she was feeling a little stunned. Once she'd dropped the flyers at the post office and her mind had slowed long enough to comprehend exactly what had happened earlier in her kitchen, a sense of disbelief had taken over her.

Last night, seducing Adam had seemed like the right thing to do. Now, just the memory of his heated kiss aroused her to distraction. What had she done? He wanted a wife and *kids*. If she gave in to this budding attraction, how would she encourage him to walk a different path with her?

Yet, now that they'd crossed that line, could they go back? The memory of his tongue stroking hers, the heat of his body warming her and his fingers taunting her nipples to hardness, rolled over her. Would his friendship ever be enough now that they'd experienced this new passion between them?

She just couldn't think about it right now. She had to keep busy, and helping at the clinic wouldn't involve any brain work. She'd figure out what to do about Adam later. Shifting, she adjusted the weight of her book bag in her lap, all too aware of the cookbook resting inside.

Don't forget that cookbook.

Kamira cast her a sideways glance. "So, heard anything more from this secret admirer of yours?"

"Um, I did get another gift."

"You did?" Her housemate's eyes rounded. "What was it this time?"

Lauren hesitated a moment, then withdrew the cookbook and held it up. "It came in yesterday's mail."

Kamira's jaw dropped as she scanned the title. "It came to the house?"

"The office."

"So whoever sent it knows both addresses."

"It wouldn't be hard to figure out. I leave my business card everywhere I can."

"So?" Kamira's eyes took on an expectant gleam.

"So what?"

"So what does Adam say about it?"

"Well, first he said that whoever sent the flowers was ultimately after an intimate relationship."

Kamira shrugged as she slowed for a light. "That's a reasonable assumption. Kind of like what he said *he* was looking for the other night."

And you think I've never thought of you in that way? His surprising words drifted back over Lauren.

"Yes, it sort of seems that way, doesn't it?"

"You think I'm right? He's your secret admirer?"

Lauren's cheeks warmed. After that kiss, how could she doubt it? Adam wanted her. She couldn't hold back the smile that curved her lips.

"Well, he does seem a likely suspect," she said.

"What? Did something happen between you two?"

Lauren's smile widened. As uncertain as she was about the direction she and Adam were headed, she couldn't hold back the wave of joy that filled her at that moment. "He dropped by this morning and we…kind of started something.''

"Oh my God!" Kamira's wide grin matched hers. "I'm so excited. So, you guys kissed?"

"Oh boy, did we.''

Kamira gave a delighted shout. "I knew it! You've got to give me that."

She held up her hand and Lauren laughed as she slapped her five.

"So, now what?" Kamira asked. The light changed. Sidewalks and various businesses swept by.

Lauren's joy waned. "Hell if I know."

"Aw, hon, are you worried about his whole settling-down thing?"

Groaning, Lauren covered her face with her hands. "I can't even think about it without my stomach tying up in knots. I have no idea what I'm doing."

"You've got to play this out. This is *Adam*. If you walk away now, you'll always wonder what might have happened."

"But a wife and *kids?*"

Kamira waved her hand. "You know how he is. He was probably just talking off the top of his head again. You haven't had much time for him lately. He's just restless, needing attention. He wants something new, and if the two of you getting together isn't new and exciting, I don't know what is. Even *I'm* excited!"

Lauren heaved a sigh. Maybe Kamira was right. Maybe Adam would be distracted enough by their new adventures that he'd forget his resolve to marry and start a family.

She forced a smile. Like Scarlett O'Hara, she wouldn't think about that right now. She'd go crazy if she did. "I can't wait to see what kind of progress you've made at the clinic. It's hard to believe you're ready to paint and wall-paper.''

"You paint. I'll do the wallpaper. You'll be forever matching every flower.''

"Don't worry. I'm perfectly happy on paint duty. There's something numbing about manual labor.''

Kamira pulled into the clinic parking lot, then turned to her. "Now, no fretting. It's all going to work out. You'll see.''

Lauren sighed. "I just hope you're right and he forgets this whole wife-and-baby scheme.''

"Babies. As I recall, he wants a passel of them.'' Kamira's eyes gleamed.

"Thank you. That's helpful.''

"Anytime.''

"Let's just go paint. I'm not talking about this anymore.''

A beat-up truck pulled in beside them. Mark Patterson, the landlord's son, emerged from the vehicle as they exited theirs.

"Good morning, ladies.'' He offered them a sweeping bow, along with his dazzling smile.

Lauren couldn't help but grin. Seeing him induced memories of Rusty. Her brother exuded the same youthful charm. It had certainly saved him from numerous scrapes that had aged her more than she cared to admit. She did miss him, though.

She shook her head and focused on Mark. His dark skin and hair contrasted with the bright blue of his eyes. Kamira was right. If he was a few years older, he'd be very appealing. As it was, he surely drove all the college girls to distraction.

"Marco, my love, you came to aid a couple of helpless damsels.'' Kamira clapped her hand on his shoulder.

His gaze swept over them as they headed up the clinic's

front walk. "Neither of you is the helpless type. I'm here to install the new light in the hall, but I can swing a paintbrush, too, if needed."

"We might take you up on that." Kamira pulled out her keys to unlock the door.

Half an hour later, Lauren stared at a spatter of blue on the drop cloth below her. Seemed she was getting more paint on the floor than on the wall. Getting Adam off her mind had proven impossible.

"Need some help?" Mark peered through the door.

She twisted around on her ladder. "Oh, I think I can manage. Thanks."

He moved into the room. "You looked like you were a hundred miles away."

"I've had a lot on my mind lately."

"Guy trouble?"

She smiled at him. He was really a nice kid. "What are you doing slaving here on a Saturday? I'm sure you've better things to do."

"Can't think of anyplace I'd rather be."

"*You* are a charmer," she said, shaking her roller toward him.

"A babe like you should be used to it. You must have tons of guys after you."

She snorted her amusement. "That's a good one."

"Come on, bet you have them lined up."

She pursed her lips.

"Fess up. How many?"

"That's confidential, and I hardly think you'd find it interesting."

"At least one, then. One in serious pursuit."

With an exaggerated sigh, she ran her roller through the paint tray. "Could be."

"I see, and you aren't certain if you return his affections?"

"Let's just say I'm not sure I need this kind of complication right now."

"Want some advice?"

She smiled indulgently. Who knew? Maybe this young man could offer some insight. "Okay. What's your advice?"

"Believe in the secrets of the heart."

For a moment, she stared at him, then she laughed. "You're one of those hopeless romantics, right?"

"Guilty."

"And is there a lucky young lady in *your* life?"

His gaze warmed. "There's someone."

"Well, she's very fortunate. Guys like you are way too rare."

Kamira stopped in the doorway. "Mark, could I borrow you for a minute? I need an extra pair of hands."

"Sure." He turned to Lauren. "Don't forget what I said. Give love a chance."

She smiled as he left. The memory of kissing Adam that morning flowed over her again. Love or not, something was happening between them.

"Yes." She glided the roller over the wall. "Whatever it is, I'll definitely give it a chance."

ANTICIPATION ROLLED OVER Lauren late that afternoon. A day of painting had done her good, but now she had to hurry. Adam would be by any moment to pick her up.

She frowned as she stood in one of the clinic's bathrooms and scrubbed a stubborn spot of blue from the back of her hand. Sounds filtered through the open doorway—a deejay from 99X cracked a joke, while Kamira rustled around in a room down the hall and Mark kept up a rhythmic hammering from somewhere in the original section.

For the first time ever, Lauren felt the need to primp for Adam. Looking like a manual laborer tonight didn't fit her plans. She moved to another speckling of paint on her other hand.

She stood firm in her decision. She couldn't forget that kiss. And if his response had been any indication, he wouldn't be able to, either. If he still wanted to pursue their new course, she was certainly willing.

"Hey, sunshine, ready to go?" Adam's neat baritone sounded near her ear.

She started, her heart racing. "You shouldn't sneak up on a person like that."

He bumped up against her back, pressing her to the sink. Her heart quickened as his body spooned hers, his arms wrapping around her. Nerve endings she hadn't known she possessed jumped to attention.

"Sorry," he said. "I was just anxious to see you. I've been thinking about you all day. Here, let me do this."

With gentle movements he removed the rest of the paint dabs. She leaned into him, aware of the brush of his cheek against hers, the muscles of his chest at her back and his hard thighs bracing her. His scent surrounded her, while his breath stirred her hair. Was it because he'd always been forbidden fruit that this simple act of cleaning her hands sent heat ripping through her?

When the last speck of paint had disappeared under his ministrations, he set aside the washcloth. "Did this morning really happen, or did I hallucinate that little episode in your kitchen?"

She turned to face him, feeling the boldness she'd previously experienced only in the boardroom blossom inside her. She'd certainly never felt this brave with Todd, or anyone before him. But this was Adam. And though butterflies stormed her stomach, she somehow still felt comfortable with him.

"You mean the little episode that went something like this?" she asked.

Leaning closer, she kissed him. If she thought too much about what she was doing—what *they* were doing—she'd never go through with it. Diving in seemed the best option.

A low rumble rose from his chest as he gathered her closer and married his mouth to hers. All the delicious sensations from earlier flooded back. The warmth of his breath. The insistent stroke of his tongue. The tingling that took over her entire body, sending desire spiraling through her. She couldn't get enough. Never had a kiss so consumed her, so excited her. For long, hazy moments she indulged. She could spend eternity in this embrace, this kiss.

His hands smoothed slowly down her back, then up her sides. He broke away and she drew a deep breath, while her pulse beat in her ears.

"Yeah, that's about how I remember it," he said.

"Really? I seem to remember it a little differently." She still craved his mouth, yet suddenly it wasn't enough. With her new boldness guiding her, she moved his hand to her breast. "As I recall, you touched me here, too."

"Lauren," he whispered her name as he again claimed her mouth. Heat built inside her while he caressed her breast through her T-shirt.

Her nipple hardened as he strummed the aching bud. Her sex swelled and pulsed with each pass of his fingertips. Wetness pooled between her thighs, while he stroked his hand down her back to cup her bottom. He squeezed and parted her, pressing his fingers along her cleft. She moved against him, tilting her hips to fit that aching part of her against his hardness, cursing the clothes that kept her from meeting him skin to skin.

The radio wound down Creed in the distance, then the hammering stopped. Adam broke the kiss to bury his face in the nape of her neck. "Woman, you make me forget where I am."

He chuckled softly, the sound swirling through her. "You make me forget *who* I am. I feel like the king of beasts, ready to beat my chest and drag you off into the woods."

"Don't apes beat their chests? I thought the king of beasts was a lion. You must be some kind of combination." For good measure, she rotated her hips, rubbing against him until pleasure shivered through her. A small moan escaped her.

Adam grabbed her hips and stilled her. "Have a heart, sunshine. I'm about out of control here. Do you want to shut this door and have our first time together right here in the bathroom?"

She actually considered that possibility. Her craving for him was so acute in that moment, his threat held a certain appeal. "It's a tempting idea, but when you're deep inside me I want to be where I can hear your unhindered roar, King Beast."

He leaned back to look at her, his eyes round with surprise. "You have a wicked streak."

She dropped a kiss on his nose. "You bring out my wild side."

"I never knew you had one."

"Neither did I."

He smiled, but his brief amusement fled. His gaze probed hers for a long moment. "Lauren, I really want you, but we can end this here. I don't want to do anything to screw up what we already have. If there's a chance I might lose your friendship if we go any further, I don't want to risk it. I don't know what I'd do if I didn't have you in my life. I swear to God, I can't even picture it.''

The depth of sincerity in his gaze and the seriousness of his tone tightened her throat. She blinked to clear the moisture from her eyes. He'd never seemed more dear than in that moment, and though she harbored the same fear, the vision of what they had to gain etched itself clearly across her mind.

She took his hand and held his gaze, confidence blooming inside her. "I want to risk it, Adam. We can be so much more.''

His jaw tightened and he straightened away from her. "Okay, then let's go home.''

THE DRIVE HOME proved to be an exercise in restraint. Adam gripped the steering wheel as the memory of that first kiss washed over him—Lauren's mouth hot on his, her nipples, taut and beckoning, and the heat of her sex driving him to distraction as she ground against him.

He glanced at her as she leaned toward him over the gearshift. The seductive promise in her eyes sent his pulse pounding. He'd been right. His blurted confession had intrigued her enough to start them on this path. He never would have thought it possible.

He slid his hand along her thigh, aching to touch her again. His heart pounded in anticipation as she nuzzled his neck and rubbed her hand across his chest.

"You smell good," she murmured as, at last, he pulled into his driveway.

Moments later, they fell through his kitchen door, their mouths locked in another heated kiss. She pulled back, gasping for air and dropped her purse and book bag on the table that dominated half the room. The cookbook spilled onto the polished surface.

Laughing, she slid into one of the chairs. He dropped down beside her, nuzzling the sweet curve of her ear, while she flipped through the pages. He didn't need the recipes in that book to turn him on. He was so turned on right now, he nearly vibrated.

"Here's one," she said. "Ants on a log."

"Ants on a log?"

She angled her head and he moved to her neck. "You remember, Mom would make a batch, then bring them up to the tree house."

"Right, she insisted on a healthy snack once in a while."

"She filled celery sticks with peanut butter, then topped them with raisins."

"I never liked the celery."

"So I always ate your log." She cocked her head and ran her hand across the glossy page. "They improvise on the log here, though."

"Exactly what do they use instead of celery?"

Her eyebrows arched suggestively.

A vision of her eating his log imprinted itself in his mind. His sex stirred. "You're pulling my leg."

"You know, this is an *illustrated* cookbook." She scooted the book closer and gave the page her undivided attention.

"Let me see." He tugged on the book, but she clamped her arm over it.

"I wouldn't want you to feel, uh, diminished by this particular log. The model is rather well endowed."

"Give it here." He reached again for the book, but she leaned over it, half lying on the table to cover the pages with her torso.

"It's not in there. You're making it up." Grinning, he reached around her and started tickling her.

She laughed and twisted sideways as his fingers found the sensitive areas along her sides. "Stop. No fair."

As she squirmed, her thigh wedged between his knees. Her T-shirt rode up, exposing her soft belly. The vision of her tracing her fingers over her tender flesh as she'd stood in her window that morning washed over Adam.

His tickling turned into a caress as he explored the area around her navel. Her laughter quieted and her gaze met his. Light burned in her eyes. Did she desire him with the same intensity he desired her?

God, her skin was soft. He marveled at the feel of her. Slowly, he pushed up the thin cotton, until the lacy edge of her bra peered from beneath the fabric. He smoothed his hand over the silky plane of her stomach, following the same path her own fingers had traced earlier that day.

"You were driving me crazy this morning at your window. I wanted to do this." He lowered his head to place a kiss over her navel.

She drew a quick breath as he dipped his tongue into the little indent. The warm scent of her skin teased him. She shifted and her knee rubbed his erection through his jeans. Desire shot through him. He traced his tongue in a wide circle around her stomach, then kissed his way up to the edge of her bra.

She cradled the back of his head with one hand and slid her top higher with the other, revealing her lace-bound breasts for his exploration. He drew a sharp breath as he followed the swell of one breast with his finger. Her lovely mounds rose and fell with her breath. He nuzzled her through the lace, toying with her nipple until it pressed against his tongue.

When she reached for the front clasp, he stopped her, his blood pounding through his veins. "Are you sure?"

Her head tilted and a smile played across her lips. With

a quick twist she freed her breasts. They were round and firm and almost too full to fit in his hands. A deep rose tinged her areolas and her erect nipples beckoned him.

She scooted upward, so she sat on the kitchen table, then yanked off both her shirt and bra. Eyes shining, she cupped her breasts in offering. "An appetizer for you, sir?"

"Very appealing, but something's missing."

He moved away from her to rummage through the pantry, smiling when he found the small jar. "Luckily I had the impulse to toss this into the cart today. Let's make this a healthy snack."

Her eyes widened as he moved between her thighs and removed the lid. A sweet, nutty scent filled the air. Pink blossomed in her cheeks. "I was joking about the ants on a log. I hadn't gotten past the table of contents."

He glanced at the page she gestured to as he dipped his finger into the jar and scooped out a measure of peanut butter. The page indeed showed the table of contents. "It's a great idea, though."

Her breath caught as he spread the creamy substance over her nipple. With a tilt of his head he moved to her other breast, coating that nipple, as well. "Now, you're ready."

He met her gaze and she laughed. "I've never been anyone's appetizer before."

"You're the appetizer, the main course, and if I'm lucky, dessert."

"Oh…well, looks like you just might get lucky."

Gathering her close, he ran his tongue across one jutting nipple, laving the peanut butter from her sweet flesh until he'd cleaned her thoroughly. "So beautiful," he murmured before taking her into his mouth.

He wanted to suckle her forever. When had he taken such pleasure in a woman's breasts? The combination of the peanut butter and her own sweet taste kept him enthralled for long moments.

At last he moved to her other breast and with quick passes of his tongue washed her nipple, while he strummed his fingers across its twin. Shifting from one breast to the other, he savored the firm roundness, the weight of her in his hands, and the erotic thrust of her nipples as she moaned softly and moved against him. Like a man intoxicated, he cupped and massaged her, letting his mouth run rampant over her tender mounds.

"Oh, Adam, you're driving me wild." She threaded her fingers through his hair and pressed her cleft to him, grinding against his thigh.

He pulled back far enough to see her. Her eyes were dilated, her cheeks flushed and her rosy nipples, glistening from his loving, stood taut and erect. Desire surged through him and he closed his eyes in an effort to regain some control.

"Damn, Lauren, you're incredible."

"You're making me feel self-conscious. You have to take off your shirt, too."

He tugged his shirt over his head. She grinned, her eyebrows rising suggestively as she scooped a fingerful of peanut butter from the jar. "I need a little protein."

Somehow, he withstood the pleasurable torture as she slathered the substance over his own nipples. Her warm breath brushed his chest as she leaned forward to flick her tongue over him.

"Mmm, I like that," she said, then bent to her task, her sweet mouth flaying him with relentless lashes of her tongue.

He ground his teeth, the sensation almost too much to bear. "Sweetheart..."

She sighed and moved to his other side, where she continued her gentle assault. Her lips closed over him and she suckled him, pulling on his nipple with her talented mouth. He rolled back his head and moaned. When she finally drew away, he pulled her toward him to take her into his arms.

"Enough of that," he said. "A guy can only take so much."

He brushed his lips across hers, then kissed her. The peanut butter tasted even better from her lips. The kiss was the same as before, a breathless ride into oblivion. The insistent stroke of her tongue sent heat licking through his veins. If just holding her and kissing her affected him this deeply, what would making love to her be like?

Her breasts rubbed against his chest as they rose and fell with her breath. She skimmed her hands over his chest, then down his sides. He reached between them and undid the snap of her jeans. "Let's get you out of these."

She wriggled out of the garment, then quickly discarded it on the floor. She sat before him in nothing but a lacy pair of black panties and a smile ripe with promise. Heat surged through him.

"You next." Her fingers hooked his waistband, pulling him closer. With deft movements, she first unbuttoned, then unzipped him, the metal teeth rasping as her gaze met his.

"Let's move to the bedroom."

"I'd rather not."

His heart plummeted. "You don't want to make love?"

"Of course I want to make love, silly. I just kind of like this table." Her palm smoothed over the polished surface. "It only seems fitting that if we're really going to make a meal of this, we should do it on your kitchen table. What do you think?"

Excitement filled him. "I think it'll do."

5

BEING WITH ADAM had always made Lauren feel more daring. When they were kids she'd climbed trees, jumped fences and dived into lakes with him at her side. Things she'd never have had the nerve to try on her own.

Now, the desire burning in his eyes inflamed her new-found sexual boldness.

"Anywhere, any way you want it, sunshine," he said.

She reached inside his pants to cup him. "I want you here and now. Like this."

His mouth again covered hers. Her heart pounding, she caressed him through his briefs. His heat warmed her through the soft cotton as she traced her fingers along his rigid outline.

"You're a little cramped in there," she said, easing his jeans back so she could slip her fingers past the cotton to his hot skin.

He touched her in kind, stroking her swollen flesh through the lace. Capturing her lips again, he ravaged her mouth and strummed the tips of his fingers over her sex, until dampness soaked her panties. Desire coursed through her. She leaned back, taking him with her onto the wide table.

"Let's get these out of the way." Shifting to his side, he tugged the black lace over her hips, down her legs, then off her feet. To her surprise, he held the garment to his nose, inhaling deeply, a look of pure indulgence on his face.

"There's just something about your scent—your aroused

scent.'' His eyes gleamed as he tossed aside the scrap of lace.

She shuddered when his fingers found her wet folds and he began his first intimate exploration of her. He parted her, then circled her opening. After dipping into her moistness, he spread her liquid honey across her nether lips and clitoris, drawing tiny circles of arousal with his fingertips.

He left her mouth to trail kisses to her breast. Suckling her hard, he pressed two fingers deep inside her, while she skimmed her hand over his erection. She moaned and pulled her knees up, spreading her legs to give him full access. As he stroked his fingers in and out of her, she rolled her bottom against the cool wood.

His erection pulsed hot and hard in her hand. He grated his teeth against her nipple and groaned as she squeezed him. Then all she could do was hold on as he continued his tender assault, his fingers moving in a steady rhythm. The tension inside her built with each pull of his mouth and thrust of his fingers.

''Oh, Adam…Adam…yes.''

Pinpoints of fire danced around her, inside her. Her body tensed, on the brink of release. Then his fingers withdrew to again trace a path along her swollen lips to her clit, sending the tension spiraling in a new direction. With circular movements that grew smaller and more focused with each pass, he brought her again to the brink.

''Please don't stop.'' She was nearly overwhelmed with need.

''Not in this life.'' He kissed her neck and strummed her aroused flesh with new intensity.

She gasped and ground against him, the frantic undulation of her hips driving the pace. Heat burst through her. She stiffened. Wave after wave of sensation rippled through her, convulsing her body until she lay breathless and filled with wonder.

"How did you do that?" she asked when she could find her voice. Her inner muscles shuddered—mini orgasmic aftershocks.

A smile curved his lips. "I just let my fingers do the walking."

"But it was like you pushed all my buttons at the same time."

She realized then that she still held his erection. Even though she wasn't quite recovered, she wanted to give him what he'd given her. She ran her hand up, then down his hard length, marveling at the vibrant feel of him. "You're so hot."

A hoarse laugh burst from his throat. "Not that I'm complaining. I'm enjoying myself, but not all of us have been satisfied here."

"Oh, then we'll have to remedy that. I still haven't seen your tattoo."

He raised his eyebrows. "Now, there'll be no making fun of my tattoo."

"I won't make fun." She shoved his jeans farther aside, then peeled back his briefs, so she had unhindered access to him. "Now, that's better."

"Definitely, though, you won't find my tattoo there."

"No." She grinned. "You said it was on your backside. We'll get to that." Her eyes widened. "My, you *are* King Beast."

"Wanna hear me roar?"

"First, I'm still hungry." She reached for the jar of peanut butter.

"Ants on a log?" His voice came out in a hoarse whisper.

"Do you have any raisins?"

He shook his head, his gaze intent on hers.

"Well, we'll have to make do."

She swirled her finger in the jar, coating it with a layer of peanut butter. With long, slow strokes, she slathered the substance in a strip along his length, taking care to cover the rounded head.

Adam fell to his back with a stifled moan. "You really know how to torture a guy."

"Shall I stop?" She paused, her mouth a breath from his makeshift log.

His lips parted and he shook his head. Without taking her gaze from his, she traced her tongue down his length, marveling at her own audacity. "Ah, that's good."

"I'll never look at peanut butter the same way."

Again, she laved a path down him, savoring the nutty taste and the feeling of power flowing over her. His hips rose as she nipped him. "Sorry, I couldn't resist. You're just so tasty."

"Maybe we should go into the bedroom now."

"Not so fast, bud. I'm not done."

His teeth clamped down on his lower lip. He was velvet-encased steel beneath her tongue. She savored the taste and feel of him as she nipped and licked and kissed away another swath of peanut butter, stopping short of the rounded tip. Taking her time, she ate away the rest of the creamy substance, running her tongue down him a few extra times for good measure. Her passage tightened and moistened. She'd never known this kind of pleasure.

As his penis moved in her hand, desire coursed through her. At last she circled her tongue around his tip, catching the salty taste of his desire. Her own sex swelled and pulsed as Adam threaded his fingers through her hair.

"You're a goddess, Lauren."

"Do you wish to mate with the goddess?"

"Hell, yes." He started to rise, but she shoved him back down.

"Not yet. I'm still not finished."

"Sunshine, I don't know if—"

She took him in her mouth. For one long moment she relished the feel of him as she traced him with her tongue and suckled him. His fingers tightened in her hair and her nipples beaded when she rubbed them against his thigh. Cupping him by the soft sacs nestled at the root of his sex, she drew him deeper into her mouth, then pulled slowly back before repeating the process.

"Sweet…"

As her own arousal grew, she tongued another salty droplet from his tip. His hands moved to her shoulders and it took a moment for her to register that he was tugging her upward. Reluctantly, she released him, then slid up his torso to place a kiss on his lips.

"I'll be right back," she said.

"Oh no you don't. You're not leaving me now."

"I'm not going anywhere. I just need to get something out of my purse."

"Got it already." He held up the small packet he'd extracted from the pocket of his pants.

A moment later he took her mouth by storm, ravaging it with a hunger that sent renewed heat flaring through her. With a twist of his hips, he nestled himself between her thighs, his erection probing her entrance.

"Yes." Shifting, she arched against him and his shaft slid into her, stretching her, filling her with his heat, his excitement.

Lauren couldn't speak. Heat shimmered through her as Adam planted himself firmly inside her, then immediately withdrew only to plunge back in again.

"Oh, sunshine…yes."

He set a fast pace from the start and her desire built quickly along with his steady movements. She rocked against him, meeting him stroke for stroke, while exquisite pleasure curled through her. Harder, deeper, faster he drove.

"Adam!" His name tore from her lips. She clung to him, seized by a heart-rending orgasm.

He thrust once, twice more, then collapsed beside her, locking her in an intimate embrace, his hand planted firmly on her bottom. Eyes closed, she nestled against him as more aftershocks rippled through her.

Gradually, his breathing evened out and her own pulse seemed to steady. He squeezed her buttock and rubbed his nose against hers. "How come we never played doctor before?"

"Maybe it was better this way, after saving it up all these years." Was that why it had been so good? Had she held hidden desires in check, desires she hadn't even admitted to herself?

He kissed her, and to her dismay she felt herself wanting him again.

"I really like your breasts," he murmured as he flicked his thumb over her nipple.

Liquid pooled between her thighs and she squirmed against him. "You go pushing my buttons again and you might never get fed."

"Don't move." He tugged his pants in place, then slid off the table, standing for a moment, staring at her. "I want to remember you just like this."

Heat rippled through her and she wasn't sure if it was from embarrassment or arousal. She stretched along the tabletop. "Now I know why you ordered such a long table."

"Actually, I *was* thinking of you when I bought that, hoping you'd be tempted to come over and cook sometime.'' He smiled. ''It never occurred to me we'd be cooking up such a...hot meal together.''

''Ah, but we've only just had the appetizer.''

''I can make a feast of peanut butter...and you. But first hold on. I'll be right back.'' He left, heading in the direction of the bathroom.

She lay back on the table, amazement swirling through her. She was lying naked on Adam's kitchen table. Where they'd just made love. And it had been wonderful. For the first time in a long time, she felt incredibly free. And wicked.

Her cell phone rang. It took her a moment to find where her purse had gotten kicked under one of the tall stools by the counter. Frowning, she pulled the phone from her bag.

''Lauren Bryant.''

''Something's missing from this script, Lauren. It isn't just the other couples...I can't put my finger on it, but it isn't right.''

She sighed and glanced in the direction of the bathroom. If she did some fast ego stroking, she could hopefully end this call before Adam returned.

''I trust you, Elliot. You've always been able to figure these things out in the past. You were brilliant with the Forester campaign. Remember how you figured out how we needed to bring in the whole melon thing? And Forester literally ate it with a spoon. That was following your gut. So, what is your gut saying now?''

The soft pad of footsteps sounded across the tiled floor. She glanced over her shoulder, flustered to have Adam catch her on a business call, while standing naked in his kitchen. This was certainly a first.

''That's the problem,'' Elliot said. ''I left the boa at the office and you know I can't create without it. My gut isn't working. I *need* the boa.''

Adam quirked his mouth to one side, then reached for the discarded jar of peanut butter. To her dismay, he scooped a fingerful from the jar, then headed toward her.

"Um, Elliot, I'll stop by the office in the morning and get the boa, then I'll come by so we can go over the script together. Why don't you try to get some rest? We'll start first thing tomorrow."

"You're a doll. I'll do that. I'm getting stressed. I'm going to go lie down and listen to Tony Bennett. He always soothes me."

"Okay, I'll see you tomorrow." She disconnected.

Adam took the phone from her and laid it on one of the bar stools. Without a word he advanced on her, until his chest brushed up against hers.

"But, remember, you already had your healthy snack," she said.

"You didn't let me finish." He leaned back until his gaze fell on the juncture of her thighs.

Her mouth went dry. "Oh, no. I don't think so."

His eyebrows arched. "Getting squeamish on me now? I let you have your way with me. It's your turn. This is only fair."

"I don't know."

"Come on. Just a taste."

"As long as I can touch you, too."

He shook his head. "This round's for you."

A measure of unease settled over her. "You really don't have to."

"But I *want* to."

She stared at him a long moment, then nodded. She could do this. "Just that little bit, then."

"That's my girl." He guided her back to the table. "Now hop back up and get comfortable."

''I can't believe we're doing this.'' She climbed onto the table, then rolled to her back, her stomach tightening.

As he dabbed the creamy substance over her, she did her best to relax, drawing up her knees and closing her eyes. Each touch of his fingers sent a measure of desire spiraling through her, though her gut twisted. She fisted her hands as he pressed his fingers into her and caressed the spot inside that escalated the building pleasure.

Then he lowered his head. His warm breath fanned her a moment, before his tongue stroked a wide circle along her swollen flesh, following the path his fingers had taken over her lips and clit. He laved the creamy substance from first one side, then the next, dipping into every crevice and fold.

The nervous tension inside her reached an almost unbearable level. He centered on her clit and began to work it with steady sweeps of his tongue. She shifted away from him. ''Stop.''

He raised his head, surprise on his face. ''We're just getting to the good part.''

''I just…'' What was wrong with her? God, she felt like an idiot. ''I want to pleasure you, too.''

''Sweetheart, this is *very* pleasurable for me. There's nothing sweeter than kissing you there. Believe me, I *really* enjoy it.''

Her cheeks warmed. She needed her head examined for sure, but somehow she found it impossible to lie there and not touch him, kiss him in return. ''But I *need* to touch you, too.''

A frown flitted across his face, then he grinned. ''Who am I to argue with a lady? I do want to finish what I started, though.''

''You can.'' She patted the table. ''Just get up here and give *me* what I want.'' She unzipped his jeans again. ''Why am I the only one naked here?''

Smiling, he slipped off his pants and briefs. He climbed onto the table beside her, stretching so his blossoming arousal was within her reach, while he nuzzled her thighs apart.

"My, you're quick on the recovery," she marveled as she closed her fingers around him. "I love the way you feel."

"I love the way you make me feel." He watched her with hooded eyes as she glided her hand over his pulsing heat. Then he ran his fingers through the springy curls guarding her womanhood. "Now, where was I?"

He focused again on loving her, his wicked tongue stroked along her engorged lips, making long, sweeping passes over her tender flesh. She shuddered, giving in to the pleasure as she circled her fingers around his penis. As he laved her, she stroked him, taking pleasure in the thickness and vibrancy of his growing erection.

When he centered again on her clit, she bent forward and pressed her lips to his penis, running her mouth along his length.

"Yes," she murmured. She rocked against him as, with his tongue and teeth, he worked her once more into a rapturous frenzy.

"Ahh…ahhh…oh!" The tension broke and she stiffened, gripped in another intense orgasm.

After a few last comforting strokes, he nuzzled his way up beside her. "I believe that was three."

"And don't you look proud. Yes, you have most thoroughly pleasured me, but I haven't yet heard you roar."

"Haven't you? We'll have to remedy that."

"Yes, we will." She slid her hand down his stomach, to grasp him again. "I can't say I'm quite recovered, but I think I can see my way to accommodating you."

His gray eyes glittered as he rubbed his erection against her cleft. "That would be *really* nice."

"Wait a minute." She pushed him aside, then rolled off the table, feeling self-conscious as his gaze swept over her. She found a condom in her purse, then hurried to help him roll it on.

Her sex pulsed with excitement.

This time, she climbed on top of him and impaled herself on his thick organ. Shivers of delight ran up her spine. "You *do* want me."

"Baby, you'd better believe it." He grabbed her buttocks, parting and massaging her as she began to ride him. His hands skimmed up to caress her breast, then he took her in his mouth, teasing her taut nipple as she moved rhythmically over him.

Pinpoints of desire shot from her breast to her sex. She tightened her passage, riding him harder as he groaned softly, still suckling her. Closing her eyes, she let her head roll back as an involuntary moan escaped her. Pleasure built and swelled between them and time seemed to collapse into one long moment of heat and ecstasy.

Her breath grew fast and heavy. Adam moved to her other breast, his teeth grazing her sensitive nipple. His hand slipped to her hip, urging her to increase her pace as the pleasure peaked. Sounds of desire tore from her throat as her body drew closer to its climax.

She ground feverishly against him. He cried out his release, gripping her closer. And her world shattered.

For long moments she lay on top of him, her pulse pounding, her lids too heavy to lift. After a short while, he moved, stroking her hair with the light touch of his fingers. "I tried for so long not to think of you like this."

She felt almost too lethargic to answer, but her curiosity got the better of her. "But sometimes you did."

"Yes, sometimes I indulged in a fantasy or two."

"Really?" She shifted to look at him. "Such as?"

He chuckled softly. "Well, that was pretty close. But there were others and the reality is so much more fulfilling."

"But fantasies can be fun."

"And arousing." He kissed her forehead. "I'll share more with you another time. For now I had better pace myself, or I'll never make it to dessert."

"Dessert?"

"Yes…but first we need the main course."

"You want to cook?"

"I don't know about you, but I've worked up an appetite." She frowned and he added, "Don't worry. We've only just begun this night."

He shifted away from her, rolling to a sitting position. "Let me clean up a little, then we'll check out your cookbook. You stay here," he said when she scooted off the table.

"But shouldn't I clean up, too?"

"By the time we're through, you'll need a thorough scrubbing from head to toe and I plan to oversee every minute of it. But for now I love the smell of sex on you."

He kissed her soundly and any argument flew from her head. She feasted her eyes on him as he walked away, catching her first glimpse of the rose tattoo adorning his left buttock. Somehow, amidst his golden skin and corded muscle, the small flower seemed right in place.

She retrieved the cookbook from where it had landed on the floor sometime during their lovemaking. Smiling, she perused the table of contents while waiting for Adam to return. A moment later, his light tread sounded across the tile.

His eyes took on a smoky sheen at the sight of her. "If we're going to make any progress with this meal, we're going to have to cover you up. The sight of all these luscious curves is too much of a turn-on.''

He tugged his shirt over her head, pulling the hem down around her thighs. Then he slipped into his jeans, before taking the seat beside her at the table.

"What did you have in mind?" she asked.

Flipping idly through the pages, he paused every so often. "Here's one. Honey garlic chicken. I think I picked up most of the ingredients today. And the way they suggest serving it up looks pretty enticing. See how they use the hollow of her stomach as a receptacle for the sauce?''

"Ah, yes, but I'm in the mood for Italian.''

"Sounds messy.''

"But tasty.''

"Let's see…" He flipped a few more pages, then with a glint in his eyes, slid the book in front of her.

She tilted her head. "Are those…"

"Meatballs.''

"I see, served in a bed of…pasta, though that—'' she drew her index finger along the picture "—is no wet noodle.''

"Neither is this." He clasped her hand over his own noodle.

"Log or noodle, this is my favorite delicacy.'' She leaned in to kiss him, but he scooted away.

"Pacing," he murmured as he opened a cabinet door. He pulled out a pot for the spaghetti, then began filling it with water.

Laughter bubbled from Lauren, but this was laughter of delight. All nervousness had left her. Adam was her lover. Her best friend and her lover. All was right with the world.

"Worried about keeping up with me?" She slid her arms around his waist and pressed herself to his back.

"I'm game. And I'm keeping track. Two for me. Four for you. It's my turn."

"No argument there. I'm happy to oblige." She ran her hand down past his stomach.

He twisted away, toward the refrigerator. "I'm pacing myself, remember?"

"But I didn't get a good look at your tattoo."

"All in good time."

"Spoilsport. Okay, where's the ground sirloin? Guess I'll start cooking."

"No question about it." His gaze rolled over her. "You're cooking all right."

She took the meat from him and smiled. Yes, this would be one night to remember.

LAUREN WOKE the next morning with the first rays of dawn. For a startled second, she couldn't figure out where she was, then the slow breathing and the warmth of a body beside her brought the previous night flooding back.

Rolling to her side, she let her gaze travel over Adam's restful face. She'd seen a whole new side of him yesterday and discovered an alternate personality in herself, as well. A smile played across her lips as she recalled her brazen behavior. He did bring out her wild side.

He smiled and reached for her without opening his eyes. "What are you doing way over there?"

With his strong arm, he scooped her against his body. The crinkly hair on his chest brushed her nipples, his belly pressed into hers and his leg wrapped around her thighs. "You weren't thinking of escaping?"

"Who could escape?" She breathed in his clean, soapy scent. After indulging in all their culinary delights last night, they'd scrubbed up together in a lengthy bath. It had been every bit as stimulating as their feast.

His eyes peeked open. "I have captured you. You are now my sex slave."

She ran her hand down his chest, past his belly to that part of him that was beginning to stir between them. Her palm skimmed over his flesh to the soft sacs nestled at the root of his sex. She took him in hand and squeezed.

"Yes, master. You are in total control. I am here to obey," she said.

His eyes opened wider as she intensified the pressure. "Maybe King Beast was mistaken and *he* is sex slave to the Wild Goddess."

Grinning, she gentled her hold. The heat of his sex warmed her hand as she slowly stroked him. "I like touching you this way."

"I like touching you this way, too." His fingers found her soft folds, already moist again with new desire.

He parted her, then began circling her clitoris. "I like watching you when you come. You're so beautiful, Lauren. I'm so happy you want to be with me like this."

Her throat tightened at the sincerity in his eyes. "How could I resist, when you followed my advice?"

"What advice?"

"My advice about wooing the woman of your choice."

He frowned and she kissed his forehead. Sweet Adam. Did it disturb him that she knew? Did he still want to play the part of her secret admirer? Well, she could play along.

Before he could say another word, she pressed her mouth to his. For once she didn't worry about morning breath or bed head. This was Adam. *Her* Adam.

Her tongue met his with long, languorous strokes. She shifted closer, then rubbed his engorged head along her cleft, savoring the feel of bare skin on bare skin, with nothing between them.

"Aw, sunshine," he murmured in her ear. "That feels just a little too good."

Delight shivered through her. She ground against him. "It can never be too good."

She slid her clit along his length, bringing the head of his penis within a fraction of her opening. He sucked in a breath. "I might come."

"Oh." She stilled, her heart racing. Never had she wanted a man the way she wanted him. "Sorry. I guess I got a little caught up in the moment."

"No apology needed." He shifted his lower body away from her, stroking his fingers once more over her sex.

He let her indulge in a long, wet kiss, before pulling back. Ducking his head, he took the tip of her breast in his mouth. He teased her nipple to attention, then suckled her. "Mmm...the peanut butter, marinara and chocolate sauce were all very tasty, but I like the taste of just you even more."

He moved to her other breast while he stroked her clitoris. She squirmed against him and moaned, heat flaring through her. "Make love to me, Beast."

She turned to feel around for a condom on the nightstand.

Adam drew a deep breath. His heart thumped. Never had he dreamed they could spend a night like last night together. How foolish he'd been to think he had to go looking for a serious relationship, when Lauren had been there all the time. Exactly what had she meant about him taking her advice, though?

She moved against him, condom in hand, and the thought swept from his mind. "I can't get enough of you," he said.

"I never thought we'd use all these."

"I had hoped." He grinned as he readied himself in all haste. "I think we're setting some kind of record here."

She guided his hardness to her entrance and he pressed

into her. With his gaze locked on hers, he began to move, savoring the curve of her face, her hip, her breast. She was an incredible lover, holding nothing back and letting him enjoy her in almost whatever way he wanted, though she'd seemed uncomfortable when she alone was the focus of pleasure. They'd have to work on that.

"Oh, Adam, it's never felt so good."

He withdrew, then slid back into her. Her tight passage gloved him. "Not even last night?"

"It was wonderful last night. I never knew…eating could be such fun."

Her muscles tightened around him as he glided in, then out. Pleasure built within him, but he drew a deep breath and continued the leisurely pace.

"Oh, that's…that's nice." She braced one foot against the mattress, and with the tilt of her hips and the pressure of her hand on his thigh, urged him to a faster pace. That delicious tension wound through him as each thrust heightened his pleasure. Her eyes widened and her breath came in sexy little pants.

Heat spread from his very center, radiating out through every inch of his body. He was on fire. His own breath came in halting gasps. "Come for me again, sunshine."

Pink blossomed along her chest and cheeks. Her mouth rounded in a wordless moan. She surged against him, gloving him, squeezing him with the muscles of her sweet passage. His chest swelled as he tried to suppress the yell of triumph rising in him, the pleasure almost too intense to bear.

The orgasm tore through him, hitting him with such force that he threw back his head and yelled. Lauren convulsed beneath him, her own climax following his. He collapsed on top of her, afraid he might be squashing her, but too drained to move.

Her fingers lightly traced his back, while he drew deep breaths and tried to calm his pounding heart. The woman would be the death of him. But what a way to go.

The faint summons of her cell phone drifted in through the open door. Adam rolled off her as she said, "That's Elliot. I promised I'd meet with him this morning."

"I know, I heard, but it's Sunday," he complained to her retreating back. She'd gathered the sheet around her and was already scurrying down the hall.

He lay back and blew out a breath. So much for whipping up Sunday brunch. He'd been hoping they'd cook up another batch of eggs Benedict. Instead, Lauren meant to spend her day with Elliot. Was there no justice in the world?

A few moments later, she whisked back into the room, her wadded-up clothes in one hand and a pleading look on her face. "I just have to go meet with him for a little while. He's having a crisis over the script for the commercial we're shooting next week. I know exactly how to pacify him. It'll be all right. I'll call when I'm done."

He folded his arms and frowned as she struggled into her clothes. "So, we'll have tonight together?"

She straightened, one shoe dangling from her fingertips. "Well, I…um, have a couple of contracts to review before tomorrow…"

What had he expected? He had to admire her determination, even though he wanted her to himself. He shouldn't have hoped that one night of ecstasy with him would rid her of her workaholic tendencies. He hated the frustration building inside him.

"I hope this isn't an omen for all our morning-afters," he complained halfheartedly.

"It's not so bad. We spent the entire evening and the whole night together, and we even had a little time this morning."

She sat beside him on the bed. "Think of all the decadent memories we have from just that time together."

He was no match for the seductive tone of her voice, or the soft brush of her lips across his. He reached for her, but she slipped away.

"But I want more," he said stubbornly. "I want you for an entire weekend."

"I wish I could stay, truly. I'll make it up to you, though. I'll really try for this evening. I'll cook you something special."

"Will you schedule me for next weekend, then? The entire weekend. We can make it extra special."

He tried to avoid sounding needy by resisting the urge to remind her that his birthday fell on the following Saturday. She hadn't mentioned it. Could it be she had forgotten?

She hesitated for a long moment. "I'll try."

A twinge of disappointment flashed through him. "Okay, I'll drive you home. We'll shoot for this evening."

She granted him a loving smile that melted his reservations. He dressed quickly, then drove her home. Before she slid out of the car, she gave him one last, long, drugging kiss that left him with no doubts.

"Don't worry," she said before closing the car door, "you haven't seen the last of me. I really want a closer look at your tattoo. You kept me so distracted I didn't get to explore it properly."

"I might let you check it out."

"Oh, I will." With one last smoldering gaze, she turned, then headed up her front walk.

He blew out a breath. He was in trouble for sure. By now she'd guessed how completely she could control him with just the promise of one of her home-cooked meals.

Especially now that they'd spiced up the menu.

6

ADAM HUMMED SOFTLY as he rinsed a lipstick-stained glass. In spite of the fact that Lauren had left him for Elliot, his mood had never been better. She'd been right. His mind was filled with decadent memories of their night together. They'd certainly made the most of that brief time.

The doorbell rang as he loaded the last dish in the dishwasher. He smiled. Had she changed her mind and come back to him?

A moment later he yanked open his front door to find her brother standing on the porch. "Rusty!" Adam greeted him with surprise and genuine pleasure.

"We didn't know you were coming. How are you, bro? You just missed…breakfast." Adam stopped himself before saying he'd missed Lauren. How would Rusty feel about her having spent the night?

After a quick back-slapping embrace, Adam ushered him into the den. "Look at you. I let you out of my sight for a year and you grow your hair and sprout a little muscle."

Twelve months ago Rusty had been a clean-cut college grad. Now his sand-colored hair hung in a ponytail down his back and dark stubble covered his jaw. The sleeves of his T-shirt stretched to accommodate his rounded biceps.

His green eyes, so like his sister's, took in the spacious room. "Nice digs. You must be doing all right."

"I'm getting by. Business is good. What are you doing here? Get tired of those oil rigs?"

"The money was great. Just can't say I want to work like that for the rest of my life."

He kept his tone light, but something in the shift of his eyes sent suspicion creeping through Adam. He'd seen that look too often in the past. "I've never known you to back down from a little hard work."

"Ah…well. Truth is, I didn't have much choice. I quit."

"You quit?"

"Yeah. It was that or get fired. Guess the foreman didn't appreciate me dating his daughter."

Adam shook his head. Rusty had a knack for getting into trouble. More times than not, some female was inevitably involved.

"Well, he trumped up some phony excuse. Blamed me for some equipment failure. Honestly, Adam, I didn't do anything wrong. It happened on my day off."

"Yeah, I know trouble just seems to follow you. Like that time when that sassy brunette fingered you as the father of her child and wanted all that child support—"

"But you got the truth out of her. And without the DNA testing—"

"Or when her sister took you on that wild gambling binge and you lost half your college fund—"

"Those two were no good. I should have known to stay away from them. It was brilliant how you got their old man to go in on that investment so he made such a killing he paid me back half the money I lost."

"What is this one costing you?"

"That fat paycheck. Plus my references."

"So you need a job."

"And a place to stay now that Lauren has a housemate." Rusty glanced around, a hopeful gleam in his eyes.

Adam pursed his lips. The kid was like a brother to him,

but the last thing Adam wanted was Rusty hanging out around here, infringing on his time with Lauren.

"I think we can handle that. I have a friend who has a duplex. He lives in one side and rents out the other. I think it's vacant. I'm sure you can get the place for a reasonable price. I'll give him a call."

"Thanks."

Adam rose, then walked over to the large oak desk that dominated the far corner of the room. He pulled his company checkbook from a drawer, and began filling out a check.

"You've done it before, so you know I run a tight crew. I expect you to be where you're supposed to be when you're supposed to be there, doing what you've been told to do. Expect long days and hard work. Your hands are good and calloused, so that won't be a problem."

Rusty had moved beside the desk. Adam tore out the check, then handed it to him. "Here's an advance on your pay. It should be enough to set you up in that duplex."

"Thanks, Adam. I knew I could count on you."

He shifted and his eyebrows arrowed down. "Um, you're not going to say anything to Lauren about the trouble with the foreman, are you? She seemed a little at her wit's end the last time anything like this happened, and I don't think I could take another lecture from her on how I need to grow up."

Adam crossed his arms across his chest. He'd always managed to help Rusty out of his scrapes without worrying Lauren or her mother too much. Lauren had plenty on her mind with the agency and Delores always seemed at her limit.

"I suppose we could keep the details to ourselves," Adam said.

The smallest measure of guilt crept over him. He'd never

liked keeping anything from Lauren in the past. Now, suddenly it seemed somehow wrong not to tell her about Rusty's trouble. No doubt she'd be upset if she found out.

He clapped Rusty on the back. "Come on, let's call Sid." At Rusty's questioning look, he added, "The guy with the duplex."

Adam blew out a breath and mentally shook himself as he lifted the receiver from its phone. Everything would be all right. After all, he was only helping the kid. What harm was there in that?

It HAD TAKEN most of the day, but somehow Lauren had smoothed Elliot's ruffled feathers and helped him work out the problems with the script.

She stopped on her front porch on her way in after their meeting. Kamira and Mark Patterson had been lounging in a swing hung at one end of the structure. "So, what have you two been up to?" Lauren asked.

Mark sprang to his feet, sending the swing, along with Kamira, swaying precariously. His face reddened. "Lauren, hello. We were…talking. Just…talking."

Stopping the swing with her toe, Kamira said, "Mark was sweet enough to spend the afternoon helping me at the center. We've got most of the painting and wallpaper done, by the way." She heaved a sigh. "My dratted car wouldn't start, though, when we were ready to leave, so I had it towed to my mechanic's shop."

His hands shoved deep into his pockets, Mark scuffed one sneaker-clad foot across the old planks. "I offered to drive her home and she gave me some lemonade."

He gestured to the side table with the pitcher, half-filled glasses and a plateful of muffins.

"I was going to offer him a beer, but figured we'd stick

with a healthy snack.'' Kamira lifted the plate, offering Lauren a muffin.

Lauren choked back a laugh. ''No thanks, I've had my healthy snack.''

''A beer would have been okay.'' A frown crinkled Mark's forehead. ''I *am* of legal age.''

''I don't want to be responsible for corrupting you,'' Kamira said.

''You're too late. I'm wise to the ways of the world.'' His glance skimmed over Lauren.

He seemed nervous. Did he have a crush on Kamira? Lauren's heart gave a little squeeze. Though Kamira was a couple of years shy of Lauren's own twenty-eight years, she was still a good four or five years older than Mark. Cute as he was, he was in for heartbreak.

Surely Kamira would let him down easy.

''Why don't you join us?'' he asked.

Kamira patted the empty spot beside her on the swing. ''Yes, Lauren, take a load off.''

''I really can't.'' She hefted her briefcase. ''Got work to do.''

With a shake of her head, Kamira made a tsking sound. ''Well, at least you didn't work last night.''

Heat warmed Lauren's cheeks. ''That's right. And I have to get these contracts done so I can take some time off this evening.''

Mark swigged back a shot of lemonade from one of the glasses. ''Guess I'd better get going. Let you ladies get on with your day.''

Kamira rose and gave his hand a squeeze. ''Thank you for driving me home. I really appreciate it.''

''No problem.'' After a quick smile at Lauren, he hurried down the steps.

''Sorry, didn't mean to scare him away.''

Kamira waved her hand in dismissal. "He's a sweet guy, but I've got to get ready for Greg."

She lifted the lemonade tray, then followed Lauren into the house. "So?"

"So, what?"

"You know, you and Adam. And how you spent the night over there."

"I probably should have called. You weren't worried, were you?"

"Ha. I was ecstatic. So, how was it?"

"I won't kiss and tell."

"It was really great, wasn't it?"

Lauren wiggled her eyebrows in answer, a smile curving her lips.

Kamira squealed in excitement. "I knew it. You two were made for each other. I could tell from the start. So, go get busy so you can see the man again. Adam's one hunk I wouldn't keep waiting."

Excitement thrummed through Lauren. "You're right. I'd better get going."

Smiling, she raced up the stairs.

LATER THAT EVENING, Lauren hit the print command on her computer, then rose from her desk, stretching to relieve the ache in her back. She ached in other, more private, areas, too. Her night with Adam had worked muscles she'd left to atrophy. And some she'd never used before.

She smiled. They must have set some marathon record.

With a light step, she headed toward the kitchen for a quick drink of water and maybe a snack. Her contracts should be ready for her review by the time she returned.

The doorbell rang as she ran down the stairs. She bit her lip. Had Adam arrived early?

To her surprise, Rusty stood on the doorstep, holding a basketful of laundry. He grinned sheepishly. "Hi."

"Adam told me you were here." She ushered him in, happy to see him, but feeling slightly annoyed. "I can't believe you stopped by to see him first. I bet I just get to see you because you have laundry to do."

"Well, kill two birds. I did want to say hello." He set down the basket, then swept her up in a big hug.

"Don't guess it occurred to you to take your laundry to Mom's?" she teased. She'd never been able to stay upset with him.

"No way. She's always so stressed. I just hate burdening her."

"Ah, but it doesn't bother you to dump your laundry on me."

"I'll do my own wash. I just want to use your machine. And your detergent. You always did have the freshest-smelling laundry."

She shook her head, but grinned. "You're just piling on the charm again, huh? Okay, this way."

He followed her to the small stack unit off the kitchen. "So, when are you going to get a full-size unit?"

"When I need one. With just me, it doesn't make sense to buy anything bigger."

With a shrug, he lifted the lid of the washing machine. "Adam seems to be doing all right. Bet he has a nice big washer and dryer."

"He does. Why didn't you ask if you could do your laundry there?"

"Didn't want to push my luck. He gave me a job. I wasn't about to ask for any more favors."

"So, you get tired of the oil rigs? Or did you just miss us?"

He didn't answer right away as he loaded his clothes into

the machine. Then he turned to her. "Who wants to be around a bunch of guys all the time? I don't care how much they pay me. It just isn't enough."

His eyes held that hint of guilt she'd seen too many times in the past. "Rusty, don't tell me you got into some kind of trouble."

He busied himself adding detergent. "No. Of course not. Okay, I admit it. I missed it around here. I didn't like being so far from home. Satisfied?"

She pursed her lips and regarded him a moment. "Sure. Welcome back. Hungry?"

"Always."

With a nod, she moved to the refrigerator, where she pulled out sandwich ingredients. How many meals had she fixed for him over the years? She knew his preferences as well as she knew her own. Taking care of her brother came as second nature. She'd been doing so ever since their father had died and their mother had gone to pieces on them.

She frowned as she spread mayonnaise on Rusty's bread. He wasn't telling her everything, she could feel it in her bones. But she'd let it rest for the time being. He'd changed a lot physically. Maybe he'd matured some, too.

Her stomach knotted as she layered turkey and cheese on the bread. She drew a deep breath, the too-familiar tiredness claiming her. Her life was complicated enough already. She didn't know what she'd do if she had to worry about getting him out of more trouble. The way she felt right now, she just didn't have the energy to deal with one more thing.

"DID YOU SEE that brother of yours?"

Lauren looked up from the contract she'd been poring over as Adam entered her bedroom. Night had long fallen as she'd buried herself in her work. She drank in the sight of his broad shoulders and beautiful face. Her pulse quickened.

How indeed had she spent all these years with him and missed the blatant sexuality oozing from him?

She offered him a smile. "He stopped by for a quick visit. He looks great, doesn't he? He's really bulked up. It was such a great surprise to see him."

Adam strode to where she sat in an old armchair by her desk. He dropped to his knees beside her, resting his arms along her thighs. "Yeah, I couldn't believe it when I opened my door. I hadn't realized how much I'd missed him."

"I understand why he's back, though."

"You do?"

"You know...the girls."

Adam straightened. "The girls?"

"They're in short supply on those oil rigs."

"Oh, right."

"Atlanta has its fair share. Plus we're here. I never thought he'd be gone as long as he was. But I'm jealous that he went to see you first."

"Ah, well, we've done that guy-bonding thing, you know. We're bro's."

"Thanks for taking him on one of your crews."

"He helped out that summer before he left. He'll do a great job. I'm happy to have him."

She brushed his hair back off his forehead. "I'm glad you're there for him."

"He deserves a break. It'll be good having him around again."

"I didn't...tell him about us."

"Neither did I. You think he'll mind?"

She hesitated a moment. "Oh, I'm sure he'll be fine with it."

The papers in her lap slid and she caught them with one hand.

"I thought you said you'd have all your work done before I got here."

"Just a few more pages."

"It's after ten. It can wait until tomorrow." He leaned forward and started nuzzling her neck.

"I'm scheduled to meet with the client first thing to finalize the deal. We really need this account."

"What is it?"

"It's that carpet cleaner you sent to us."

"Morris Cleaners?"

"Yes, and thanks for the referral. Looks like we'll be doing business."

"Great. They'll be a good account. Clyde Morris is very reputable."

She nodded, then concentrated again on the contract. She had just found her place when Adam took her foot into his hand and pulled off her sock.

"What are you doing?" she asked.

"Don't mind me. Finish up. I'll just occupy myself until you're done."

With his strong hands, he kneaded first the ball of her foot, then each toe in turn, before moving along her instep to her heel.

"We're going to get you good and relaxed," he murmured as he finished up that foot, then moved to the other.

The words on the page seemed to run together and she reread the same paragraph five times before she gave up and tossed the papers onto the pile on her desk. By then he'd worked his way up her calf to her thigh, stroking her leg through her jeans.

"I'll just have to trust I got it right the first time. It's all pretty standard, anyway," she said.

''Nothing standard here.'' He smoothed his hand over her leg.

She wore her favorite jeans and a light sweater in deference to the chillier fall temperatures. Though she had taken a few moments to brush her hair and freshen her lipstick, it was nice knowing she didn't have to get all dressed up to please him. The light in his eyes showed he didn't mind the old jeans and sweater at all.

He ran his hands over her hips, then under her to cup her bottom. ''These jeans are almost as soft as your skin. They fit nice, too. Hug you in all the right places.''

He squeezed her buttocks for emphasis.

''So, you like my backside?''

''Mmm-hmm, among other things.''

Lifting her slightly, he pulled her close and kissed her. She looped her arms around his neck and gave in to the hungry stroke of his tongue. If she'd known kissing Adam would be so thrilling, she'd have tried it long ago.

''So, we missed dinner and you promised to make up for abandoning me on the morning after the most significant night of our lives to date.''

''I'm so sorry.''

She kissed him again, then drew back to look at him. Excitement vibrated through her as he ducked his head to nuzzle her breast. Even with them both fully dressed, he made her feel...decadent.

''How can I make it up to you?'' she asked.

''Well, there *is* one way.''

''What?''

His mouth curved into a slow, seductive smile. ''Come walk with me.''

Surprise and a small measure of disappointment shimmered through her. ''I thought you had something else in mind.''

"Oh, we'll get to that later, not to worry. It's just, well, I love exploring this new sexual angle to our relationship, but I don't want it to overshadow what we already have."

Her heart warmed at his thoughtfulness. "It won't. It will just make that part so much more special."

"Right. But I want us to still do the things we used to do as just friends."

"We haven't been walking in forever."

"I know. Don't you miss it? Remember how we used to go for long hikes up by the lake?"

"But that was before we became responsible citizens."

"Having a successful business doesn't have to come at the sacrifice of your personal life."

"A little sacrifice is necessary, at least when you're getting started."

"Lauren, you are the most determined woman I know. I love that about you, but you don't always have to work so hard. You can work smart. It's all about networking and planning. I can show you."

"I can't afford membership in a fancy country club, or to take time away from work to kiss up at parties or other social gatherings."

"It doesn't have to be like that."

She placed her finger over his lips. "I don't want to argue. Thanks for the advice. Let me get my cell phone and shoes and we'll go for that walk."

Adam nodded. No, he didn't want to argue either, so he kept quiet as she pocketed her cell phone. Why was it so hard for her to leave it behind? He hated seeing her bust her butt just to make a living. He hoped to show her that life had so much more to offer.

A few moments later they headed down the driveway to the sidewalk. The moon shone brightly overhead, lighting their path along the tree-lined street. He twined his fingers with hers and they walked a ways in silence.

He wouldn't trade the last couple of days for anything. The new direction of their relationship pleased him more than he could say. It was like a missing piece of a puzzle had slipped into place. Why he hadn't seen it before escaped him. He and Lauren had always been together, now they'd be together in a way he'd never dreamed.

She smiled at him and warmth expanded his chest. He'd made his desire for a committed relationship very clear and she'd chosen this time to open their friendship to this new level. Did she mean for them to share a lifetime of loving, and eventually, marriage and a family?

The cool air swirled gently around them, lifting a flock of birds from a nearby tree as they passed. The houses tapered into a landscaped slope that ended at a small footbridge leading to one of the many nature trails scattered throughout the neighborhood.

"This is nice." She drew a deep breath as they reached the center of the bridge. "The air smells so fresh. I love this time of year."

"Remember when we camped by the lake that one summer?"

Her eyes took on a faraway look. "That seems like a lifetime ago. It was right before Dad passed."

He swept his arm around her. "I just know that wherever he is, he's really proud of you."

She nodded and moonlight glinted off the moisture in her eyes. "He always thought of you as a son, you know."

"He was more of a father to me than my own old man."

"Adam, I'm sorry."

"For what?"

"Well, for never realizing how much it really bothered you that your parents weren't ever around. I always thought you were…happy. It never occurred to me that you wouldn't be. I guess I should have paid more attention.''

The scent of rose petals drifted from her hair as he hugged her closer. ''I was always happy when we were together.''

She tilted her face up to him. ''Me, too. I still am. Even more so now.''

Crickets played their night melody and tree frogs joined them in chorus as he brushed his lips over hers, then kissed her with all the joy in his heart. She was his. Life was as simple as that. She was his to kiss and to pleasure. She was his to love and plan a future together.

With a soft sigh, she looped her arms around his neck and opened her mouth in welcome. Her tongue parried his with a sweet gentleness that left him breathless.

They walked and talked farther along the path, taking time to enjoy the busy sounds of the night insects, the swooping glide of a lone bat and the crunch of leaves under their feet as the trees shed their golden coats.

Much later, moonlight stole in through her window as Adam snuggled her close. It felt so right to be there with her.

She smiled, well satisfied and half-asleep after a thorough loving. ''Thank you.''

''Always here to please.'' He brushed a lock of her golden hair from her cheek.

''Yes that, too. I meant earlier. The walk.''

''We've a lifetime to enjoy the simple pleasures.''

She shifted to face him more fully and her eyes lost their sleepy haze to focus more clearly on him. ''You're so sure we'll be together a lifetime?''

''Why not? We've made it this far, haven't we? And tonight, you put your work aside to spend time with me. That's important. When we have kids your life will change. Work won't be your priority then.''

"Wait." She scooted up in the bed, her eyes wide. "I never agreed to kids. I'm glad you feel so sure about things, but I can't say where we'll be next week, let alone next year. We can't be talking kids already.

"Besides, haven't we seen how life can be pretty satisfying with just the two of us?"

He shifted upward to face her, unease tightening his stomach. "I like what we have, but will it always be enough? You were going to help find me a wife so we could have this wonderful life and kids. I was hoping you would decide to try the part."

She squeezed her eyes shut. When she opened them, a storm of confusion swirled in their green depths. "Yes, but I said from the start, marriage and kids don't work for me."

His chest tightened, the earlier warmth dissipating. "I guess I misunderstood."

She stared at him a long moment. "I'm sorry. Someday, I might want those things, but I can't say for sure. I…I don't know."

"It's okay." Drawing her into his arms, he stroked her back. "I can wait. As long as I have you, that's all that matters for now. There's no hurry."

In time she'd find she wanted the same things. Surely she would.

"Maybe we shouldn't have started this."

He stilled. "You mean us?"

"I don't want to hurt you, Adam. I know you want more from life. You did make that clear. It's just that suddenly there you were…well, wooing me—you were suddenly interested and mysteriously interesting. I just couldn't help myself."

"Wooing you?" A feeling of foreboding stole over him.

"You don't have to pretend. It wasn't hard to figure out after you made such a big deal over the blatant gift-giving issue. I was a little surprised by the cookbook at first, but as you know, I've grown rather fond of it.''

He opened his mouth to respond, then shut it again. Good God, she thought he was her secret admirer. Was that why she'd seduced him? He'd completely forgotten about the guy.

''Lauren—''

''Shh, let's not say another word about it. I don't want to spoil the mystery. If you want to keep pretending, I'm happy to play along. I never dreamed you had such a poetic nature. I love those romantic quotes.''

''Right.''

He should set her straight. He should tell her he'd been so caught up in being with her he hadn't even thought to send her any gifts.

But now their new relationship was founded on a misunderstanding. Lauren had mistaken him for her secret admirer. Was that why she'd started them on this path? Would she regret their new status if she knew the truth?

And who *was* this secret admirer? Adam would have to find out and find out quickly. He couldn't risk having some nut stalking her.

''What are you thinking?'' Lauren asked.

''Just thinking about you. I guess I've been having these secret fantasies from time to time over the years. It's nice not to have to stifle those impulses anymore. I'm glad we're together. We'll work it out. You'll see.''

With that he kissed her again, before she could utter another uncertainty about their future.

Then he made love to her once more, to ease the shadow of doubt that had fallen over them. They *would* work it out. They had to, because the alternative was unthinkable.

7

LAUREN'S HEAD ACHED. After her late night with Adam, she'd gotten up early to go over the contract and put some finishing touches on the marketing proposal for her meeting this morning.

The buzzer on their office door sounded, alerting them to a visitor. Elliot stepped out into the hallway. "Hey there, Rusty. Come on back. I heard you were back in town. Good to see you."

The two exchanged a friendly greeting, then a moment later Rusty entered Lauren's office. He wore an old pair of jeans and a T-shirt. Dirt caked his knees and sweat stained the front of his shirt. "Um, Manuel's in the truck. We're on our way to replant another entryway."

He glanced at Lauren. "Actually, I was hoping I could have a private word?"

"Oh, sure." She moved around her desk. "Elliot, do you mind?"

"No. Of course not." He waved at them, then backed out of the room and shut the door.

Lauren turned to her brother. "Is everything okay?"

"Oh sure. It's just…" His gaze skidded to the side. "Well, I'm a little short on cash. I was hoping you could float me a loan."

"Oh. No problem. Let me get my purse. How much did you need?"

"Um, could you spare a couple hundred dollars?"

Her heart dropped. "Two hundred dollars?"

"The move cost me a little more than I had anticipated."

She frowned. "I don't know, Rusty. You know how I hate spending it if it isn't really necessary."

The worry lines in his forehead deepened. Her stomach knotted. He had never asked to borrow money from her in the past. Surely he wouldn't have asked now if he didn't absolutely need it.

"Look, I guess I can swing it. Can you stop by tomorrow and I'll have it for you then?"

He relaxed, granting her a smile. "Thanks, Lauren, I knew I could count on you. I'll make it up to you, I promise."

"No problem. Now get back to work. I don't want to get you in trouble with your new boss."

"Adam? He's great, the best boss I've ever had."

"Yeah, he's a good guy. The best. Stop by tomorrow after lunch."

"Will do. See you then." With that he hurried from the room, a loud whoop following him down the hall.

Lauren sighed. She'd put a dent in her savings, but she couldn't turn down her younger brother. Besides, she could always cut herself a paycheck. She'd held off, trying not to drain the company's funds, but with luck, Bennett would pay them next week after the commercial shoot.

And hopefully she'd land another contract with her meeting this morning. After checking her watch, she hurried to gather her things. She didn't want to be late.

Forty-five minutes later, she gripped her briefcase and headed down the carpeted hallway toward Clyde Morris's office. She hadn't had a full night's rest in too long and had been tempted to reschedule, but Morris had sounded most anxious to get started on the promotional plan they'd discussed briefly over the phone.

And she was always up for signing on a new account.

She found the correct door, then entered, stopping in a small outer room that opened to a larger work area. A movement to her left drew her attention to a young girl of about six or seven, who was sprawled out on the floor, an assortment of toys and books scattered around her.

The child straightened, her blue eyes wide. "You're the advertising lady?"

"That's me. Is your father here?"

"He's in the back. I'll show you." She rose and beckoned Lauren to follow her.

Lauren eyed the child with curiosity. Children were foreign creatures to her. Motherhood was something she hadn't contemplated since her days of playing house with Adam. All her misgivings from the previous night flooded back to her with a vengeance.

When we have kids your life will change.

What an idiot she'd been. Adam had been right. She'd known full well his intentions before they'd gotten involved. Somehow, she hadn't quite believed he'd been serious about the whole wife-and-baby thing. By the hurt look in his eyes last night, the prospect of having a family had become very important to him, though.

Could she give him one?

Mr. Morris rose from his desk as they approached. "Ms. Bryant?"

She extended her hand in greeting. "Mr. Morris, I'm pleased to meet you."

"Thanks for meeting with me here." He gestured to the girl. "I would have come to your office, but Meggie's out of school today. Teacher's workday. My wife's working, so Meggie came along to keep an eye on me here."

"See, I helped my daddy clean his files this morning." Meggie pointed to a haphazard pile of papers sitting on a nearby chair.

Morris grinned and squeezed the child's shoulder. "You'll be a fine businesswoman one day, sweetheart. Now, run along and let me talk to Ms. Bryant. She's going to help us rustle up some more business."

The look of pride on the young girl's face warmed Lauren's heart. "She's a lovely child," she said as the girl scurried away.

"Ah, can't imagine life without her. We're trying for number two. Wish me luck."

Lauren settled into the chair he indicated. "Well, good luck."

"Don't mind my saying so, but you look like you could use a cup of coffee. I brew it strong."

"That would be wonderful."

He walked over to a worktable that housed an assortment of hoses and attachments, as well as the coffeemaker. "How do you take it?"

"Sweet and light. Milk, powdered creamer—anything that'll do it will work."

A moment later he handed her the steaming coffee. To her dismay, her hand shook as she took the cup. Tonight, after her dinner with her mother, she'd rest. A good night's sleep would set her right.

Gripping the cup with both hands, she sipped the soothing brew. "If you can clean carpets as well as you make coffee, we won't have any trouble."

With a satisfied grunt, he resumed his seat. "I like to think so. Now, let's talk a bit more about this direct marketing. I've an idea or two I want to run by you."

They spent the next half hour finalizing a possible marketing strategy, then to Lauren's relief Morris signed the contract with a flourish.

"I have a good feeling about this. You tell Adam I owe him for putting me on to you."

"We'll do everything in our power to put Morris Cleaners on the local map."

"Indeed we will." He shook her hand, then rose to see her out.

"Come see." Meggie rushed to them as they reached the outer office.

To Lauren's surprise, the girl grabbed her hand, and tugged her toward a makeshift dollhouse she'd made from books and magazines and furnished with assorted items she'd found around the office.

Lauren swallowed at the warmth of the small hand in hers. "That really is something." She knelt beside Meggie to examine the structure closer. "That empty tape dispenser makes a unique lounge chair."

"Do you want to play?" Hope gleamed in Meggie's eyes.

"Ms. Bryant has work to do, sweetheart." Morris took the child by the hand.

Her crestfallen look tightened Lauren's throat. "I'm so sorry, Meggie. I *do* have to get back to my office. I have to get to work on your daddy's campaign."

"That's okay, I understand. No one has time to play with me. Everyone's busy."

Morris ruffled his daughter's hair. "We'll go out for lunch in a bit."

"Pizza? Pepperoni with stuffed crust?" Meggie's eyes brightened.

"If that's what you want."

"Yes, Daddy. Thanks. And remember you said we'd go home early today." She turned to Lauren. "'Cause even grown-ups need to play sometimes."

"Right." Eyebrows raised, Lauren nodded to Morris. "We'll talk later in the week."

She left, Meggie's words fresh on her mind. Out of the mouths of babes.

"WHERE ARE YOU?" Elliot's voice crackled across Lauren's cell phone connection as she breezed along the interstate.

"I just left Morris's."

"Are we a go?"

"It's a go. Apparently Adam wowed him with some of our previous successes. He was familiar with the campaign we did last fall for Love Lists, that dating service. Said he trusted our judgment."

"Great. Listen, don't come back to the office. I just made us a lunch date."

"I hope there are clients involved, Elliot. Otherwise, we can't afford it."

"Not just any clients, doll. I'm talking our bread and butter."

"I'm listening."

"I ran into an old college buddy of mine last night. In the grocery store of all places, but there she was by the frozen foods. Norma Whitfield, but she's Craig now. A real looker. If ever there was one to turn me, she was it. Really knew how to dress, you know—all elegance. Rubbed shoulders with the high rollers.

"Anyway, she married one of them, a wealthy widower with a fortune at his disposal. She's got him opening a string of lingerie shops."

"A string? Wouldn't they be better off starting with just one?"

"This guy's got the Midas touch. He made his money starting profitable businesses all across the country, then selling them off. This time the shops are for her, though, and she plans on keeping them and running them herself. Of course, they need advertising.

"I suggested we all get together to get to know each other, see if anything meshed. She called just now to see if we could meet them for lunch. Of course, I said we'd be there."

"Where?"

"Bones, in Buckhead."

Lauren grimaced. She hated putting so much on the company's credit card. Maybe if she stuck to a salad and the rest didn't order too heavily off the expensive menu, they'd keep the bill at a reasonable figure.

"Lauren?"

"I'm here. Okay, I'll meet you there."

She disconnected, then moved into the far lane. Fifteen minutes later she pulled up to the restaurant's parking valet. The Craigs proved a study in opposites. Norma, an attractive woman of forty-something had statuesque, though shapely, proportions. Confidence radiated from her.

She wore a flaming-red dress and spiked heels. The dress's front took a daring plunge to reveal her abundant cleavage. As if to balance the rest of her body, her hair was piled high atop her head in a mass of bold swirls, in a shade so black it appeared almost blue.

In his plain brown, though expensive suit, Charles Craig seemed small and retiring beside her. How did such a seemingly mild-mannered man amass his fortune in the way Elliot had said? Perhaps he was all quiet brain behind the heavy-rimmed glasses. A bean counter of the first degree. They could be the most ruthless.

"Laurel, darling!" Norma grabbed her hands and planted an air kiss above her cheek. "Any friend of Elliot's is a friend of mine. He's told me so much about you."

She dropped Lauren's hands and pursed her lips as she

surveyed her from head to toe. "Hmm, you look a little run-down, dear, but you have such…potential."

Lauren opened her mouth to reply, but Elliot cut her neatly off. "That's Lauren, not Laurel. I think they're ready for us. Shall we sit?"

"Well, she looks like a Laurel." Norma cast her one last glance as Elliot steered her away.

"She's really just a pussycat." Charles offered Lauren his arm. "She keeps her claws sheathed…most of the time."

Lauren forced a smile as they headed after the others. The headache that had threatened earlier began to pound in her temples. The waiter apparently knew the Craigs and greeted them with much enthusiasm. Norma ordered a bottle of champagne and several appetizers before Lauren even opened her menu.

"You get whatever you want, love." Elliot hooked his arm over the back of Norma's chair. "Entice is picking up the bill. You know we're here to wine and dine you and get you to sign on the dotted line."

Lauren stretched her smile farther and somehow refrained from kicking him under the table.

"I like this 'entice' business," Norma said, leaning in closer to Lauren. "Sensuality is key in marketing Secret Temptations."

"That's right up our alley. And your shops fit all our concepts. We won't even have to fudge anything," Elliot said.

"I'm sure we'll love whatever you come up with. Won't we, dear?" Charles patted Norma's hand. He turned to Lauren. "She was so thrilled to have run into Elliot last night. Quite serendipitous."

"Time will tell." Norma gave Lauren a warm smile. "Anyone can come up with a decent ad campaign. What

I'm looking for is someone I can work with on an ongoing basis. To me, that interpersonal relationship is more important than anything else.''

Lauren returned her smile. ''Certainly—''

''Don't you worry about a thing,'' Elliot interrupted. ''You're going to love Lauren. She's a real doll. Now, tell me about this cruise you just took.''

Lauren relaxed a little as Norma filled him in on their recent trip to the Virgin Islands. She painted a colorful picture of long strips of beach, sparkling water and enough food to please even a king. Charles sat quietly, nodding on occasion. Every so often he glanced Lauren's way and she smiled her interest.

The appetizers arrived and everyone hurriedly glanced over the menu to order their meals, while Lauren kept a running tally in her head. She ordered a Caesar salad and water, then sat up straighter as Norma launched into a description of the shops' start-up schedule.

Elliot waved in Lauren's direction as he leaned toward Norma. ''Piece of cake. Lauren's a whiz at making schedules work. Just give her the dates and she'll work up a plan that'll have the public panting on your front step on opening day.''

''Well, we want them panting all right. *Enticed,* shall we say?'' Norma giggled at her pun, then sipped her champagne. ''Oh, did I tell you what my dear husband bought me for our anniversary?''

Eyes wide, Elliot glanced from Charles to his wife. ''What did he get you?''

''His-and-hers spots at a cryogenics center.'' She beamed expectantly.

''Oh.'' Elliot's eyes grew rounder. ''Cryogenics?''

''We're just so in love…'' Norma clasped Charles's hand. ''We can't bear the thought of losing each other. So when our times come, it's the big freeze for us. Isn't that romantic?''

Lauren bobbed her head at Charles's expectant look. ''Why, that's the most romantic thing I've ever heard.''

''That is so *cool*.'' Elliot laughed and the couple laughed along with him.

He nodded to Charles, who popped a crab cake in his mouth. ''As long as she doesn't give you the big freeze before your time.''

After wiping his mouth, Charles grinned. ''My Norma's too hot for that. She knows how to keep a man's blood warm.''

Lauren blinked. Maybe the man wasn't as mild as she'd thought. Either that or he'd been sipping too heavily on the champagne.

''I just can't help myself.'' Norma shifted in her seat. ''I put on that sexy lingerie and I get so turned on. I'm designing my own line of erotic wear. I'd like it featured in any advertising we do.''

Lauren cleared her throat. ''Of course, that wouldn't be a problem.''

''Wonderful.'' With a clap of her hands, Norma warmed to her subject. ''I think there's something irresistible in the dominatrix concept. Part of the line contains some very naughty leather wear.''

''Yes, well…'' Lauren glanced at her partner. ''I'm sure Elliot could do his usual magic. Depending on how you want to present it, we may have a more limited market—''

''Limited?'' Norma frowned.

''We could broad-base it if we present the line in just the right way,'' Elliot said.

A spark of unease passed through Lauren. ''Possibly, if it isn't too adult in nature—''

"We can work details out later. Let's talk concept." Elliot tossed her a sideways glance.

"You work something up for us." Waving the conversation aside, Norma turned to her champagne. "I'm getting a little low. We need another bottle."

Lauren suppressed a groan as Elliot flagged down their waiter. Giving in, she raised her own glass and drained the contents.

CHILDREN'S LAUGHTER drifted on the afternoon breeze. Adam straightened from inspecting the walkway Rusty had just helped Manuel lay. After Adam's night with Lauren, he'd woken alone in her bed, a vague sense of unease settling over him. He'd thrown himself into work, hoping to banish the feeling.

He turned to Manuel. "I think Rusty's taken to brickwork better than pansies."

"Leave him with me, boss. I'll have him laying a herringbone by the end of the week." Manuel nudged Rusty playfully. "Not that that's all he's laying."

Rusty's eyebrows furrowed. Before he could respond, Rick Ashby, the owner of the walkway and acreage surrounding it, rounded the back corner of the massive brick house. His son, a boy of about six, and daughter, who seemed a year or two younger, trailed in his wake, pumping their shorter legs to match his long stride, laughing as they vied for a place by his side.

He grinned at the pair as Adam shook his head. Rick, one of the landscape architects he often worked with, had it all—a picture-perfect life, complete with this beautiful home, a loving wife and the two towheaded youngsters who obviously worshiped their father as he swung them one under each arm, then ran the rest of the way laughing with them.

A feeling of envy Adam had never known rose up inside

him. Lauren's words from the previous night rolled back to haunt him. He'd been a fool to think she'd so readily fall in with his plans. She didn't want children. She wasn't sure if she'd *ever* want them.

"Miranda's bringing iced tea," Rick announced.

He deposited his offspring in a grassy spot near Adam. The two scampered in a circle, then took off running across the wide expanse of yard.

Adam smiled. "I see why you need the fence."

"They're a handful, but worth it." Rick beamed after his kids.

His pretty blond wife rounded the corner and they raced after her as she balanced a tray in both hands. The youngsters ran circles around her as she advanced to where Rusty and Manuel gathered together their tools.

The scene struck a chord deep within Adam that resonated outward, filling him with warmth. "You've got it made, you know."

Rick smiled, a satisfied light in his eyes. "Yeah, I know."

"Look how nice that turned out." Miranda nodded toward the walkway as she set the tray on the corner of a nearby planter. "You men look thirsty."

With murmured thanks, Rusty and Manuel accepted glasses of the cool beverage. Adam also took a glass. "Much appreciated, Miranda. I was just telling your husband how he has it made."

"He does okay." She pressed a glass into her husband's hand as he swept an arm around her and tucked her against his side.

With their children darting around their legs, the two formed a picture of marital bliss. The longing inside Adam intensified. He took a long swallow of the tea.

"Oh, I played around with the design some. Let me get

you the latest printout,'' Rick said, straightening away from Miranda.

"As long as it doesn't affect the walkway.'' Adam gestured toward Rusty and Manuel. "Don't think these two would care much to redo it.''

"No, not the walkway. I've adjusted the placement of the play area to better suit that slope. That means I had to shift the flower garden.'' Rick waved toward the sunny patch to their left as he headed back toward the house.

"I tried to tell him from the start he needed to shift that garden.'' Miranda lifted her daughter, resting her on one hip.

Adam shrugged. "It's his vision. We're just here to bring it to life.''

"It's about time. All these years of working on other people's houses, I'm so glad Rick is finally concentrating on ours.''

"It's a great place you have here. He's been tinkering with that design for some time. He's certainly talked about it enough.''

"Oh, yes, he's a big talker.''

"Uh-oh, do I sense trouble in paradise?''

"No, not really. It's just that he's been talking forever about hiring a nanny to help with the kids so I can go back to work part-time, but nothing ever seems to come of it.''

"You're not happy staying at home?''

"I've been home for almost six years now. Sometimes…it just isn't enough. I miss working.

"Don't get me wrong. I love my kids. I love being here with them. I have days, though, when I just need to be around adults. I need to feel I'm doing something more meaningful—not that raising my kids isn't meaningful. It's just, I don't feel like I'm doing enough for *me*. Does that make sense?''

Was that what Lauren feared? "I guess so. You don't

want to sacrifice your own needs for the sake of your family.''

''Exactly. I don't want Christie growing up thinking she has to be self-sacrificing. I want her to be self-empowered.''

''I never really thought of it in that way.''

''There's a balance, of course. I still feel the kids are my priority. But I'm not just a mother.''

He regarded her a moment. He'd always assumed Miranda was happy at home. Was it too much to expect a woman of today to want to give up a life of her own to concentrate on raising a family?

''So, it's hard—this balance?'' he asked.

''Extremely. I've been juggling family time with volunteer work I do for the community. If I go back to work, it'll be even harder.''

''But you still want to do it?''

''Sure.''

''So, tell me, are you sorry you quit working to be a stay-at-home mom?''

''Honestly?'' Christie squirmed and Miranda set her down. ''Some days, I'm just not sure.''

''NEED SPICE, think Entice. Lauren Bryant here.''

''Hello, sunshine.'' Adam's neat baritone resonated across the phone line.

A shiver ran up Lauren's spine. She smiled. ''Hi. Sorry I had to cut out early this morning. You looked so peaceful, I didn't want to disturb you.''

''You should have woke me. It would have been nice to start the day with you, instead of abandoned and alone.'' He drew the last out in dramatic tones.

She laughed. ''Poor Beast. I'm so sorry.''

His voice took on a seductive drawl. ''You can always make it up to me.''

"I will. What can I do?"

"How about dinner? I'll take you somewhere nice where you don't have to cook. Then we'll come back to my place for dessert."

"I wish I could, but I promised to take Mom to dinner at Ippolito's. You know how she loves that place."

He gasped. "You mean you're having Italian...without me?"

The memory of sucking spaghetti from his chest sent warmth to her cheeks. "You know I'll be thinking of you the whole time."

"Ah, I guess I'll have to entertain myself then. Maybe I'll whip up some of that salmon with truffles."

It was her turn to gasp. "You wouldn't. Not without me. According to the notes in that recipe, those truffles are a potent aphrodisiac. They drive male pigs to distraction. They simulate the female pig hormone or something."

"Oooh, yeah, I can see what a turn-on that might be."

She giggled. "It really did say that. That's how they hunt truffles. They turn the pigs loose."

"Hmm, well, who are we to argue with pigs? Maybe we should give it a whirl sometime."

"I'm willing."

"So, you could still make dessert tonight."

She shifted in her seat, frustration welling. "I just can't. I have so much to do. After dinner I have a pile of work that has to be done by tomorrow, ads to be approved—"

"It's okay. Do what you've got to do."

"I'm so sorry, Adam. I do want to see you, but I know I won't finish until late."

"And you need to get some rest. You didn't get much sleep last night. I'm sorry I kept you up so late."

"It was wonderful. I wouldn't have missed a minute of it."

"Me neither."

Silence hummed across the line. She glanced at her computer screen, needing to get back to her current proposal, hating to say goodbye.

"So, how's your day going?" she asked.

"Catch any big accounts?" he asked at the same time.

They both laughed.

She said, "You first."

"Did a few inspections. That brother of yours does good work. He helped lay a brick walkway today. I think he prefers that to the flowers."

"I'm glad he's working out. With Rusty, it's like always waiting for the other shoe to drop."

"He's doing a great job. So what about your day—I mean, aside from missing me and wishing you were with me?"

She smiled. "Signed with Morris, then Elliot and I had lunch with a potential client. A chain of lingerie shops. Could be big."

"Sounds like a match made."

"I hope so."

Silence again hummed across the line. She closed her eyes, imagining the shape of his face, the hot urgency of his kiss, the feel of him deep inside her.

"Well, I guess I should let you get back to work. I just wanted to hear the sound of your voice." He paused. "Say something sexy before you go."

Her pulse quickened. She drew a deep breath. "I love the way you kiss me, the way your tongue strokes mine while you're touching me between my legs, making me hot—making me come."

"I love the way your skin's so soft and the feel of your nipples beading against my tongue. God, I love your breasts.

I love how you get so wet when I slip my fingers inside you. I wish I was inside you right now.''

"I wish you were inside me, too." She squeezed her thighs together against the sexual ache his words evoked. She slid her hand low, over her belly.

"Are you touching yourself?"

A loud knock sounded on her door. Without waiting for a reply, Elliot poked his head in. "I've got a few ideas for Secret Temptations. Want to come take a look?"

She straightened in her chair. "Sure, Elliot. Give me a minute."

Speaking into the phone, she said, "I'm sorry, Adam. I have to get back to work. Maybe we could pick this up another time."

"It's okay. I have to run, too." He chuckled softly. "At least I'm leaving you wanting me."

"I *do* want you. I don't know how I'll make it until I can see you again."

"Tomorrow night?"

"Yes. Tomorrow night."

She hung up the phone, her heart thrumming in anticipation. Suddenly tomorrow seemed an eternity away.

FRANK SINATRA CROONED an old tune over the soft murmur of the Ippolito's dinner crowd as Lauren waited for her mother that evening. They'd planned this outing to their favorite Italian restaurant weeks ago and Lauren couldn't bring herself to cancel, even though she was watching her budget and she was so tired, all she wanted to do was crawl into bed.

She took a long swallow of water, willing away the soreness that had crept into her throat. The last thing she needed was to get sick.

Elliot had given her a file of marketing ideas for one of

their accounts. She'd also started a rough draft on a proposal for the Craigs, but thinking back on their lunch, she wondered how hard it would be to pin them down to another meeting. She'd stuffed Elliot's folder, along with her notes, into her briefcase to look over should she need to kill some time.

For once, though, she couldn't bring herself to work.

The throbbing in her head had steadied to a dull ache. Her eyes felt dry and gritty. She couldn't keep burning the candle at both ends. Something had to give, but she couldn't see giving up either her work or Adam.

Closing her eyes, she let the memory of their lovemaking flow over her. When she was with him, she felt vibrant and alive, but was she getting in way over her head with him? He believed she'd eventually come around to his way of thinking. If only she could be so sure.

Delores Bryant, a petite woman with fading blond hair, swept through the entrance, lines of worry etched in her forehead. Lauren waved to her mother and Delores's expression eased as she made her way through the crowded restaurant.

"You look like you need this as bad as I do, dear." Her mother sank into the seat opposite Lauren.

"I do."

The long-buried desire to lay all her troubles at her mother's feet rose up in Lauren. Her mother had been through the struggle of child rearing. Certainly she'd understand Lauren's reservations.

"My property taxes are due, Claire's been laid off, I won't be able to count on her coming up with her share of the bills, and this new district manager is driving me nuts," Delores said in one long breath.

With a sigh, Lauren tamped down her own worries. "Okay, let's take these one at a time."

Their waiter, clad in a green apron, stopped by to take their order. After they'd requested a couple of the specials, Lauren turned back to her mother. "If I remember correctly, your taxes should be paid out of your escrow account. Check with your mortgage company to make sure they received the bill."

"Oh, that's right. I'd forgotten we set it up that way. I just got the bill in the mail and panicked."

"Have you spoken to Claire about her situation? Maybe she has some funds set aside for an emergency."

"She has some money saved, but it won't last long."

"Does she want to look for another job?"

The worry lines deepened in Delores's forehead. "She's like me. Never went to college and depended on her husband for way too long. What a pair we are. How I made it to management level at the store still eludes me."

"You worked hard and proved you could do the work."

"Sometimes I miss the old sporting-goods store. Things were so much less complicated there."

"You've moved onward and upward."

Her mother nodded, the lines of worry still etched in her face.

"There are several personnel agencies that will place her with their fee paid by the employer. They're easy to find. She can look in the Yellow Pages or online. She may want to start looking for temporary work. That might lead to something permanent if the layoff goes on. She does secretarial work and that should be easy enough to place."

"Good idea. I'll suggest that."

Their waiter returned with a basket of rolls. Lauren pinched a bite from one, savoring the pungent garlic taste. "So, things aren't going well with the new district manager?"

"He's set up home base out of our store."

"How's that working out?"

Delores's gaze shifted to her iced tea. "It's unheard of. They have offices downtown for that, but sales are up forty percent. Corporate is thrilled."

"You don't seem so impressed, though."

"The man is impossible, really." Her cheeks flushed. She took a long draw from her tea. "He's always underfoot wanting to know what I'm doing every minute I'm there. I can scarcely turn around and he's breathing down my neck."

"Well, it's good that the store is doing well." Lauren cocked her head. "If he's really paying attention, he's seeing how your hard work is contributing to that."

"I suppose. He did like my suggestion for implementing a friendlier sales-training program. I just cannot tolerate pushy salespeople. I'm so glad you encouraged me to mention it. I'm outlining some of the resources you told me about."

"I'm glad it's working out for you."

They paused awhile as their waiter reappeared and served their entrées. Lauren savored a bite of linguini smothered in a marinara sauce with shrimp and scallops.

"So, you never did say. What's going on these days with Adam?" Delores asked.

Lauren paused with her fork halfway to her mouth. A memory of licking marinara sauce from Adam's chest swept over her. She set down her fork.

"Um, we're…dating."

Her mother's eyes rounded in excitement. "I knew it. Rusty's probably thrilled—his two favorite people hooking up."

"I don't think he knows yet."

"Oh, he'll be thrilled. I am. So, everything's going well then?"

Lauren forced a smile. "Sure. Everything's just peachy." Before she could say another word to dispute that statement, she took another bite of pasta and forced herself to chew.

Her mother had enough to worry about. There was no sense in burdening her further. Lauren would find a way to work out her own problems. Just as she always had.

8

ADAM PULLED UP to the curb beside the newly replanted entrance to one of Roswell's newer subdivisions. His conversation with Miranda earlier had increased his feeling of unease. He knew his notion of a stay-at-home wife might be somewhat dated, but he'd always thought most working mothers worked as a matter of necessity. With today's economy, sometimes it took two incomes to keep a family afloat.

In his case, though, that wouldn't be necessary. If only Lauren wasn't so tied up in her work.

He blew out a breath and got out of the car. Since Lauren was seeing her mother, then working at home, he wouldn't be seeing her tonight. He was too restless to go home, though.

He glanced around the elaborate stone marker emblazoned with the name of the subdivision. Pansies in purple, burgundy and white hues winked at him from their fresh bed of soil. A car rolled past him, heading toward the first row of brick-fronted homes.

He waited for the car to pass, then crossed to the island where Rusty and Manuel worked. "Hey, Rusty, it's quitting time. I'll buy you a beer. You, too, Manuel."

Rusty closed the tailgate on the truck he'd been loading with the plants he and Manuel had apparently pulled. He walked slowly toward Adam. "I don't know."

"Thanks, but I've got to get home." Manuel slipped into

the loaded truck. "You guys have a good time. I'll see you tomorrow." With a wave, he headed out of the subdivision.

A dark car turned the corner, before sliding to the curb behind Adam. Rusty straightened, his eyes shifting to the young redhead behind the wheel. "Uh, I've got to go, Adam. That's my ride."

"Rusty, wait." Adam followed him back to the new arrival, his internal alarm sounding. "Why don't you bring your friend along?"

"Hey there, hot stuff." The redhead slipped from behind the wheel. She wrapped herself around Rusty, who glanced apologetically at Adam.

"Adam, meet Sherry. Sherry, my boss."

"Sherry. Nice to meet you."

Smiling, she acknowledged Adam with a nod, but kept her hold on Rusty. "I've heard lots about you. It was really great of you to take Rusty on and help him get his place. My daddy was just terribly unfair. I'll never forgive him for forcing Rusty to leave like that."

"Your father?" Adam threw Rusty a questioning glance. Had the girl followed him all the way from Texas?

"Uh, Sherry, we've got to run, sweetie." Rusty tried in vain to pry her arms from around his waist, but she seemed to cling even tighter.

"Hey, bro, could I see you a moment?" What kind of trouble had Rusty brought to town?

With a pout, Sherry loosened her grip. Rusty cupped her cheek reassuringly and gave her a quick smile before following Adam a short distance away.

"Look, Adam, I swear I didn't know she was coming. She called and said she needed to borrow some money, so I sent her a wire. The next thing I knew, she was knocking at my door, with her bags in hand. What was I supposed to do?"

"Send her home?"

"I…couldn't."

"How old is she?"

"Eighteen."

"You're sure?"

"I made her show me her license before we started going out. I didn't want any of *that* kind of trouble."

"Does her father know where she is?"

"I'm not sure."

"From what you've told me, he doesn't seem the type to just let her run off without knowing where she's going."

Rusty shifted uneasily. "I don't think she told him she was leaving."

"She ran away?"

"She's eighteen. She's not a minor. She's got a right to live her own life."

"Granted, but what are you going to do when her father shows up?"

"I don't know. I haven't done anything wrong."

"I'm not saying you did." A horn blared in the distance along the busy road fronting the complex. Adam shook his head. "Is she living with you?"

Rusty's shoulders heaved. "Yes."

"And that's all right with you?"

"I guess." He blew out a breath. "She rearranged everything—the furniture, the kitchen. I go to shave this morning and I can't find my razor. It's in the shower, where she'd been using it."

A deep furrow formed between his eyes. "She's been reading bridal magazines."

Adam whistled softly. "That's serious."

"What am I going to do?" A note of desperation colored Rusty's voice.

"Well, we're just going to have to send her home."

"How?"

"I don't know." Adam patted him on the back. "I'll take care of it. Don't worry. We'll work something out."

"Thanks, Adam." His eyes shone with relief. "I should have come to you right away."

"Rusty?" Sherry called from the car. "Can we go?"

"Coming."

A slight breeze scattered golden leaves across the road. Adam shook his head. He had to get Sherry safely home before Lauren caught wind of this. The last thing she needed was to worry about her brother. Somehow, Adam had to fix this and fix it fast.

THE STOCK FIGURES blurred before Lauren's eyes. She blinked. Normally, she had no trouble concentrating on the numbers that often reflected whether or not their campaigns had impacted a client's business. Tonight, however, she couldn't keep her mind from wandering.

Rusty's return, then dinner with her mother had Lauren obsessing over events she'd thought she'd long put to rest. Her father's illness had been a frightening time. They'd all been distressed to learn her father had known of his cancer for a while but had chosen to keep it from them until he could no longer hide his condition. The shock of it, combined with his imminent death, had sent them all reeling.

After his death, she'd come close to losing her mother, too. The memories of those dark times rolled over her—trying in vain to wake her mother, scavenging for food for Rusty and holding creditors at bay with the promise of payments she knew they couldn't make.

Though Adam had been there for her, she'd kept the extent of her mother's despondency from him.

Responsibility had dropped on Lauren's shoulder like a lead cloak. Through necessity, she'd taken matters into her own hands. She'd called a friend of the family who owned a small sporting-goods store, then roused her mother, dressed her and driven her to the store for the interview.

Like a lost child, Delores had followed Lauren's instructions. She'd taken the job and Lauren found part-time work after school, waitressing at a family-run diner. Somehow they'd struggled through the following years.

All the while, Lauren was the one to patch Rusty up when he got into fights—and there were plenty of those—to wait up all night worrying about him when he missed coming home by curfew, then to drive across the state to pick him up when he'd been stranded after a night of partying with the wrong crowd.

She shook her head. She'd had a year of peace while he'd been gone, but now he was back, and if the knot in her stomach was any indication, trouble wasn't far away.

If she worried like this about her brother, how could she possibly take on the responsibility of a child?

She glanced at the clock. It was late, but not too late to see Adam. She just had to talk to him. She had to make him understand that she didn't want children—that she might never want them.

And if that meant she had to let him go in order for him to pursue the life he wanted, then so be it. Her throat tightened as she headed out her door. The sooner she got it over with, the better.

ADAM SMILED as Judith McDougal took a seat across from him. He'd expected a P.I. to have a harder look. With her short brown curls, rosy cheeks and warm smile, Judith presented a picture of wholesome goodness. He liked her immediately.

She'd asked him to meet her at Blarney's, a tavern not far from his house. A waitress hurried by with a tray of drinks for a table near them. The chatter of myriad conversations mingled with a steady rock beat.

Judith leaned toward him over the table, raising her voice so he could hear over the noise. "I hope you don't mind. I have to make this pretty quick. I've got some baking I'm doing for my troop."

"Troop?"

"I'm a Girl Scout troop leader." She shrugged. "My niece wanted to join Brownies, but there weren't any openings in her area. My sister is just too busy, so I volunteered to lead a new troop."

"Oh. Well, you certainly aren't what I expected."

"I get that a lot." She reached into her purse. "My company's licensed and bonded. I've got a four-year degree in criminal just—"

"I'm not questioning your qualifications. You've come highly recommended."

She sat up straighter and favored him with a smile. "So, you'd like me to ascertain the identity of your girlfriend's secret admirer?"

"That's right."

He handed her a manila envelope. "Like I said, she doesn't know I'm doing this. And it's very important we keep it that way. I wasn't able to get much. There's Lauren's business card, and the card that came with the roses. Then I made some notes about the dates she received the gifts."

He cleared his throat. "And the title and publisher of a cookbook I think he sent her. I just want to be sure this isn't some wacko."

"He sent her a cookbook?"

"Right."

"Odd. That doesn't sound like the kind of gift a secret admirer would send."

"Well, it's um…an erotic cookbook."

"Oh." Her eyes rounded. A pink flush crept up her cheeks. "Yes…that's…noteworthy."

"Adam?" Lauren's voice sounded behind his shoulder.

With a start, he turned to face her. His pulse pounded in his ears. "Sunshine, what are you doing here?"

Lauren stiffened as Adam rose to place a kiss on her cheek. The awful feeling in her gut intensified at the guilty look in his eyes.

Her gaze swept over the dark-haired woman. "I was coming to see you and happened to notice your truck in the parking lot."

"You were coming to see me?" A look of surprise with an unexpected measure of delight flickered across his features.

"I wanted to talk." Lauren fisted her hands, too aware of the strain lacing her voice.

Her gaze shifted again to the strange woman. Who was she? What was she to Adam? Who was Lauren to him, for that matter? She was more than his best friend, but they were far from life partners at this point. There were just so many issues between them.

She tamped down her jealousy as he gestured to the woman. "Um…this is Judith, a…friend of mine. Judith, this is Lauren, the one I've been telling you so much about."

The woman rose and extended her hand to Lauren. "It's a pleasure."

"Judith has some baking to do, right, Judith? So we're all done."

"Right. I think that's it." Judith hefted her purse onto her shoulder. "Like I said, I do need to run. I'm baking brownies for my Brownies."

"Girl Scouts. She's a troop leader," Adam explained to Lauren.

"Oh."

Judith nodded. "Well, it was really nice meeting you, Lauren. Adam, we'll talk soon."

"Right." He pulled out his wallet, then dropped a number of bills on the table.

"You want to head over to my place?" he asked Lauren as Judith retreated into the crowd.

"No, I don't have much time, either. I really have to get back to work."

A look of unease passed over his face. He gestured toward the booth. "Then, please have a seat."

She hesitated for a moment before dropping into the space the woman had vacated. He was lying. This Judith woman was more than a friend. Lauren stifled the horrible urge to cry. She was losing her best friend.

Instead of returning to his seat, he slid into the booth beside her. "Look, that wasn't a date or anything. Judith is just—"

"A nice wholesome girl who looks like she'd fit your new life plan."

"Lauren, sweetheart, you're the only woman I want fitting my life plan. You *are* the plan."

"No, I'm not. You want a wife and kids, remember? I want a career and stability."

He gritted his teeth. "You would have stability. Don't you see? I *want* to provide for you. I'd like to take care of you. You don't have to do all this on your own. I hate watching you kill yourself over your work. You look so tired and I have to wonder if it's really necessary.

"You've made it through your first year. I know you have a strong client base. You're not sleeping, are you? Unless I'm around, you don't eat right, either. Sweetheart, you're making yourself sick."

The table before her blurred. "I *am* tired. I know I can't

keep this up, but it's so hard to get everything done that I need to do in a day.''

''And seeing me has really complicated things.''

''Yes.''

''Talk to me.''

She hesitated. If only they could go back to the way they were. She'd never had trouble talking to him before.

His warm hand closed over hers. ''Lauren, it's still me, Adam—your best friend. Tell me what's wrong.''

''I understand that you want to take care of me, but don't you see that I will never allow myself to be so dependent on another person?''

''I know how rough things were back when your dad died—''

''You don't know all of it. You don't know that my mom didn't get out of bed for weeks. That I had to force-feed her because she wouldn't feed herself, let alone me and Rusty. That Dad left us in debt, with no money coming in. That if I hadn't dragged Mom down to Mr. Forester's store, she wouldn't have gotten that job and God knows what would have become of us.

''And even then we were lucky to keep a roof over our heads. He never told us. We never had time to prepare. It was hard, Adam. It was damn hard.''

Adam swallowed. A mixture of emotions raced through him—surprise, guilt, anger that she'd kept so much from him for all these years. Of course he'd known things had been difficult after Lauren's father died, but she was right. He never knew the extent of it.

How could he have not known? Had he been so absorbed in his own misery, he hadn't noticed hers?

He resisted the urge to take her in his arms and soothe away the hurt. She sat stiff and straight beside him. ''Why didn't you tell me?'' he asked.

She wiped a stray tear from her eye and stared at a candle flickering on the table. "I don't know. Family pride? She was always such a great mother. I thought she was invincible. Maybe by not admitting what was happening, it somehow wouldn't make it real."

"But, how?"

"It was easy to make things seem okay on the surface. And I guess it was a little like what you said before. When I was with you, it was like that was all a bad dream. I was always happy around you."

"Was?"

She finally turned to face him. The torment in her eyes sent a shaft of apprehension through him. "It's so hard now. It's just...I saw you sitting there with that woman—the baker of brownies and leader of young girls—and there's part of me that's really...hurt and jealous that you found another woman to spend *any* time with, even if it was all innocent. But then there's this part of me thinking you look perfect together and if I really care about you, how can I possibly keep you from pursuing someone who might want the same things you want?"

"Whoa. There is nothing going on with me and Judith. You have it so wrong."

"She's just a friend."

"Right."

"Who likes children and baking."

"That doesn't have anything to do with anything. Besides, you cook."

"That's really not the problem."

"You think we want different things."

"We do."

"I want to be with you. You want to be with me. The rest will work itself out."

"I need some time."

He squeezed his eyes shut and drew in a deep breath. When he opened them, she was again fixated on the candle. "How much time?"

"A few days. I don't know."

She looked up at him and it was all he could do not to crush her to him. Somehow, he spoke past the lump in his throat. "You get some rest. Everything will seem brighter when you're not so tired."

She nodded as she scooted out of the booth. He moved to follow her, but she held her hand up to stop him. "I'll see myself out."

For a moment, she stared down at him as if she might change her mind, then she turned and walked away.

"RUSTY ISN'T HERE. He's visiting his sister." Sherry leaned against the half-open door, her eyes wary.

A wave of empathy moved through Adam. He felt as left out as she did. He had done his best today to give Lauren all the space she needed. It hadn't been easy. He'd caught himself punching in her number at least half a dozen times yesterday.

He shrugged. "They need some time to catch up. Besides, I came to see you."

"Me?" Her eyes widened in surprise, then narrowed, her chin coming up defensively. "Why? I'm not even good enough to introduce to his family."

"You've met me, and I'm like family."

The door eased open a fraction more. "I think that was an accident. He wouldn't have introduced us if you hadn't happened to be there when I came to get him. He seemed a little upset about it."

"Why don't you let me come in? You look like you need someone to talk to."

She hesitated, then swung the door open. "I don't understand why he's acting so uptight all of a sudden."

Sniffling, she led Adam to the dimly lit living room, where she flopped unceremoniously onto the couch. "He's so cranky. I can't seem to say or do anything right. I gave up my whole life to come here—quit school, my job at the nail salon, left my sister."

"You have a sister?" Adam perched on a nearby chair. The furniture was old, secondhand and sparse, a reminder of the rough times Rusty and Lauren had gone through.

"Becca. She's younger. Still living with Daddy. I wanted her to come, too—to get away from that tyrant, but she was too softhearted to leave him. Plus she wants to finish up high school."

"So, she knows where you are?"

Sherry's eyes widened. "I wouldn't just desert her."

"Does your father know?"

"Hell, no."

"Your sister won't tell him?"

"She wouldn't rat me out."

"What do you think your dad will do?"

Her shoulders shifted. "Who cares? He can drop dead. That would just suit me fine. I'm on my own now. I don't need him bossing me around."

"So you're going back to school?"

"I need to establish residency first, so I probably won't go back until next year."

"You're working in the meantime?"

She straightened. "Rusty's taking care of me. And I'm taking care of him. I bought groceries and made us pot pies for dinner last night. He said it was really good. He ate every bit, too, so I think he meant it."

"You know, Sherry, Rusty's trying to get himself established. I have a feeling he may have borrowed that money he sent you. He's already in debt and working really hard to stay afloat.''

''Well, I tried to get a job. I put in an application at that nail place in the strip mall around the corner. I don't have a car and I'm trying not to use his too much. Not that he minds,'' she added hastily, her chin jutting higher. ''He wants to help me. He wants me here.''

Adam leaned forward and softened his voice. ''Did he ask you to come?''

Her eyes widened, shimmering with all the trepidation of a young girl out on her own for the first time and realizing how frightening the world could be. ''No.''

''But he was happy to see you when you showed up on his doorstep?''

''He said I could stay. He said it was okay.''

''And I'm sure he meant it.''

''Then why is he so moody? I think he went to his sister's to get away from me.''

''Did the two of you live together before?''

''No. I was still at home. We only went out a few times. He didn't even know who my dad was.''

''But you followed him here, without asking him first, and moved in with him, expecting that everything would just work out.''

''I thought he liked me.''

''I'm sure he does.''

''But he doesn't love me.''

''Do you love him?''

The question seemed to take her by surprise. Her eyebrows arched. She opened her mouth to respond, then closed it and looked away. ''I don't guess so.''

She swiped her hand across her eyes before turning back to Adam. ''Maybe I shouldn't have come.''

''That's not for me to say.''

"But that's why you came here. To talk me into going back. Because Rusty's too nice to tell me to leave."

"Would going back be such a bad thing?"

"I'm not living with my father anymore. He thinks I'm still a child. He thinks he owns me."

"I'd be willing to bet you've gotten his attention by now. Maybe he's willing to listen."

She leaned forward. "You think I could maybe negotiate the terms of my return?"

"If he's like most parents, he thinks he's doing the right thing. That's all he really wants. I'm sure he loves you, or he wouldn't be so worried about you all the time. I doubt he wants to see you miserable."

"Will you stay while I call him? For moral support."

"Sure." Adam settled back in the chair. At least something was going right. If only he could solve his own problems as easily.

9

ADAM TURNED OFF the stove. Two days. He'd given Lauren two days away from him. It was Wednesday and he hadn't seen her since Monday night. Though they'd spent weeks apart in the past, these had been the longest two days of his life. He'd meant to give her more time—to wait until she called him, but suddenly he'd found himself headed in her direction.

He glanced at her kitchen clock. With luck, she'd be home any minute now. Even when she worked late, she was usually home by nine and it was almost that now.

A shiver of apprehension crept through him. Kamira had been enthusiastic in helping with his impromptu plan to cook a surprise meal for Lauren, but would Lauren feel the same way? She hadn't made any attempt to contact him since that night she'd walked in on his meeting with Judith.

Since then, he wasn't sure where he stood with her. After two long days and two agonizing nights, he simply couldn't wait anymore. Either she booted him out, or they found a way to make things work. One thing was for sure. He meant to remind her just how good they were together.

Maybe he wasn't her secret admirer, but it wasn't too late to start wooing her. If she wanted romance, he'd give her romance.

If only he knew what she was thinking right now. Had he been wrong to think she might eventually want the same life he now wanted? Funny how he'd always been able to read her every thought, but now that they'd become lovers everything suddenly wasn't so clear.

The front door clicked open then shut. "Adam? Are you here?" Lauren called.

He set down the pan he'd been stirring, then found her in the entryway. His chest tightened at the sight of her. She looked frail and run-down, with dark circles under her eyes. How long could she keep up the pace she'd set for herself?

She pulled a slightly wilted rose from the vase on the table. "Hello," she said and handed him the flower. "I was surprised to see your car out front."

He took the rose, then wrapped her in his arms, relaxing some when she melted against him. "Hello, sunshine. I hope you don't mind. I couldn't wait to see you any longer. Kamira let me in."

"No. It's okay. This is a nice surprise."

"I missed you."

Her eyes held a sadness when she looked at him. "I missed you, too. I'm just so afraid we're making a mistake."

"No. No. Don't even think it. I can wait forever if need be. No pressure. No hurry."

"But that's just it. I may never want the things you do. I just don't know if I have it in me."

He couldn't help the small laugh that tore from him. "It's there, sunshine. Remember our old clubhouse? You were a regular Susy Homemaker. I wanted a he-man fort, but you made it a little haven for us. The curtains, the tablecloth, all those little touches."

"You're talking about games we played as kids. I'm talking about having the guts to live up to the responsibility of raising children. You know I've had a taste of it with Rusty, and to be honest, I'm not sure I'm up to raising children."

"I have never met a single soul who is more responsible than you."

"I just don't know if I can do it. I don't know if I *want* to. Look at all the trouble Rusty's gotten into over the years. Do you know what a load it's been to keep worrying about him? I don't know if I'm cut out for that kind of stress. Maybe I just need to worry about *me* for a little while."

"Ah, what would you worry about? You're not the type to get into trouble."

"That's just it. How can I be sure? I've been so busy taking care of everyone else, I never had the chance to get into trouble myself."

"You *want* to get into trouble?"

"Well, not like my brother."

"Rusty's doing okay." Adam's stomach tightened. She didn't know the half of her brother's shenanigans. Hopefully, Sherry would run home to papa before anything bad happened, like the man coming after Rusty.

"So far. I'm keeping my fingers crossed, though. See, even though he's my brother, it's almost like I've already had a child to raise. How much worse would it be with my own child? I'm not sure if I want to go through this again."

Heaviness weighed Adam's heart. She wasn't sure if she wanted to have his child. The minute she had made it clear that she wanted to be the significant other in his life he had known he wanted to have a family with her. Why couldn't she feel the same way?

Would it be enough to just have her—to not have children? "Who knows? Maybe I'd be a lousy dad."

"You'd be a terrific dad. Look how well you've done with Rusty."

Guilt tugged at his conscience. "Maybe I could live without children."

"Do you really think you could?" She eyed him doubtfully.

Suddenly, he felt more tired than ever. "I honestly don't know. But if it means jeopardizing my life with you, then I'm not so sure."

"Adam, you—"

"Let's not talk about this now. I want to show you something."

He took her by the hand, then led her into the kitchen. "I tried to clean up as I went, but I'll get the rest later."

Dropping her hand, he moved to where he'd been arranging a dinner tray for them. With quick movements, he transferred the sauce from the pan into a small bowl, then set it on the tray beside a dish of strawberries.

She glanced over the tray, lifting lids, sniffing the tantalizing smell of curry, tasting a dip of chocolate. "You cooked."

"I threw the meal together without a recipe. This was my own creation. *Not* from the cookbook. I kind of sautéed everything. I sampled as I went. It's not bad." He couldn't bring himself to use the cookbook her *real* secret admirer had sent.

A twinge of guilt pierced him. He couldn't tell her the truth yet. Maybe once their relationship was on firmer ground he'd explain how he hadn't sent the gifts.

Her eyes misted. "This is the sweetest thing you've ever done for me. I'm sorry I'm so late. We have this new account we're trying to get…and the last thing you want to hear about is work."

"I want to hear about everything that has to do with you." He lifted the tray, then led her back to the den off the far side of the kitchen.

"That's okay. I need a break from it. Oh my." She drew up short and stared.

He held his breath. He'd made a small haven of pillows and a couple of fluffy comforters on the floor, put on soft music, then lit the dozens of candles he'd bought earlier and placed them all around the room. To set the mood further, he'd banked a roaring fire in the fireplace.

"Is it...all right?" he asked.

Slowly, she turned to him. Taking the tray, she set it on one of the comforters, then she turned back to him. "It's wonderful."

Her mouth was sweet and warm, her lips incredibly soft. He delved into the richness of her kiss, pressing her to him and savoring her honeyed taste. Her tongue parried his with the same longing he'd felt for the past couple of days.

"Hungry?" she asked when at long last she pulled back.

"Yes." He made a pass for her mouth, but she ducked and broke away from him, slipping off her shoes as she headed for the pile of pillows.

"I take it Kamira is spending the night at Greg's?"

"She and Nala hightailed it out of here when I showed up. Said we could have the house to ourselves."

"Now, that's a good housemate. And you are a most considerate lover. You worked extremely hard on this meal. I can tell. And we won't let it go cold. We'll enjoy every bit of it." She sank to the makeshift bed on the floor, stretching languorously across the pillows.

With a seductive smile, she patted the spot beside her. "Come now, you need to eat your dinner so you can stay strong and fit for me."

He lay down beside her and she plucked a bite of chicken from the tray. After dipping it in the spicy curry sauce, she ran the morsel over his lips, before letting him bite it from her fingers. Then she brushed her mouth over his, removing the sauce with tiny flicks of her tongue.

"Mmm...delicious. Maybe this didn't come from the

cookbook, but we can still copy their serving instructions.''
She swiped a stray drip from his cheek, then sucked it from
her finger.

''I think you've got the gist of it. Would you like to try
the chicken?''

''Yes, please.''

''First we have to get you out of this. Don't want to get
it messy.'' He slipped her silk scarf from her neck. One by
one he undid the buttons on her blouse, kissing each inch
of newly exposed flesh, stopping to run his tongue along
the swell of each breast.

Lauren wriggled out of the blouse as soon as the last
button came free. As always, her tiredness left her in
Adam's presence. Anticipation washed over her. ''If mine's
coming off, so is yours.''

He let her perform the same slow removal he had done,
and she kissed her way down his hard chest. As he pulled
off the shirt, she ran her hands over him, threading her fingers through the springy black curls that arrowed down to
his belly. ''All mine.''

Her pulse quickened as he tilted her back to drizzle the
yellow sauce in the hollow of her throat. A shiver of desire
rippled through her and he dipped a morsel of chicken in
the spot, then held it to her lips. She chewed the tender bite
as he lapped the sauce from her skin.

''Take off your bra. I want to eat from your breasts.''

Fingers shaking slightly, she unhooked her bra, then
tossed it aside, while he pulled off his shoes. She swept
back her hair, then stilled at the heated look in his eyes.
Warmth suffused her skin and she'd never felt more wanted.

She skimmed her hands over his chest while he caressed
her, seeming to momentarily forget about their meal. After
weighing her breasts in his hands, he kneaded them, then
teased her nipples until they stood proud and erect. With a

sound of satisfaction, he took her into his mouth. Heat shot through her. He suckled first one breast, then the other, laving her nipples to attention, while the fire crackled and the candles sent shadows flickering across the walls.

Moaning softly, she ran her palms across his chest as she pressed her lower body against him, delighting in his guttural response.

At some point he raised his head. "I almost forgot."

With his fingers, he painted the sauce over her nipples. After popping another bite of the meat into his mouth, he licked the sauce from her skin, circling first one nipple, then the next with the pointed tip of his tongue. He again suckled her long and hard, eliciting that sexual ache in the juncture of her thighs.

"Adam," she murmured. "You're getting me so hot."

In answer, he gave her breast one last pull while he undid her belt and slacks. At last raising his head, he yanked the garment from her.

"These have to go, too." Her panties followed the rest of her clothes and she found herself on her back. "I want to kiss you all over," he murmured in her ear.

He started with her face, pressing gentle kisses to her eyes, her cheeks, her lips. She skimmed her hands down his chest, then over his belly, but he stopped her from progressing lower. "This is all about pleasuring you right now."

His words sent a nervous shiver through her. "But I want to touch you—to pleasure you, too."

A slight frown formed between his eyebrows. "Is it so hard for you to just relax and let me pleasure you without you giving anything in return?"

"But it shouldn't be just about me. It should be about us."

"It *is* about us. It pleases me to love you like that." He paused, then continued, "Tell me, if I asked you to kiss *me* all over, would you enjoy that? Say my hands are tied and I can't touch you in return."

Her heart thrummed at the thought. "Is that one of your fantasies?"

His eyes sparkled. "Actually, my fantasy is that I get to tie you up, then have my way with you, but I can see the need to work up to that. I think I can suffer through the new version. If you think you'd enjoy it."

"I could touch you anywhere—kiss you anywhere—for as long as I want?"

He nodded.

She drew a deep breath. "Yes, I'd like that."

He slipped out of the rest of his clothes, then stretched across a satin comforter. Her heart thrumming, she lifted her silk scarf from the pile of discarded clothes. "Are you sure you want to do this?"

In answer, he held his arms toward her, wrists together. She wrapped the scarf around his wrists, knotting it loosely so he could get out of his bonds if he wanted. The soft tones of a violin drifted over her as she let her gaze wander along his muscled length. God, he was beautiful to look at, from the angles of his face to his proud erection.

She stroked her hand over his chest, to his stomach, then down his hard thigh. The man didn't have an ounce of fat on him. He was all golden skin and hard muscle. Smiling, she stretched out on top of him, rubbing her sensitized nipples across his chest and grinding her cleft against his erection. He moaned softly and she brushed her mouth across his. She indulged in one more long, wet kiss, her tongue caressing his with slow strokes, before shifting upward to sprinkle smaller kisses along his forehead, cheeks, nose.

Cupping his jaw, she nibbled his earlobe, then traced his ear with her tongue. He squirmed and she kissed her way down his neck to his collarbone.

"Mmm, this could take a while, you know," she said.

A hoarse laugh escaped him. "I'm not going anywhere."

She reached for the bowl of curry sauce. With slow strokes, she painted the sauce around his nipples, then licked him clean. He blew out a ragged breath as she suckled him, reveling in the taste and feel of his taut bud against her tongue.

He banged his fists against the floor above his head and groaned. "This is torture."

"You want me to stop?"

"God, no."

She held his gaze. "Then maybe I should move on."

His eyes darkened and his lips parted as she trailed her mouth down his torso to the washboard of his stomach. She drizzled more sauce in his navel, dipped a bite-size piece of chicken in it, then held it to his lips. He ate hungrily, watching her as she repeated the process for herself.

"Mmm, that's good," she said, bending to lave the rest of the sauce from his stomach.

Her hair slid over his groin and his erection moved of its own accord. "Sunshine, you're my fantasy woman—my goddess—forever."

"You like the feel of my hair on you?"

His gaze remained intent on her as she brushed a lock of her hair along the length of his penis. His hands still bound, he threaded his fingers through her hair. "Like spun silk," he murmured.

"Shall I kiss you here?" she asked, her lips a breath away from him.

"Please."

Taking him in hand, she pressed kisses down his hard length, savoring the hot, velvety feel of him. With slow strokes, she laved him, her own desire building. Her sex grew moist and swollen. After thoroughly exploring the rounded head, she took him in her mouth. It did indeed please her to pleasure him.

He held his bound hands over his chest and rocked against her, rotating his hips in rhythm to the pull of her mouth. Sounds of pleasure rumbled through his chest and she exalted in the feeling of power surging through her. She closed her eyes and savored the salty taste of his desire. The sexual ache between her thighs intensified.

"Stop. Sunshine, you have to stop." Adam's breath came in halting gasps. "I can't…I can't hold it."

She placed one last kiss to his quivering manhood, then found a condom in a nearby bowl. "I see we're well stocked for the evening."

"Sweetie, could you hurry?"

With sure movements, she rolled the rubber in place, then stretched on top of him again. Shifting her hips, she rubbed her cleft along his length, up, then back again. Heat surged through her veins.

She made another pass. This time, when she drew forward, Adam twisted his hips and slipped inside her. "Ohh…" She levered up over him, her breath catching at the feel of him, the fullness. "This…this is good."

"Ahh, Lauren…" He closed his eyes and bit his lip. He wouldn't last much longer.

"Almost." Fire flared through her. She rode him fast and hard. "Almost." She gasped as the sexual tension neared its breaking point. "Al-*ahhhh.*"

He pressed up into her and it seemed her very womb convulsed in pleasure so exquisite, she felt for a moment they'd transcended their earthly existence.

She collapsed on top of him, his heart pounding beneath her ear. He lowered his arms around her, the scarf tickling her back.

When his breathing evened out, he murmured, "My goddess."

Smiling, she shifted up to meet his gaze. "My beast."

He kissed her, a long languorous joining of tongues and teeth that sent her blood thrumming. She pulled back and drew a deep breath. "We're so good together."

His gaze darkened. "And that was only half the fantasy."

She closed her eyes, fighting back the nervousness. She couldn't quite say herself why the thought of being the object of such pleasure made her uneasy, but she'd said she'd give it a try.

"We won't tie your hands."

She opened her eyes and the gentleness of his gaze soothed her. "Okay."

He lifted his arms over her, then presented his wrists to her. Fingers fumbling, she untied him, then tossed the scarf aside. He'd never hurt her, but the thought of giving him complete control over her sent a tremor of foreboding through her.

One step at a time.

He fluffed a pillow, then patted it. "Now get comfortable. I want you to relax."

With a funny feeling in her stomach, she settled where he'd indicated, forcing her muscles to relax. "All right, I'm ready."

He chuckled softly. "The rule is that I do all the touching. You're receiving pleasure here, not giving it." He shrugged. "Not that having you at my mercy isn't an incredible turn-on."

His palms swept down her arms. "Now, where did I leave off? Was it here?"

He nuzzled her neck.

"Yes, I think so."

He massaged her breast as he kissed a path down her

neck, then across her collarbone. She gripped the pillow to keep from touching him, the need to do so almost overpowering. Drawing a deep breath, she forced herself to lie still.

As his mouth covered her breast, she closed her eyes. Why was it so difficult to accept this from him?

Again, he laved her nipple with the pointed tip of his tongue. She gasped and he moved quickly down her belly, parting her thighs as he skimmed over her springy curls. Anxiety rose up in her. His fingers parted her, delved into her moist crevice. She stiffened and caught his hand. "Maybe we should try this some other time."

His disappointment was clear in the set of his mouth and the furrow of his eyebrows. He nodded, then moved up to take her in his arms, spooning her with his body.

"I'm sorry."

"You don't have to apologize. It's okay."

She laughed nervously. "I guess I'm just some kind of control freak. I like being in charge."

"There's that, but I think there's more to it." He was quiet a moment. "You've spent so much time nurturing others, you've forgotten what it's like to *be* nurtured."

"But you do things for me all the time."

"Yes, but if the action isn't reciprocal, you're uneasy with it. Think about how you harp on me for sending you clients."

Could he be right? It sounded simplistic put that way, but the emotions swirling through her held a complexity she couldn't begin to fathom.

"Don't worry." His breath stirred her hair. "We'll work this out, along with everything else."

She closed her eyes and focused on the warmth and solidity of his body. In spite of all the issues they faced, she drew such comfort from him. Adam was stable, strong and enduring. He knew her and accepted her with all her quirks. A contented quiet fell over them.

After a moment, he shifted. "So, I gave you two days. Did you get it all figured out?"

"You mean us?"

He nodded.

Closing her eyes, she let the memory of seeing him at Blarney's with that Judith woman wash over her. It had taken her all this time to understand what the sick feeling in her gut had been. She feared she was falling in love with him.

But she had no idea what that meant. Their paths were still so far apart. What they needed was time, something she never seemed to have enough of these days.

"No. But I think I managed to get caught up enough to give you that weekend you've been wanting."

"The entire weekend?" His eyes twinkled in anticipation and she laughed.

"Yes, if you still want me."

"Oh, I want you all right."

LAUREN DREW a deep breath and faced her partner the next morning. The solitude and peace she'd felt with Adam last night had evaporated as soon as she'd stepped through her office door. She'd left their world of fantasies to enter a world of harsh realities—a world of deadlines and budgets and dealing with people who didn't always see eye-to-eye.

No doubt Elliot was a genius when it came to artistic execution, but he could be so fickle. And, unfortunately, bottom line had no meaning for him.

"Elliot, I think we'll be fine with just the one couple for this commercial. They play well off each other. There was lots of sexual tension in the auditions. And, most importantly, it fits our budget."

"But it isn't big enough for what we're saying here. What's our theme? Bennett's is the better bagel, right? Well, how can we show that with just one couple? We want to show *everyone* eating at their sandwich shops. *All* the beautiful people are there, enjoying those bagels and each other. We have to show it's a happening place. We cannot accomplish that with just this one couple."

"But Bennett *liked* the one-couple version. Besides, the budget doesn't have room for extras."

"But they're not extras. Don't you see? They're necessities."

Her head throbbed. "Please, Elliot, I know it goes against your better judgment, but could we try it this way? If it really doesn't work, then we'll think of something else."

"If we do it that way, I have to insist we go full color on the Sunday insert."

She heaved a sigh. The phone at the end of the conference table rang.

Elliot reached it first. "Need spice, think Entice. Elliot Star here... Norma, doll! I was just thinking about you...probably working. My partner's a driven woman. I try to keep up... Florida? For the weekend? Sounds exciting. I think I can swing it... Yeah, like old times."

His eyebrows arched as he glanced at Lauren. "Well, you'll have to ask her. Here, I'll put her on."

Lauren gave him a questioning look as he passed her the receiver. "Hello?"

"Lauren, dear, Norma Craig here. I trust I'm not interrupting."

"No, Mrs. Craig—"

"Norma. Call me Norma. All that Mrs. stuff makes me feel old."

"Okay, Norma, what can I do for you?"

"Well, I was just telling your partner that my husband

and I are heading to West Palm Beach this weekend. We would love for the two of you to join us. We could mix a little business with pleasure.''

"West Palm Beach?'' Lauren repeated, stunned.

"We have our own little Beech Baron. It's a twin engine that seats four comfortably. Charles pilots it. We've got room for two more, if you pack light. I know it's short notice, but I won't take no for an answer.''

Short notice? She'd say. It was already Thursday. "Well, I—''

"Humor me. I have this thing about getting to know everyone before I work with them. It's really important to me that we mesh well, that we're of like mind.''

"Well, I'm sure we won't have any trouble—''

"Wonderful! I'll take that as a yes. We'll pick you up in the limo on our way to the airport. Shall we say Friday evening around seven?''

"Mrs.—Norma, this weekend really isn't good for me.''

"I would really hate to have to look elsewhere for Secret Temptations's advertising needs. We've got plans for six more stores in the next four years. We want to saturate the market. We'll have some heavy advertising needs.''

Lauren gritted her teeth in frustration. "Friday at seven will be fine.''

She hung up the phone in a daze. How would she explain this to Adam? With a resigned sigh, she dialed his number.

ADAM PRESSED his cell phone to his ear and turned his back, walking away from where a backhoe carved a neat strip from the side of a hill. "Hi, sunshine, sorry I couldn't hear that. You said something about this weekend?''

Her voice came across a static-filled connection. "I said I wanted to get together for lunch so we can talk about this weekend.''

"Can't get away for lunch today, but I'll stop by to-night."

"I have that dinner with the bagel people. Don't know when I'll get home."

"I thought the wining and dining was over once they signed the contract."

"They're spending lots of money and we have to keep them happy. I'll feel a lot better once this commercial is shot."

"So tell me now what you have in mind for the weekend. Just give me a hint, though. I like surprises."

"Well, I wanted to tell you in person..."

"Tell me what?"

"Promise you won't be upset."

"I don't like the sound of that, Lauren. Don't tell me you have to work. We talked about this. You said you were going to start cutting back on the weekends."

"I know. You're right. But this couldn't be helped."

"It can never be helped with you." He hated the anger burning through him.

"Adam, please. This is for a potential account we're courting. It could mean the difference in us scraping by this year, or really making something of ourselves. It's really important."

Frustration welled up inside him. "Right. And your business is more important than anything else."

"You know that isn't true. I'll do everything I can to try to get back early enough on Sunday to see you."

His stomach clenched. "Get back?"

"I'm going to West Palm Beach for the weekend. This couple has a place there and they're flying us—"

"You're going away?"

"Yes. I'm sorry."

He gritted his teeth against all the old memories—his parents leaving, the feelings of abandonment, Lauren always by his side to make everything better. She was his touchstone.

It was juvenile to be upset over a single weekend. It wasn't as though he needed her here, holding his hand all the time. Any other weekend he wouldn't have objected, but she'd never once missed celebrating his birthday with him and he hated the thought of turning thirty without her.

But more importantly, even after their bout of incredible lovemaking last night, he wasn't so sure they stood on steady ground. He had wanted this weekend to make everything right again. Now she was leaving and he hated to feel slighted, but he did. It hurt that she clearly had forgotten his birthday.

"West Palm? That doesn't sound like a business trip to me."

"I'd much rather stay. You know that."

"Yeah, well, I'd much rather you stayed, too."

"I'm so sorry. I'll make it up somehow. We'll do something next weekend."

"Sure. Call me when you get back."

Without waiting for her response, he disconnected. A heaviness settled over his heart. Would she ever quit putting work first?

LAUREN GLANCED UP from her laptop as Kamira knocked at the bedroom door. "Come in. You just getting home?"

Kamira nodded as she plopped down on the bed beside a scattering of papers and files. Her silver tabby jumped up beside her. "Working?"

"Always."

"Not always. You didn't work last night. How did your evening with Adam go? Things are really heating up between you two, aren't they?"

Lauren closed her eyes, thinking of her earlier conversation with him. He'd sounded so hurt. "I don't want to talk about it. What's up with you?"

Lips pursed, Kamira eyed her a moment, then shrugged while she scratched the cat's ear. "Same old, same old."

"You've been spending lots of evenings at the center."

A quizzical expression crossed her housemate's face. "Yeah, we're just about ready. We should start using the new section next week. I'm telling you that cute little Mark has been the biggest help. I don't know how we would have gotten it done without him."

"He's not so little."

"Well, he's young."

"Just a few years younger than you."

"Lauren," Kamira's eyebrows rose. "Are you insinuating something?"

"Well, you did make that comment about him the other night and you two seemed so cozy when I got home the other day. I felt like I was interrupting something."

"Please. I told you I'm no cradle robber."

"And you've got Greg."

Kamira hesitated. "Right."

"Something wrong?"

"No. Maybe. It's gone a little flat."

"I'm sorry. Want to borrow my cookbook?"

"Hmm, maybe."

"So seriously, was I interrupting?"

"No, it's just…"

"I think Mark has a crush on you. He seemed nervous the other day."

"Really, you think so?"

Lauren shrugged. "I'm no love expert, that's for sure."

"Me neither. So what's the problem with Adam that you

don't want to talk about? When I saw all those candles this morning I figured things were great with you two.''

Tears welled in Lauren's eyes. ''I don't know. As long as we concentrate on the moment, we do all right. It's when we talk about the future that we get into trouble.''

''Uh-oh. He's still talking bambinos?''

''I can't even manage to plan a single weekend with him. How could I ever hope to plan a lifetime?''

''Well, you *have* been working an awful lot lately.''

Unease rose inside Lauren. She was so tired. ''I…need to.''

''Really? I thought you guys were on steady ground now and maybe you could start easing up.''

Lauren drew a deep breath. ''It's just necessary to keep us there.''

Kamira paused a moment, then she shrugged. ''Well, Adam understands that, doesn't he?''

''I think he tries to. Everything comes so easy for him, though. He thinks I should work smart and not hard, but he doesn't realize all the little details that have to be taken care of. It just isn't that simple.''

''But you have been making more time for him.''

Guilt filled Lauren. ''I promised him I'd spend the entire weekend coming up with him. I was going to give him my undivided attention.''

''Uh-oh, something came up at work?''

''An invitation to West Palm Beach with some prospective clients. It's a potentially big deal. It would make all the difference. Once we get them on board I might not have to work all the time.''

''Ouch, so you're going away on this great weekend get-away and he's upset.''

''Practically hung up on me.''

''He'll get over it. You'll see. You just have to plan

something extra special for him to make up. That's always the fun part.''

"I don't know. Sometimes I think maybe we should have just stayed friends."

"Really?"

Lauren shrugged. "No. Maybe."

"It kind of complicates things that you were best friends before, doesn't it?"

"Yes. You know, I think I always loved him, but not in a romantic sense. He was just always there for me. Maybe I was just too attached." She shook her head. "I'm so confused. I had all these old feelings and now there are all these new feelings and I can't tell what I want anymore."

A small laugh worked its way from her throat. "I'm having sex with my best friend and it's incredible, the most fantastic sex I've ever had. I should be ecstatic."

"But he doesn't want to just have sex."

"You know, I can put him first. I can commit to a lasting relationship, but I don't know how I feel about having children. I don't know if I'm up to that kind of responsibility. Honestly, it scares me."

"And he's serious about being a family man."

"Yes, I really think he is, though he seems open to not having kids. How can I force him into a compromise like that?"

"And the longer you're in this relationship, the harder it will be to go back to the old one."

Lauren sat back and thought for a moment. What would it be like to not be Adam's lover? Could they still be best friends? Her vision blurred. "I don't think we *can* go back. If we can't work this out, then I've lost my best friend."

10

"DON'T FORGET your suntan lotion. With that pale complexion of yours, you're likely to burn," Elliot said to Lauren as he entered her office, his arms full of the day's mail.

"We're shooting the Bennett Bagel commercial next week. This really isn't a good time for both of us to be leaving." She held out her hand for her share of the assorted envelopes and packages.

"It's all set. Besides, if you need to, you can handle most anything by phone."

"I suppose so." She scanned a couple of the return addresses, sorting the mail into stacks as he handed it to her one by one.

He paused, perching one hip on her desk. "I can't believe you're not even a little enthusiastic about this trip. White beaches, beautiful sunsets. If I know Norma—and I do—this will be mostly play and very little work. She really hates to talk business."

"If we're not working, then why are we going?"

"Because Norma wants to get to know you better. Trust me, once you're in with her, we're set."

"Great. No pressure. What if she doesn't like me?"

"She's going to love you. I'll bet you get to be her new best friend."

"Well, there may be an opening for that."

Elliot's eyebrows drew together. "You and Adam aren't best friends anymore?"

"It's complicated, since I listened to everyone's advice about taking it to the next level."

"So what's the problem?"

"He wants a serious relationship."

"And you don't?"

"I don't think I *can* have one and still pull my share around here."

"You don't see me cracking a whip. Take some time off. You could use it. I don't understand why you have to work all the time. We're doing okay."

She stared at him, her frustration building. If only Elliot understood how precarious life could be. How the rug could get yanked out from under them at any moment. "You know, we'd be in big trouble if we were to lose just one of our accounts."

As he always did when she broached the subject, he waved her concerns aside. "Why all the gloom and doom? We're way too busy to be on the brink of collapse. I refuse to hear it. What you need is to just relax. Everything is going to be fine. I'm telling you, in a week's time we'll be adding Secret Temptations to our list of accounts. I can feel it in my bones."

He just couldn't understand. Obviously, he'd never had to rebuild his life from scratch. He just didn't have the same perspective she had. "I just don't like cutting things as close as we've been."

He held up his hand to silence her. "Not another word. Let's try for a positive attitude from here on out."

After giving her a pointed look, he returned his attention to the mail.

"Okay, Mr. Positive. So what am I going to do about breaking my promise to spend the entire weekend with Adam?"

Elliot glanced up. "You sure he's so upset?"

"He hasn't spoken to me since I told him I was going away."

"Well, maybe he's communicating through other means." He handed her a thin package. "No return address, but looks like the same kind of label that was on that cookbook. Could be another gift from your secret admirer, who maybe isn't so secret anymore."

"He doesn't believe in blatant gift giving." Hope whispered through her as she turned the package over. The postmark showed he'd mailed it after that phone call. Could it be a peace offering?

With unsteady hands, she tore open the seal. A small wrapped rectangle tumbled out along with the standard folded note. She opened the note and read:

> How delicious is the winning
> of a kiss at love's beginning.
> —Thomas Campbell (1777–1844)
> *Freedom and Love*

"Doesn't sound like he's too upset." Elliot leaned forward as she ripped off the same flowered paper that had covered the cookbook.

Lauren lifted the deep-green and gold scarf, its silky surface shimmering in the light. A shiver ran through her as the memory of Adam's silk-bound wrists floated over her. "It's beautiful."

"See? Everything's all right. Why don't you call him and thank him?" With an encouraging nod, Elliot left.

She rubbed the soft fabric between her fingers.

You've forgotten what it's like to be *nurtured.*

Could she learn to give up control and allow him to nurture her—pleasure her the way she'd pleasured him?

A moment later, she waited with bated breath as Adam's

cell phone rang on the other end of the line. To her disappointment, his voice mail picked up. She hesitated for just a moment.

"Hi. It's me. Just wanted to say thanks for understanding about this weekend. I've been thinking about what we talked about…and you might be right. I really miss you. Please call me."

She hung up. The scarf was soft against her fingers. Closing her eyes, she imagined the feel of it gliding over her naked body—imagined the softness circling her wrists. She owed it to Adam to get over her inhibition. She owed it to herself.

THE SUN SHONE DOWN the following afternoon, glinting off the white sand of the beach. Lauren adjusted her sunglasses. Her surroundings seemed surreal. How could she be here, soaking up the sun? It didn't seem possible. She longed to be back home—to see Adam, make up for ditching their weekend plans.

She sipped her umbrella-topped drink while Elliot and Norma continued their rehashing of "the old times." Apparently they had run around with a wild crowd.

"Do you remember that pajama party we had and the police came, but instead of breaking it up, they joined right in?" Norma chuckled with the memory.

"As I recall, you answered the door in some scanty little black thing. And they went easy on us because you had such a *pleasing* attitude." Elliot pursed his lips in mock censure.

"I vowed my life to sexy lingerie right then and there." The two of them engaged in a round of laughter, while Lauren and Charles grinned along with them.

Charles leaned forward and patted his wife's hand. "That's my girl."

Norma's face brightened. She turned to Elliot. "What do you think about a campaign centering on men in uniform? You know, with scantily dressed women falling all over them?"

"I can see that." Elliot tossed his partner a sideways glance.

She straightened. At last they were getting around to business. "Men in uniform certainly have mass appeal."

"Draw something up." Norma waved her hand.

"Actually, Norma, I've jotted down some ideas—"

"I can't think about it now, Elliot. I'm in a rum buzz. No more business. It's time to play. Come, Charles dear, let's go for a swim." With that, she set down her drink, tossed aside the big straw hat, then threw off the frilly pink cover-up.

Beneath it, she wore a shockingly scanty one-piece, which she wore with great aplomb. Charles made an enthusiastic grunt beside Lauren and rose to chase after his younger wife as she lured him with seductive glances over her shoulder toward the sparkling water.

"Ah, well. We won't be seeing them for some time." Elliot tossed the little umbrella from his drink and gulped back a long swallow.

Lauren sighed as Charles caught his wife in the breaking surf and her excited laughter drifted to them. "What must it be like to lead such a carefree life? Sometimes, I wish I could be like that."

"You could, if you quit all your worrying."

He gestured toward the wide expanse of beach and the vast home behind them. "We're in paradise, a place where time stands still. Worries aren't allowed here."

As he settled back for another long draw from his drink, she tried to relax, but something nagged at the back of her mind. "I'd better call to make sure we're set for Monday."

"You already did that. The shoot is scheduled. Everyone will show up. It's all set. We don't even need you. You know how boring those things are. I could handle it blindfolded. Quit obsessing."

She closed her eyes. He was right. She usually felt in the way at shoots. Since she always bowed to Elliot's judgment, should intervention on their part be needed, her role was superfluous. However, she still wouldn't miss the shoot.

The waves crashed and retreated in an endless rhythm. Drawing deep breaths, she forced herself to relax her muscles one by one. Still, a sense of impending doom crept over her.

After another quick check on her cellular phone, she let out a frustrated sigh. No messages. Why hadn't Adam returned her call?

"Put that thing away." Elliot adjusted his chair to face the sun. "You're making me nervous. The best thing you can do is recharge, so you hit next week fresh."

"Something's wrong. I can feel it." She dug around in her bag and found her Palm Pilot.

"I can't believe you brought that to the beach."

Ignoring him, she punched up her calendar, then scrolled through the days. "I just have the nagging feeling I've left something undone. Let's see, confirmed with Bennett, sent out invoices, paid bills...oh...my...God."

Horror filled her. "I can't believe I forgot."

"Forgot what?"

She stared, stricken, willing the dates to change on the digital display.

"Lauren, you're scaring me. What did you forget?"

Her throat constricted as she focused on her partner. "Today is Adam's birthday."

"Ah, I knew it." Norma's voice startled Lauren.

She turned to find the woman dripping and smiling broadly, Charles by her side.

"I told Charles you weren't all work. Now, who is Adam? Someone important, by the look on your face."

"Her best friend turned lover," Elliot supplied and Lauren choked.

She opened her mouth to comment, then shut it. Had it been any other time she would have been mortified at how her professional relationship with the couple seemed to be deteriorating. But all else paled next to abandoning Adam on his birthday.

Charles beamed and rubbed his hands together. "Oh, a mission of love."

"Yes." Norma squeezed his arm. "We'll need to return right away so you can fix this whole thing."

"Oh, no." Lauren rose to her feet. "I wouldn't dream of asking you."

"But we insist. Don't we, dear?" Charles turned to Norma, who nodded enthusiastically.

"It's just the opportunity I was looking for," she said.

A measure of relief flowed over Lauren. If she could return home in time, maybe she could make things right with Adam. "I would be eternally grateful."

Norma patted her arm. "There's just one thing I ask in return."

"Oh, of course. What would you like me to do?"

A light danced in Norma's eyes. "I've been dying to test out this new lingerie line."

"OKAY, breathe." Norma gripped Lauren's shoulders as the limo stopped in front of Adam's house well after dark that night. The trip home had seemed to take forever for Lauren. Her anxiety had grown with each passing mile, until she felt like a huge bundle of nerves.

"Look, the light's on," Norma said. "It looks like he's home, but we'll wait until he answers the door, just to make sure."

"Maybe I should try to call one more time." A fit of trembling overtook Lauren. How would she ever make it up to him?

"You're here. You might as well ring the bell," Charles coaxed.

Lauren gripped her coat tighter. "I can't believe I'm doing this."

Charles straightened her collar. "He's going to love it. What man could resist?"

Lauren turned to Norma. "I hate that you cut the trip short for me."

"All for the sake of love." Charles scooped his arm around his wife.

Lauren's heart pounded. A tangle of emotions swarmed through her—guilt, worry…and what was it she felt for Adam? *Was* she in love with him? All she knew was that she had to see him.

"Thank you," she said to both of them. "I don't know how to make it up to you."

"Oh, that's easy. Come to my lingerie party next weekend. I'm looking for some feedback on the new line. It would mean a lot to me if you'd come and let me know how things worked out. I'll send an invitation, so you'll have all the details."

Lauren forced a smile. She could hardly think past the next few minutes. "Of course. I look forward to it."

"Wonderful." The other woman beamed. "Now, shoo."

ADAM DROPPED the last of his dirty clothes into the washing machine, then glanced at his watch. He'd spent the better part of the day getting caught up on laundry. He hadn't spent this much time in the basement, since, well, since the last time he'd done laundry.

Carrying a basketful of folded clothes upstairs, he tried not to feel sorry for himself. What did it matter that Lauren had forgotten his birthday? At least he was being productive.

So he was thirty. It was just another day. He frowned. And she *had* called and said she'd missed him before she left. And that she'd been thinking about what they'd talked about. His groin tightened as he envisioned her bound by silk and at his mercy.

He'd tried to return her call, but hadn't been able to get through. Of course, she'd feel awful when she realized what she'd done. Maybe she'd feel bad enough to finally carve out enough time for the two of them to get away together.

A flashing light on his answering machine caught his eye and he headed over to the unit. He must not have heard the phone down in the basement.

The loud ring of his doorbell stopped him midstride. He turned, frowning. Who could it be? The only person he was interested in seeing was soaking up the warm breeze down in West Palm.

He pulled the door open, then stood stunned. "Lauren?" he asked, not quite believing she'd somehow appeared on his doorstep.

She clutched her coat to her throat and eyed him warily. "May I come in?"

"Of course." He moved aside to let her pass.

Her heart pounding, Lauren stepped across the threshold, closed the door, then turned to face Adam. At least he looked more surprised than angry. "Hi."

"Hi." He gave her a quizzical look. "I thought you were in West Palm."

"I was."

"Oh."

"But then I remembered something important. And I can't believe I nearly forgot. And I really want to make things right." She paused and took a deep breath. She was babbling. Since words seemed to be failing her, she gathered her courage and slowly unbuttoned her coat.

Her fingers fumbled with the last button. For the briefest millisecond, she nearly chickened out. She slipped her hand into the pocket to withdraw a condom, then she dropped the garment from her shoulders.

"Happy birthday, Adam."

He stood motionless, his gaze traveling over her lingerie-clad body. Heat blossomed in her cheeks. She'd been scandalized when she'd slipped into the merry widow that Norma had insisted she wear.

The push-up bodice barely contained her breasts. If she breathed too deeply her nipples popped over the top. Narrow strips of black leather joined the lacy body, and to her dismay, she'd discovered the bottom was crotchless.

She drew a deep breath and her nipples rubbed against the barely adequate bodice. The corners of the foil packet pressed into her hand. In spite of the short expanse of leather and lace, she'd never felt more exposed.

"Sunshine," he breathed and scooped her into his arms.

His mouth anchored her, while her body spun out of control at his touch. She met every hungry thrust of his tongue, savoring his warm scent and the roughness of his calloused hands as they moved over her, fondling her hip, her breast, her bottom.

He broke away to nibble her ear and she murmured. "So, you're not mad?"

"How could I be anything but grateful when you show up like this?" He kneaded her breast, rubbing the taut peak against the leather and sending sparks of desire shooting to her sex. "Are you my birthday present?"

"If you want me to be." She tugged at his shirt and he leaned back to pull it off.

"I want." He slipped his hand between her thighs.

His eyes widened when his fingers found her exposed sex, already swelling with her desire. "Sweet. You're so wet."

He swept his fingers through her damp folds, spreading the wetness, coating her with her desire. Bending his head, he kissed her neck, while he circled her clit, beading it, coaxing it to an aching, hard point. Flashes of fire shot through her. Her fingers trembling, she massaged him through his sweats, her throat tightening as he swelled and stiffened beneath her fingers.

"Sunshine…" He thrust his fingers deep inside her, burying them in her heat, stretching the muscles of her passage. With deliberate movements, he massaged her, coaxing the first tremors of an orgasm.

"I want you so bad, Adam. I've missed you."

His sweatpants gave way easily as she yanked the drawstring. Aching with need, she tore open the square packet, then rolled the thin rubber over him. With a throaty moan, he hooked his arms under her legs, and lifted her, pressing her to the wall.

His thick organ probed her, then he entered her in one swift motion. Heat licked through her as he filled her. Each movement of his hips sent shivers of delight to all her nerve endings as he withdrew, then thrust in an ageless cadence. Time spun into an endless moment of bliss. His rhythm increased. He drove into her, fast and furious. She rocked to meet him, her breath heavy, her body responding in a spiral of desire so intense she seemed to melt into him.

She came.

Her cry of release seemed to drive him into a sensual

fervor. Again and again he thrust into her as her muscles quivered around him and waves of pleasure swept over her so intense, she opened her mouth in a silent scream. At last, he cried out and stiffened, collapsing over her.

She closed her eyes and clung to him, her pulse surging, blood pounding through her tender flesh. He nestled his head in the crook of her neck and for several long moments they cradled each other.

The loud summons of the doorbell startled them from their haze.

"Who the hell?" Adam set her down, then slipped his sweatpants in place, knotting them before glancing back to see that Lauren had scrambled into her coat.

Frowning, he pulled open the door.

"Happy birthday, dumpling!" A tall, thin brunette, wearing a slinky black dress and a sexy smile greeted him.

"Yvonne. This is a surprise." He angled the door, blocking Lauren from view.

Blood roared through her ears as she sank against the wall, mortification filling her. He didn't want this woman to see she was there. Who the hell was she?

"Aren't you going to invite me in? I've been thinking about you, Adam. I have a special birthday surprise for you."

"Actually, this is really not a good time."

Drawing a deep breath, Lauren slipped around the corner, then into the kitchen. Irrational jealousy burned through her. He'd been with that woman, made love to her. The sultry tone of her voice said that much.

Her hand on the back doorknob, Lauren fought the sick feeling in her stomach. She needed air. Straightening, she yanked open the door, then stepped out into the cool night, drawing deep breaths.

She had no exclusive right to Adam. She shouldn't be

upset if he kept other "friends" on the side. But she was. God help her, she loved him. She loved him the way a woman loved a man. She'd love him forever.

The same jealousy that had invaded her that night she'd found him at Blarney's ate away at her now. He'd claimed there wasn't anything between him and the woman. He'd probably claim the same about the woman on his doorstep.

And in spite of the guilt in his eyes the other night, he was probably telling the truth. Knowing Adam, he probably felt guilty because he realized Ms. Brownie was a better choice. If not for Lauren, would he be happily pursuing a relationship with one of these women?

What right did she have to stand in the way of his true happiness? She didn't. And she had no business hanging around if she couldn't contribute toward that happiness. Maybe her best contribution would be her absence.

Her legs stiff and unsteady, she headed down the steps, and around the corner. Belatedly, she realized she didn't have her car. Head high, she pointed herself toward home and started walking.

She hadn't reached the end of the block, when Adam's truck pulled alongside her.

"Lauren, please come back. I sent her home. I don't know what possessed her to drop by like that. Honestly, I haven't seen her in months." The truck rolled slowly along beside her.

"It's okay."

"No, it isn't. Not if it upset you."

"I'm not upset," she lied, raising her chin a notch higher and putting more purpose in her stride.

"Then why are you running away?"

"I'm giving you space."

"I don't want any space. I want you. And if I have to adjust my plans to have you, then so be it."

She stopped, turning to glare at him. "Don't put that on me."

"Why can't a guy change his mind?"

"Because…I will *not* have that kind of sacrifice on my head."

"That's up to me to decide."

"Every time I'm with you, it'll be there between us."

"Not if we don't let it. Please, get in the truck. I'll drive you home if that's really what you want. You can't walk the whole way."

She glanced down at her strappy shoes with their spiky heels, then up into his pleading eyes. She took a step closer to the truck. "Adam—"

"It's my birthday night. Please spend it with me."

Her earlier guilt over abandoning him on his birthday washed over her. "I don't know what to do."

He opened the door and held out his hand. "Come with me. For once in your life don't try to overanalyze this. Just live in the now and leave tomorrow for tomorrow."

Drawing a deep breath, she stepped off the curb and took his hand.

11

THE AROMA OF COFFEE drifted over Adam, drawing him into wakefulness. He rolled to his side and found the black lingerie Lauren had worn. He pressed the garment to his nose, inhaling her musky scent.

She'd been every man's fantasy last night.

After a long stretch, he padded nude into the kitchen. She turned from the toaster when he entered, her eyes widening as she scanned him from head to toe.

"Good morning," she greeted him.

She wore one of his T-shirts. Its hem brushed the tops of her thighs. Damn, she looked good, all rosy-cheeked and bright-eyed.

"We should make a rule," he said, advancing on her.

When he reached her, he skimmed his hands up her thighs, under the shirt and encountered only her smooth skin. He bunched the shirt up, then dragged it over her head. "When we're alone together, clothes are prohibited. Unless you're wearing something like you wore last night. That was positively erotic."

He rubbed himself against her and her nipples hardened against his chest.

"You liked that?" she asked.

"Oh yeah."

"It came from Secret Temptations. They're the ones we were courting down in West Palm."

"That was mixing business with pleasure. Maybe there's hope for you yet."

"Hope for us, you mean."

"I'll always have hope for us."

"Even though I'm a workaholic?"

He pressed his forehead to hers and smiled. "Admitting it is the first step."

"I don't know what the future holds for us, but I want to find a way, Adam. I really want to be with you."

"Then be with me, love. It's that easy."

"I'm here today."

"That's easy. It's Sunday. Everyone knows Sunday is a day of rest. Not working on a day you're not supposed to work doesn't count. And it still isn't the entire weekend I asked for."

"But it's a start."

"You'll give me the whole day?"

"Every minute of it."

"Then let's not waste a second."

"SO, WHAT DO YOU think of this one?" Lauren pointed to an elaborate drawing of a wolf. "It's beastly. I'd think of you every time I saw it."

"You'd get a tattoo for me?" Adam grinned, unaccountably touched by the thought. They'd wandered into a piercing and tattoo shop after a leisurely lunch in Little Five Points.

"I mean, hypothetically speaking. I'm not as impulsive as you. *If* I were to get a tattoo, would you like the wolf? I've always felt drawn to them."

"Wolves mate for life. I'd say I can relate to that."

Her smile faltered. "Let's walk some more."

He blew out a breath and followed her as she headed for

the sidewalk. Had the mere reference to the future sent her running?

"Why don't I buy you a cup of coffee?" he asked as he caught up with her.

She nodded. They walked without speaking for the short distance to the coffee shop. Cars passed on the street beside them, people hurried or wandered by, and a woman pushing a toddler in a stroller walked along in front of them.

Lauren seemed to relax once they settled at a small table out front, their cardboard cups steaming in the cool air. She took a sip. "That hits the spot."

A breeze swept up, ruffling her hair. She smiled and in that moment Adam could have easily committed to her for a lifetime. Why was it so difficult for her to do the same? All he wanted was to take care of her—to ease the lines of strain from her gentle face.

The woman with the stroller stopped at a nearby table. Her young son fussed as she answered the summons of her cell phone. She juggled the phone and the stroller, rocking him in a soothing way as she talked to her caller. But the longer she talked, the fussier the little boy became, until she ended the call, then picked him up.

"I just can't imagine it." Lauren swirled her coffee. "Or maybe I can. The simplest task, like answering the phone, turns into a two-handed juggling act."

"But look at him now." Adam gestured toward the child, happily playing peekaboo with his mother.

"I know. I know." She stood with her drink. "Let's just walk some more."

"Sure, sunshine, whatever you want." He took her arm and guided her back onto the walkway.

She was definitely running again, from anything that reminded her of the family life he longed for. Would he have the fortitude to keep up?

If only he could find a way to give her a taste of that life—to take her away from the hustle and bustle and let her see how stress free and happy they could be.

The way they'd been when they were younger.

LAUREN'S ALARM CLOCK jolted her awake. Swearing under her breath, she hit the off button, and rolled to her side. Adam snaked his arm around her and pulled her back beneath the warm blanket.

She snuggled into him, dreading parting from him and facing her hectic work schedule. With the shoot first thing, the day promised to be endless. God, she was tired. "Why can't every day be Sunday?"

"It can." He rolled on top of her, his body warm and heavy. Bending his head, he flicked his tongue across her nipple. One pass, two, until it beaded to a rounded point.

"Mmm, that's very nice, but we don't have time to start anything. I have to get going."

He continued to taste her, while parting her legs and delving his fingers into the folds of her femininity. She moaned and made a halfhearted attempt to dislodge him. "You'll make me late for the shoot."

"So be late," he murmured against her breast.

Time stretched and stilled as his fingers traced her nether lips, then stroked her nub to attention. She ran her hands over his chest, unable to keep from touching him. He kissed her neck, then moved again to her breast, suckling her until she sighed in frustration, torn between her growing need for him and the relentless compulsion to get to work.

He left her breast to nuzzle her cheek. She turned her head before he kissed her senseless, even as his fingers strummed her into a fine state of arousal. Her conscience prickled as she plucked at his nipples and her blood heated.

"I can't walk in late. Once they…aahhh…start shooting, the studio's…ohhh…sealed."

"Then…" As he made one last pass over her tender flesh, orgasmic tremors rippled through her. "Don't…" He slipped two fingers into her slick passage, pressing deeper as she gasped and her muscles contracted. "Go."

"Yes…ahhh…yeeesss!"

This time, when he brushed his lips over hers, she kissed him. His tongue delved into her mouth and she met him stroke for stroke, losing herself in his intoxicating spell. When at last he lifted his head, his eyes were alight with pleasure.

"There now. That wasn't so difficult. Was it?"

"Oh no. Not at all." She nipped his chin as she felt her way down his body to his erection. God, she loved the feel of him as he pulsed hot and hard against her hand.

"You did that quite well. You've never done that before, have you?"

She blinked. "You think I've been faking it before now?"

He laughed, then dropped a kiss on her nose. "I wasn't talking about your orgasm, sweet."

"Oh." She frowned, suspicion growing inside her. "Then what did I just do for the first time?"

He gave her a look that seemed to say she was pulling his leg. "You just agreed to play hooky with me today."

LAUREN DREW a deep breath as Adam opened his trunk and waited patiently. She made her way slowly to stand beside him. "I'm still not so sure about this."

"Come now, you can do it."

"This is silly, you know. I can't believe I let you talk me into taking the day off, especially with the bagel shoot this morning."

"Elliot said he could handle it. You said yourself that's his area of expertise." He held out his hand.

With a sigh, she handed him first her Palm Pilot, then her cell phone. "It is. He's in his element there, encouraging the director, fussing over the actors and watching his ideas come to life. He'll probably schmooze the client better than I could. He and Bennett have a great rapport. It'll be all right."

"Of course it will." He removed a large picnic basket and blanket from the trunk before shutting it.

Whistling happily, he shifted the blanket to his shoulder and reached for her hand. The moment his fingers twined with hers, her apprehension lifted. He always managed to instill a feeling of ease in her. Everything *would* be all right. She'd take this day and make the most of their time together.

They picked their way along an overgrown trail, one they hadn't walked in more years than she could remember. She brushed aside a cobweb. "It doesn't look as though anyone's been here in ages."

"I'll bet no one else has ever discovered this spot."

She'd always loved the privacy of their secret place by the lake, but suddenly the little inlet's isolated location took on a whole new meaning. Her body warmed as she touched the scarf at her throat. Did she have the guts to let him tie her with it? Adam's hand felt warm and strong. The heat of his body radiated out to her.

He caught her eye and awareness sizzled between them. Her heart thumped in anticipation.

Patches of sunlight peeked through the overhead branches, dappling the leaf-strewn path. They broke into a clearing that was bathed in golden sunlight. The sun's rays danced across the water on the far side of the open space.

A mixture of oaks, pines and maples formed a barrier along one side, shielding them from the outside world.

Happiness bloomed in her as she grinned up at the bright blue sky. "It's even more beautiful than I remember."

He set the basket and blanket down on a grassy spot. "Glad you came?"

"Yes."

Her pulse quickened as she turned to him. His eyes shone and the wicked curve of his mouth held a sexual promise. Why had it taken her all these years to notice him? He opened his arms and she stepped into his embrace.

The warmth of the sun played on her face as she smiled up at him. "I never realized the romantic draw of this place before."

"We were fools. Think of all the opportunities we missed."

"We'll just have to start making up for it today."

Tingles of excitement raced through her as his mouth covered hers. With deliberate slowness he caressed her lips with his, before deepening the kiss. Her blood warmed.

Long moments later he pulled back. "Hungry?"

"You know, I don't think I had much of an appetite before we got together."

They spread the blanket across the springy grass. "I've got to say, mealtime *has* taken on a whole new meaning."

She smiled as he opened the picnic basket, then began unpacking their meal. "Are those strawberries?"

"And whipped cream." He opened the container with a flourish.

"Very cliché."

He snatched the whipped cream away. "Well, you needn't indulge, then."

"I'm all for a good cliché."

He held the treat out of her reach. "I thought we had a rule."

"What rule?"

"We're all alone."

"Yes, so give me the whipped cream."

"Not until you're naked." His smile wide, he yanked his shirt over his head, then undid his belt. "First one undressed is the first to eat."

Laughing, she followed suit, excitement racing through her as the sun caressed her skin. In a flurry of flying clothes, she rushed to bare it all.

"Ah, I win."

She glanced up as she skimmed her jeans down her legs. Her breath caught. Sunlight gleamed across his broad chest. He knelt beside her like some golden god, sculpted by every woman's fantasy.

And he was all hers.

A sudden shyness crept over her. "Not fair. I had more to take off."

"No excuses. Lie back. Get comfortable. I'll take these." His calloused palms brushed her legs as he slipped off her panties.

She swallowed, her pulse racing. She leaned back on the blanket, naked, except for the scarf. The warm rays touched her in places she never dreamed they would. It was a thrilling sensation.

He stretched out beside her and fingered the silky scarf. "This is pretty."

Her heart thrummed as she slowly untied it. "It's soft and silky."

"So it is."

With the now-familiar boldness racing through her, she unknotted the square, then skimmed it over her breasts.

"'How delicious is the winning of a kiss at love's beginning,'" she recited the quote that had come with the gift.

Adam drew back and his eyes narrowed briefly, then his expression cleared. Gently, he took the scarf from her, then set it by the basket. "It's lovely on you, but we don't want to stain it."

She opened her mouth to protest, but he handed her a strawberry. "You hold this. And…this." He scooped a handful of whipped cream onto her belly.

Feeling a little as though she'd been given a reprieve, she sighed, squirming as the cool substance touched her heated skin. Goose bumps rippled down her arms. Adam leaned over her, dipping his tongue into her navel to capture a taste of the cream. She held the strawberry to his mouth and he bit almost to her fingertips, his lips warm and soft.

"Mmm, tasty," he murmured as he chewed.

"It's nice to share."

He took the rest of the strawberry from her and swirled it in the remaining whipped cream, before holding it to her lips. Sweetness burst across her tongue as she took the morsel into her mouth. "Oh, that's good."

"Let's have another."

The second strawberry he used like a paintbrush, dipping it in the whipped cream, then stroking it across her nipples. "I might have paid more attention in art class if we'd had projects like this."

He coated the strawberry again and made another pass over her nipples, circling each crest, until it budded. Heat arrowed through her, invoking a deep pulsing in her sex. She shifted against the blanket.

"Do you like this?" He ran the fruit down between her breasts, then swirled it again in her navel.

"Yes."

"Me, too." His breath fanned across her breast.

When he took her in his mouth, she moaned softly and moved against him. He laved her nipple, teasing it to a hard point.

She laced her fingers through his hair and held him to her as he suckled her for long, endless moments. When she thought she might die if he didn't move on, he lifted his head, then shifted to her other breast. A small cry escaped her as he continued the pleasurable assault, his tongue circling the aching point.

"Adam, you're driving me crazy."

He kissed his way up her neck to murmur in her ear, "Have you made more cream for me?"

"Yes, and you can eat as much of it as you want," she whispered, amazed at her own words.

A satisfied rumble rose in his chest. He shifted, his hip skimming her arm as he parted her legs. Unable to look away, she watched as he sifted his fingers through her triangle of hair, then traced the strawberry over her swollen sex.

Her fingers itched to touch him. Rolling to her side, she reached for his erection. He drew a sharp breath, but moved to better accommodate her, even as his mouth closed over her.

She clasped his hardness, pulling him closer and bending to close the gap, until her lips brushed his soft flesh. She pleasured him as he pleasured her, thrilling to his touch and the tremors of arousal passing through him.

Heat flared in her. Closing her eyes, she followed her instincts, tracing his length with her tongue, nibbling along the rounded tip, before taking him into her mouth. While he worked her clit into a point of burning need, she savored the taste and feel of him, lost in the give-and-take of their loving.

He broke away from her, his breathing rough and heavy. "I want to be inside you."

Nodding through a sensual haze, she welcomed him as he settled between her legs. "Wait, we almost forgot."

Twisting, she found a condom in the basket, then they both hurried to roll it over his length. With a twist of his hips, he planted himself deep inside her.

"Ohhh, Adam." Fire licked through her, but he held back, drawing out their joining with long, slow thrusts.

"It...feels...so...good."

"Yes." She traced her nails down his back and rocked her hips in cadence to his steady rhythm.

That place deep inside her tightened and swelled. She closed her eyes and let the blissful waves carry her even higher. He groaned her name as he pushed hard into her. She cried out and indescribable pleasure burst through her, shattering the tension and sending her over the edge.

She lay with him in the sunshine, warm and satisfied and more relaxed than she could ever remember being. No thoughts of the past. No thoughts of the future. Only now, this moment existed.

She smiled up at him. "Okay, flip over. It's high time I examined this tattoo. I've only caught glimpses of it so far and it's driving me to distraction.

"You promised you wouldn't make fun."

"I won't. I love that you're so confident in your masculinity that you can wear a rose on your ass."

Yes, this was exactly what she'd needed. A day of feasting and frolicking.

Why hadn't she thought of it sooner?

"WHAT WAS I THINKING?" Lauren pressed her palms to her suddenly aching head and squeezed her eyes shut.

Adam glanced at her from his spot behind the wheel as

they raced back to Atlanta. "I'm sure it's all fixable. You know how Elliot is prone to overdramatizing everything."

Anger boiled up inside her. "Don't make light of this, Adam. We're talking about my livelihood here. He said Bennett followed the director off the set, after yelling something about breach of contract."

She shoved her cell phone back into her bag, wishing she'd left it in the trunk and was still oblivious to the chaos that had ensued in her absence. "I should have been there."

"You couldn't have known."

"I should never have let you talk me into taking the day off."

"You were exhausted. How do you know you would have made a difference if you'd been there?"

"I would have reined Elliot in. I just never thought he'd argue with a client. He and Bennett have always gotten along—seen eye-to-eye on everything."

"Look, we'll go right now to see Bennett—"

"*We* won't be doing anything. *I'll* take care of this. You've done enough already."

"I can explain to Bennett—"

"Damn it, Adam, will you just butt out? You can't fix everyone else's problems. Can't you see where all your help has gotten me?"

His eyes narrowed. "So, this is my fault?"

"You and your great idea to play hooky."

"Up until you picked up that phone you were perfectly happy with it."

Her cheeks burned. While she basked naked in the sun, her business had nearly gone to ruin. "You don't understand. We *can't* lose that account."

"You don't know that you have."

"If that commercial doesn't air on time, which I don't see how it can after today's debacle, then we *are* in breach of contract and Bennett has every right to take his business elsewhere.'' Her voice rose to an almost hysterical pitch.

''Calm down.''

''Don't tell me to calm down! Do you have any idea how much time and money we have tied up in that campaign?''

''I'm just saying, it doesn't make sense for Bennett to walk away. He'd be better off trying to resolve this with you than to start over from scratch elsewhere.''

''He already walked away.''

''People do things in the heat of the moment.''

A dry laugh worked its way from her throat. ''Don't I know it.''

''What is that supposed to mean?''

''Just that sometimes people *do* react to the heat of the moment.''

''And then later regret it?''

She lifted her chin. ''Yes.''

''Lauren—''

''Don't.'' She held up her hand to stop him. ''Just take me home.''

What an idiot she'd been. How had she let him talk her into missing the shoot? She'd been thinking with the wrong body part, for sure. Well, she wouldn't make this mistake twice. She folded her too-pink arms. She'd been burned in more than one way today.

And she didn't intend to let that happen again.

12

"WHERE IS RUSTY?" Adam slammed his truck door, then stomped over to where Manuel lifted a small pear tree from the back of his truck.

"He...uh...had an errand to run. He'll be back."

Adam's already black mood darkened. He grabbed a second tree from the open bed. "You two were supposed to finish this job this morning. When is he getting back?"

Manuel shrugged, keeping his eyes averted. "Don't get angry, boss. I'm sure he'll be here any minute."

"Chris and Eric are busy at Town Center. Guess that inspection at Cross Creek will have to wait. I promised we'd be out of here this afternoon."

"Mrs. Edington has already come out twice, asking how we're doing. She's planning some party tonight or something."

"Then we'll just have to get the job done." Adam frowned. His day had been plenty full without having to pick up Rusty's slack.

With a shake of his head, he followed Manuel. Maybe the hard work would improve his temper. God knows, between Lauren and her brother, he needed to vent some of this frustration.

Rusty showed up an hour later, his eyes wide as he spotted Adam. "Adam, hi. I didn't know you would be stopping by."

Adam stood, wiping the dirt from his hands. "We had an agreement when you took this job."

"Right. I know. I'm sorry. It's just that…"

"It's what?"

The young man's expression hardened. "I wish you hadn't meddled in my business."

Adam stared at him, incredulous. "Meddled?"

"Why'd you have to talk Sherry into going back to her old man? I've just come from trying to convince her to stay, but she said her dad's increasing her allowance and letting her move into the garage apartment."

He stormed away a couple of steps, then stomped back. "She was perfectly happy until you butted in."

"You *wanted* her to leave."

"Well, maybe for a while, but…" Rusty's shoulders sagged. "All of a sudden she's so excited about going back and she's talking about this guy from there and he's calling, and she's saying she hopes we can still be friends…it just doesn't feel right—her leaving."

"Rusty, you can't tell me you suddenly have feelings for this girl—"

"What if I do? What would you know about it, anyway? It's not like you're some expert on love or anything."

Adam ground his teeth. What *did* he know about love? He had thought he and Lauren were headed in that direction, but now she wouldn't give him the time of day. She wasn't even returning his phone calls since yesterday.

"Maybe you have a point. I'm no expert, for sure. But I'm willing to bet I know more than you think I do."

"Ha, how? When have you ever had a relationship that lasted more than a few weeks?"

Anger simmered through Adam at Rusty's insolent tone. Had he been such a bad role model? "I've got one pretty good relationship right now that's lasted twenty some years."

"Ah, hell, Adam, I'm not talking about what you and Lauren have. I mean a *real* relationship—like between a man and a woman."

"And what are we?"

"You know what I mean."

"Yeah, I know." Adam gazed steadily at him until the youth's eyes widened.

"You...and my sister?"

"Since right before you got back."

Rusty's eyes narrowed. "Well, that's just great."

"It was until yesterday."

"Well, good. You might as well be miserable, too. It's only fair." He stalked off toward Manuel.

Adam glared after him. He didn't have time for this. "Manuel," he called. "Can the two of you wind this up within the hour?"

"Sure, boss. We're just about done. You go on."

With a curt nod, Adam turned, then headed for his truck. Meddled? Is that what Rusty thought? Obviously, Lauren and her brother did *not* appreciate his help, even though he had meant well.

So much for good intentions. It seemed all he'd managed to do was muck things up. Well, from now on, maybe they could fix their own problems.

"I'M SORRY, Ms. Bryant, Mr. Bennett is still in a meeting," Bennett's secretary recited across the phone line.

Lauren sighed. "Will you please tell him I called... again?"

"Certainly."

"When should I try him back?"

"He's booked for the rest of the day, but I will give him your message. Is there anything else I can do for you?"

Get him to call me back. Ask him to be merciful? "No. Thank you. I'll try him back later."

Elliot peeked in through her open door as she disconnected. "Still no luck?"

She shook her head, staring at the bills that had arrived in the day's mail. She had another stack she'd just paid. They had to work this out soon.

"I'm so sorry, doll. Guess I went a little too far. I'm going to fix it. You'll see. But I have to say, that director didn't know his—"

"What's done is done. I should have been there, so I'm as much to blame. We'll find a way through this."

"It's not the end of the world. We have other clients. Besides, I'm guessing Norma's about ready to sign."

"Is she ready to come in for a presentation?"

"I called her after the fiasco yesterday. Thought I might be able to soothe over the bad news with a little good news. The message on her voice mail says they're out of town, but they'll be back in a couple of days and I have a really good feeling about that account.

"I know her. I know what she likes and I'm telling you, she's going to flip over that men-in-uniform campaign. If I do say so myself, the whole hero-worship angle will have the women flocking to the store opening in droves. I know just the models to use."

"Well, you keep working on that. We'll keep our fingers crossed."

He nodded, then left. With a groan, she dropped her head to her folded arms. In spite of her long weekend, she'd never felt more drained. Why did life have to be so hard?

KAMIRA SET a steaming cup of tea before Lauren. "Drink up. It'll help you relax."

Lauren glared at her. "That's a dirty word."

"Tea?"

"Relax."

With a shake of her head, Kamira sank onto the sofa beside her. "You can't let what happened the other day get you down. Things always have a way of working out for the best. Maybe you're better off without that bagel account."

"I've left half a dozen messages over the past two days and Bennett hasn't returned one call."

"Maybe he just needs some time to cool off."

"Well, I'm heading over there tomorrow and I'm not leaving until he sees me."

"You go get him, girl."

Lauren raised her teacup. "I'll grovel, if need be. He just has to give us a second chance."

"How could he say no to you? It'll work out."

"Right." She took a long swallow of the warm brew, letting it soothe the tightness in her throat.

She could do it. She could convince Bennett to let them reshoot the commercial. And she'd be sure to be there this time to see that all went well.

"You've got that other big account you're working. That looks good, doesn't it?" Kamira asked.

"I don't know. It's hard to say."

"Well, you said this lingerie woman would sign if she decided she liked you. And if she cut her trip short to help you out with Adam, she must like you."

Lauren closed her eyes against the memory of Adam's heated gaze as she stood before him in the merry widow. She'd do better to remember how he'd coerced her into abandoning her real duties. Blinking, she refocused on her current situation.

"I guess so, but getting her to talk business is complicated. Elliot says we have to let her come to it on her own. The trouble is that she doesn't ever seem to want to discuss it.''

''Well, they're going to have to make a decision soon to advertise their store opening, right?''

''Yeah. They really need to get on the ball.''

''They'd be fools not to give their business to Entice. It's like the two were meant to work together. I think you should just quit worrying. They're bound to sign with you. I just can't see how you could work so hard and it not pay off. That would be too unfair.''

Frowning, Lauren sipped more of the tea. She wouldn't comment on the unfairness of the world. She'd get too depressed if she did.

''Enough about me and my troubles. What's up with you these days?'' she asked Kamira.

Her housemate was quiet a moment, then she sighed. ''Greg and I broke up.''

Guilt filled Lauren. Here she'd been dwelling on her own misery, when Kamira was dealing with a breakup. ''Oh, honey, I'm so sorry.''

''It's okay, really. I'm cool with it.''

''You are? So, tell me what happened.''

''Well, I liked your idea about the cookbook, but when I stopped by with a can of whipped cream, he wasn't so enthusiastic.''

''Really?''

''He was a little put out. Actually, he was a lot put out.''

''You're kidding. I thought all guys went for that stuff. Was it just the whipped cream maybe? Could he have a food allergy, or maybe he just doesn't like the stuff.''

''No. He said he didn't know I was into kinky sex and if that was what I wanted, I should look for it elsewhere.''

"No way."

"Yes. So I took my whipped cream and I left."

"I'm so sorry. I should never have suggested it."

"It was a fantastic idea. I have been wanting to try something like that ever since you showed me your cookbook. I think it's wonderful that you and Adam have that kind of relationship."

"Had."

"Aw, hon, you can't just end it like that."

"You ended your relationship over a can of whipped cream. I think it makes perfect sense to end mine over the possible collapse of my business."

"Is it really that serious?"

"It feels like it is."

"But, Lauren, you do have a tendency to expect the worst. Realistically, will losing this one account put you under?"

The old anxiety rose in Lauren. She glared at Kamira. "Expecting the worst prepares you for the worst."

Kamira sighed. "But can you really blame Adam?"

All the anger and hurt from the last couple of days crowded in on Lauren. "His work ethic and mine don't jive. Obviously, he wasn't good for me. I was right in the first place. I don't have time for that kind of distraction."

The tightness in her throat swelled to an unbearable ache. She blinked back unwanted moisture in her eyes.

I will not cry.

"You should think about it, Lauren. I wouldn't toss aside what you two have over this. It isn't as though he deliberately sabotaged your agency."

Lauren sat in brooding silence. She was still too angry to think straight. Her emotions were all in a tangle. Was Kamira right? Was she unrealistically blaming Adam? God, she missed the simpler times they'd shared. She missed having him to lean on when times were rough.

Had her fears cost her her best friend?

Desperate to change the subject, she asked, "What's that cute little Mark up to?"

Nala, Kamira's cat, took that moment to spring onto the couch between them. She preened a moment as Kamira stroked her back. "Well, actually, we had a very interesting conversation right after Greg and I broke up."

"Really? What kind of conversation?"

Kamira's eyes rounded. "One about how he has a thing for older women."

"I knew it! So?"

"So, what?"

"So, you and Mark?"

Kamira petted the cat one last time, then sank back into the soft cushions. "He's so young."

"He's twenty-two. It isn't as though you'd be breaking any laws."

"No, but—"

"And he's a really great guy, who seems awfully interested in you."

"He is very mature for his age. I'll give him that."

"So?"

Kamira laughed and somehow the sound lifted some of Lauren's tension. "I'm thinking about it. Don't pressure me. I really will give it some thought."

ADAM SWUNG. The tennis ball connected with the sweet spot on his racket. God, it felt good to hit something.

The yellow speck sailed across the net. Brad Chambers lunged. He missed. The ball touched down neatly within bounds, ending the match.

"You're killing me today, Morely. How about a rematch?" Brad stepped to the net and offered his hand.

Adam grasped the man's hand in a hardy shake. "You don't know how badly I needed this, but I really have to get back to work. How about next week?"

"Sure. I'll give you a call. That'll give me some time to work on my backhand."

They gathered their belongings, then headed for the locker room. Chambers mopped the sweat from his forehead as they walked. "Clyde Morris told me you hooked him up with a great gal who does advertising."

Adam blew out a breath. Would Lauren say he was meddling if he kept sending business her way? "That's right."

"Well, business has been a little off at those dry cleaners I've got. Do you think she could help?"

For a moment Adam walked with him in silence. In spite of the fact he was still mad at her, he still cared about Lauren and her business. Damn, he still cared a lot about her. If only the woman wasn't so stubborn.

He blew out a breath. He still saw red when he thought of how she blamed him for her current predicament. If he was at all responsible for Entice's woes, though, maybe this was one way to help make it up to her. She probably didn't deserve it, but he'd never been the vindictive type.

Besides, she was nothing if not professional. She did her job well.

Finally, he turned to Chambers. "Yeah, she can help."

LAUREN STARED at the large fish tank in Bennett's reception area. She had been to the offices here before, but had never had the chance to study their aquatic decor in such minute detail. Half a dozen fish in various colors, a small fake scuba diver and seven varieties of plants—some fake, some real—

filled the small tank. A bright-blue fish darted from behind some waving greenery.

She glanced at her watch. She'd been waiting for over an hour and still no sign of Marshal Bennett, the head honcho behind the small bagel empire.

"Ms. Bryant..." The petite blonde behind the receptionist's desk peered at her. "He'll see you now."

A mixture of relief and panic—if there was such a combination—swept through Lauren. She drew a deep breath and stood. "Thank you."

Clutching her briefcase, she headed down the endless hall to the double doors at the end. With her head high, she knocked twice. At the muffled "Come in" she turned the knob, then entered.

Bennett was a serious-looking man in his midfifties. He glanced up from his spot behind a massive cherry-wood desk. A frown drew his eyebrows into a deep vee. "Ms. Bryant. Have a seat."

Her stomach tightened as she sank into the chair he indicated. "Mr. Bennett, thank you for seeing me."

He remained silent, the frown seemingly etched in place.

"First of all, I'd like to offer my apologies for not being present at the shoot and for the subsequent trouble that ensued in my absence."

"You trusted your man, Star, to handle things for you?"

"Yes, I did. Elliot is very capable. It's true, sometimes his sense of artistic justice can get a little out of control, but I believed he would handle the shoot in a responsible manner."

"He was responsible all right. Responsible for running that director right off the set."

"I'm so sorry, Mr. Bennett. If you would just give us a second chance, I promise we'll make it up to you."

"I don't think that's necessary."

Lauren's insides heaved. He couldn't be saying what it sounded like. "You tell me what it'll take for us to keep your business. We'll make this right."

Bennett leaned forward and his eyes narrowed. "Oh, we're doing business, all right, Ms. Bryant. We have a contract and I expect Entice to honor it."

A measure of relief flowed through her, but still his expression remained stern. "Yes, sir. Thank you. I'll reschedule the shoot right away."

"As I said, I don't believe that will be necessary. We're behind schedule as it is. There simply isn't time. Besides, the last thing I want is to go over budget."

He had a point. She opened her mouth to comment, but he continued before she could utter a sound.

"I was rather impressed with the final cut Star sent."

"Final cut?"

"Your man. I knew I liked him from the start. Temperamental, for sure, but I can see now what he was after. And I think he was right. That director was a bit of a prima donna. Sorry I insisted on him."

"Excuse me. I'm missing something here. Elliot sent a final cut of the commercial?"

Bennett raised his hands and for once the frown lines disappeared from his forehead. "I was surprised myself. I wouldn't have thought it was possible, but apparently he sat through the editing process himself. They used what footage we shot that day, which was enough to come up with a passable commercial."

He rocked back in his chair. "He actually saved us money by having the shoot cut short. Ingenious. You need to hang on to that one. He's got real talent. A *star* for sure."

"Yes, sir."

"I take it you haven't seen it?"

"The commercial?" Embarrassment warmed her. Why hadn't Elliot told her?

"Yes. You've got to admire a man who cleans up his own messes." He turned to the console behind his desk and withdrew a videocassette. "Why don't I put it on?"

"That would be great. Thank you."

ADAM DROPPED his keys on the kitchen counter. He closed his eyes and rubbed his calloused hands across his face. If he was a drinking man, he'd be headed for a bar right now.

God he was tired.

He flipped on the light and the kitchen came into full view, stoking memories of that first night with Lauren. He pulled out a chair, then sank heavily onto it.

How he missed her. He missed her scent, her smile and the sassy way she spoke to him. He missed the way he lit up inside whenever she was around.

Sadness pressed down on him. He dropped his head to his arms and let it take him. If only he could go back to that night. He never would have touched her if he'd known it would come to this. How would he go on if he didn't have her in his life?

The doorbell rang. His heart thudded dully. She'd shown up that night on his birthday when he'd least expected. Could it be she'd come to make things right between them again?

He held his breath, almost afraid to hope as he opened the front door.

Rusty stood in the darkness of his front porch. Adam switched on the front light. He stood back, gesturing the young man in, disappointment tightening his throat.

"Hey." Rusty entered, then stopped in the entryway, swinging his arms stiffly.

"Rusty."

"I…um, wanted to apologize for being such an ass yesterday. I don't know what got into me. I just seem to lose my head when it comes to women. They get me so mixed up."

"Yeah, well, I can relate."

"So, do I still have a job, or what?"

Adam paused to give him a long look. "Consider yourself on warning. I can't make special concessions for you, Rusty. You want to keep this job, you'd better take it seriously."

"Yes, sir. I swear it won't happen again."

"Is that all you were worried about?"

"No, man, you're my bro. I don't want to mess with that."

The concern in Rusty's eyes melted a measure of Adam's reserve, though some of his earlier anger remained. "I'm still mad at you."

"Yeah, I guess you have a right to be."

"You have a point, though. I suppose I should have left you to work it out on your own in the first place."

Rusty nodded thoughtfully. "I'm too used to letting you step in."

A moment of silence passed. Rusty was right. He wasn't a kid anymore. And he was certainly capable of handling his own affairs. Hadn't he done so for the past year? Granted, that had ended with him scuttling home penniless, but maybe Adam was partly to blame. He'd always taken care of Rusty's problems for him. Now was the time for Rusty to learn to do this for himself.

Smiling for the first time in days, Adam clapped him on the back. "We're cool, buddy. I only wish your sister would come around as quickly."

"Man, I still don't know how I feel about that."

"Well, it might not matter now."

"You love her, don't you?"

Adam stared at Lauren's brother and suddenly all the anguish he'd suffered over the past few days made complete sense. "Yeah, I guess I do. Does that bother you?"

"I don't know. It's a little weird. Guess I'll have to get used to it."

"Only if she forgives me."

"Well, what did you do to get her so mad?"

What *had* he done? "I talked her into playing hooky, and while she was gone her business fell into chaos and she's now struggling to keep from losing her key account."

"Hell, that's one for her ego. They really need her around that bad?"

"Apparently. And she'd been telling me as much, but I guess I wasn't listening." He clenched his jaw as a wave of guilt swept through him.

"Personally, I think unless you kidnapped her or something, she went of her own free will, but, hey, I'm not the one to interpret the inner workings of any female's mind. Not even my sister's."

"Well, I never meant to cause her any trouble. I'll just have to wait for her to cool off and come to her senses."

"You never got into fights like this before, did you? The whole sex thing probably did you in."

"Thanks, I'll keep that in mind the next time I start lusting after a lifelong friend."

Rusty nodded, his lips pursed. "You know, I think I'm going to try that."

"What? Lusting after a lifelong friend? I wouldn't recommend it."

"Naw, I mean just the friend thing. I can see where it could make things a lot less complicated."

"Or not."

"Oh, right. But this girl's different. She—"

"What girl?" Was that the light, or was Rusty blushing?

"I met this girl—"

"Rusty—"

"She had a flat tire by the side of the road. I can't believe no one was stopping. She was good and determined to change it herself and I think she could have, but she was wearing this dress…" His eyes took on a far-off sheen.

"You've already got the lust going. You sure you want to keep it friendly?"

Rusty frowned. "Well, I just want to get to know her first. *Really* get to know her, you know? Then maybe later we can get into the lust part. All that stuff about friendship being a good foundation. I think there's got to be something to that. You've got to have a good foundation to weather the storms. Don't you think so?"

"God, I hope so."

This time, Rusty gave Adam a reassuring clap on the back. "You and Lauren, you've got foundation. Think about it. No way a little storm like this is going to swamp your relationship. You've got history."

The hope Rusty's arrival had snuffed earlier sprang to life in Adam's chest. The kid had a point. "So, what do I do? Wait for the storm to pass?"

"Hell if I know. But here's one thing. Have you told her you love her?"

Adam heaved a breath. "No, I don't guess I have."

"Well? It's something."

"Right."

If only he could find the right time and place to tell her. The trick would be to get her to listen to him in the first place.

13

LAUREN PERCHED on Elliot's desk. "So, why didn't you tell me?"

He peered at her over his glasses. "About the bagel commercial?"

She nodded. "I'm so grateful that you pulled it off, but I felt really foolish when Bennett brought up what you'd done and I didn't have a clue."

"I didn't know if he'd go for it. I didn't want to get your hopes up."

She leaned over and gave him a hug. "Well, thanks. You really saved our butts." Leaning back, she smoothed his boa. "I guess I've been a bit of a control freak. Maybe I can let up a little on that."

A wide smile split his face. "A little loosening up wouldn't hurt you, but I'm still counting on you to keep us on the straight and narrow."

"No problem there."

His phone rang. She gave him a smile, then headed back to her own office. A moment later he leaned around her door. "Lauren, we've got a guy out here. He dropped by to see if we can do something to perk up his jewelry business. Also, there's someone on line two. It's another potential client. Where are they all coming from?"

Lauren turned from the market analysis she had started for another new account that morning. "Beats me. Do you want the live one, or the one on the phone?"

"I'll take the phone."

She nodded. He moved back down the hall to his own office and she headed to their reception area.

Over the past two days new business had been flooding their way. Not that she minded. It was exhilarating and certainly appreciated. It was odd, though. Sure, they snagged an occasional referral, but never anything like this.

"Hello," she said to a dark-haired man in tennis clothes. Her heart gave a little pang as she thought of Adam. "I'm Lauren Bryant. How can I help you?"

"Ms. Bryant—" he flashed her a dazzling smile "—Curtis Simpson. Thanks so much for seeing me. I hope it's okay that I dropped in."

She grasped his hand in a hearty shake. "Oh, sure. No problem. Why don't you come into my office, Mr. Simpson?"

"Thank you."

He followed her back to her office, then took a seat as she settled behind her desk.

"Now, what can I do for you today?" she asked.

"Well, I guess you could help put the sparkle back into my jewelry stores."

"Has business been a little off?"

His eyebrows drew together. "Down over thirty percent this last quarter."

"I'm sure we can help. Now, tell me what kind of advertising you've been using."

Forty-five minutes later she smiled down at his signature. Another contract. And this one had walked right through their door. Somehow, it seemed too good to be true that Entice had picked up so many new clients on their own.

"Mr. Simpson, tell me, where did you hear about us?"

"Well, I've heard nothing but good things about your agency."

"That's great. From anyone in particular?"

"Actually, several gentlemen at my tennis club recommended you."

"Really?" Tennis club? Adam had to be at the root of this.

"Sure, Clyde Morris, Brad Chambers and especially Adam Morely all spoke highly of Entice Advertising."

So, Adam *was* behind this. She felt suddenly humbled by his generosity, especially in light of her not-so-forgiving attitude. Regret flooded her. He hadn't exactly forced her to take that day off. Perhaps she'd been wrong to blame him. She owed him an apology.

She cocked her head, remembering the names of some of the new accounts they'd acquired over the last few days. "You wouldn't happen to know Steve Hanks, Mitch Brewer or Rebecca Burgundy?"

"Oh, sure. They're all members at the club. You seem to have found a nice pond to fish from."

"Yes, it seems I have. Thank you so much for your business. I look forward to working with you."

"Me too, Ms. Bryant." He shook her hand before leaving.

She stared at the closed door. So, she had Adam to thank for sending her all this new business. She should have known he'd go out of his way to help her, even though he was probably still angry with her.

With a sigh, she picked up the phone, and dialed his number. Her heart thumped in anticipation. She missed the sound of his voice. She waited through four rings, then to her disappointment, his voice mail picked up.

"Hi. It's me. I...I'll call you later." Her throat tightened as she hung up the receiver.

She didn't just miss his voice. She missed him. Every

blessed inch of him. But even if they put this last fiasco behind them, nothing else had changed.

They just didn't want the same things. Wasn't it better to end their relationship now, before they both got any more attached? She blew out a determined breath. She had to at least try to salvage what she could of their friendship.

The bell on the door rang as their mail carrier entered. "Good afternoon," he said as he handed her a bundle of mail.

"Thanks, Frank. You have a good one."

He nodded as he slipped back out. She set aside the pile of envelopes without opening them, then sank into a nearby chair, her gaze riveted on the medium-size package in her hands. It bore the same labeling as her previous gifts.

Slowly, she tore away the brown paper. As before, the rose-covered gift wrap lay beneath. She smoothed her hand over the glossy flowers, then peeled away the paper.

"Oh, Adam," she whispered. "What have you sent me?"

It was a book of love poems. She traced her fingers along the gilt lettering, then opened the cover. The same neat handwriting adorned the first page.

> Love is the enchanted dawn of every heart.
> —Alphonse Marie de Lamartine

A deep sigh escaped her. He still wanted them to be lovers. Was there some way for them to compromise? Would he be willing to prolong having kids, respect her need to continue working once they did?

Her head ached. It was too much to think about for now. She set the book aside, then glanced through the rest of the mail, pausing when she came to a pink envelope. The return label bore a Secret Temptations logo.

She opened it to find an invitation to Norma's lingerie party. "I'd almost forgotten," Lauren murmured to herself.

Since she and Adam were at odds, the party didn't conflict with any plans she'd made. And she *had* promised Norma. Maybe her attendance would convince Norma to sign with them once and for all.

Determined to charm the woman, Lauren lifted the phone, and punched in the number etched in gold at the bottom of the invitation.

"Norma," she said when the woman answered, "it's Lauren Bryant. I'm calling to RSVP about your party. I would love to come."

ADAM'S STOMACH tightened as Judith McDougal slipped into the seat opposite him. Steam rose from the two cups of coffee sitting on the table between them. He'd felt a little guilty asking her to meet him in this coffee shop across town, but he hadn't wanted any repeats of their last meeting.

She looked as scrubbed clean and wholesome as before. "So, how're the cookie sales going?" he asked.

"Cookies?"

"Girl Scout cookies. Don't you guys sell cookies?"

"Oh, yes, but that's usually around March."

He nodded. "Right. So, what did you find for me?"

She handed him a manila envelope. "I believe I've determined the identity of Lauren's secret admirer."

His blood rushed through his ears. Somehow, he'd been hoping the guy didn't exist, but of course, those gifts had come from somewhere. Slowly, he opened the envelope, then drew out a photograph of a young man, probably somewhere around Rusty's age. He looked vaguely familiar.

"Who is this?" he asked.

"His name is Mark Patterson. He's a graduate student at the University of Georgia, working on his master's in En-

glish education. A really smart guy. Good grades. Doesn'
seem to get into any trouble.''

"How does he know Lauren?''

"Well, his father owns a building housing a women's
center in midtown. Seems he does some maintenance work
there from time to time.''

"That's why he sounds familiar. I've heard he's been
helping out while they've been remodeling. Lauren's housemate works there. Lauren's been down there pitching in
You're sure this is the right guy?''

"That cookbook turned out to be a key piece of evidence
There was only one local bookstore that sold them. They
sold a copy two days before she received hers. The owner
was an older woman who remembered him quite fondly
Said he was the romantic type. It was easy to trace him
from there. A florist around the corner from the women's
center also remembered him and the white roses. You're
lucky he didn't shop online. That would have made finding
him more difficult.''

"Well, thank you. You've done a great job.''

"You can rest assured your girlfriend isn't in any danger.
Mr. Morely. He's more a hopeless romantic than a serial
killer.''

"Yes, of course. That's a weight off my mind.'' Adam
sipped the strong coffee.

No, Lauren wasn't in any danger, but she had a right to
know the real identity of her secret admirer. With things as
they were, telling her the truth couldn't make matters worse
between them. He'd go see her tonight.

It was time to come clean.

A GENTLE BREEZE rustled the trees along the walkway as
Lauren and Kamira strolled back to the women's center.

"I feel so honored you could work me into your schedule.'' Kamira smiled broadly as she rubbed her belly. ''That Chinese was incredible, but I think it's going to have to count as lunch and dinner for me.''

''It *was* good. And I'm glad I slipped away. It's getting too busy around the office even for me.''

''So, you think Adam is behind this rash of new clients?''

''It looks that way.''

''And you're feeling bad about blaming him for the bagel fiasco?''

Lauren sighed. ''I think I was a little short-tempered, but I haven't been able to reach him.''

''Well, I'm sure you'll find a way to make it up to him.''

They turned the corner and the women's center came into view. Lauren pursed her lips. What *was* she going to do about Adam? Was she making up with her friend or her lover?

''We still have so much to work out,'' Lauren said. ''One thing's for sure, though. I'm not falling back into bed with him until we work out some kind of compromise for where we're heading in this relationship. If we're even having one.''

''You guys will work it out.''

They walked the rest of the way in comfortable silence.

''Oh, I almost forgot.'' Kamira stopped in front of the center and dug in her purse. ''Your mom called this morning right after you left. Something about Rusty. Here it is. She wants you to call her at work. She's there until closing.''

Lauren took the message from her. ''I hope it isn't trouble.''

''She did sound a little worried.''

A feeling of apprehension crept over Lauren. ''I'll stop by to see her before Norma's party. They're actually in same mall. Norma has insisted she send the limo for me. I think she's afraid I'll skip out. I'll see if her driver can pick me up a little earlier.''

"The lingerie party is in the mall?''

"Apparently they've leased the space, but haven't opened yet. Norma said this was a christening of sorts.''

"That means they're going to need to make a decision about their advertising pretty soon.''

"I'm hoping tonight's the night.''

The door to the center opened and Mark Patterson emerged onto the sunlit walkway. "Good afternoon, ladies. Can I interest you two in lunch?''

Kamira seemed to stand a little straighter. She fluffed her hair back. "Darn. We just ate. How about a rain check?''

He heaved an exaggerated breath. "I guess that'll have to do.''

Lauren smiled. She should probably leave the two of them alone. Kamira seemed interested, after all. "I need to get back to work.''

"Me, too,'' Kamira said. "Good luck with tonight, Lauren. I'll see you later.''

She nodded, but to her surprise, Mark turned with her as she stepped from the curb. "I'll walk you to your car,'' he said.

"Okay, thanks.'' She cast Kamira a questioning glance, but her housemate just shrugged before turning to enter the brick building.

Mark probably wanted to talk about Kamira. Lauren turned to him as they crossed the street to the lot where she'd parked. "So, what's up with you these days?''

He smiled, but there was something hesitant in his eyes. "Oh, still chasing love.''

"Come on, Mark. A good-looking guy like you? I find that hard to believe.''

"Well, you see, there's this woman I'm very interested

in. I've been thinking about her a lot, but I've been unsure about approaching her directly.''

Lauren nodded as they reached her car. ''There's an age difference and you're not sure how she'd feel about it, right?''

His eyes rounded. ''Yes. So, you figured it out?''

''Well, it's to be expected. I think she's used to men of all ages falling for her.''

''I'm sure she is.'' He was quiet a minute, then asked, ''So, she's open to the possibility of a relationship with a younger man?''

''I believe she is.''

The smile he gifted her with at that moment could only be described as radiant. He drew her hands into his. ''Lauren, you've made me so happy.''

''Well, to be honest, I think she's a little hesitant, but with a little urging, I think you'll have Kamira eating out of the palm of your hand.''

He straightened. A deep frown formed between his eyebrows. ''Kamira?''

She nodded. ''That's right. Kamira.''

''You think I'm interested in your housemate?''

''Well…yeah. Older woman to die for. You two have been spending all this time together getting the center ready.''

His eyes clouded. He dropped her hands. A ragged laugh tore from his throat.

''Mark, what's wrong?''

He drew a long breath as he held her gaze. ''I've been inventing all these reasons to work up here and getting closer to Kamira because of…you.''

A funny feeling claimed Lauren's stomach. ''Me?''

''Yes. I figured she knew more about you than anyone else and I might glean a little inside information through her. Plus, I hoped you might show up here to help on occasion.''

"Me?" she repeated numbly.

"Yes. I thought you'd figured it out, Lauren. *I'm* your secret admirer.''

ADAM PARKED his truck outside one of his job sites. They were almost finished landscaping the vast suburban property and he had stopped by for a final inspection. With luck, Manuel and Rusty had teamed with Chris and Eric to finish the job.

Before exiting his truck, Adam pulled out his cell phone to check his messages. He swallowed as Lauren's message played. The soft tones of her voice sent his blood pumping. So, she had finally called. He should be relieved. That meant she was at least still speaking to him. Of course, that might not last once she heard what he had to say.

"Hey, Adam. Could I see you a minute?" Rusty strode toward him across the side lawn. Worry lines creased his forehead.

Adam slid out of the truck as Rusty reached him. "Sure, Rusty. What's up?"

"I know we had that talk about me handling things on my own, but..." His gaze dropped away and he shifted nervously.

"What is it? Something wrong?"

Rusty rolled his eyes. "Isn't there always something wrong?"

"Well, you made it a year in Texas."

A short laugh burst from the youngster. "And you think I wasn't ever in trouble during that time?"

"But you must have handled it on your own, then, because we never heard from you."

"That doesn't mean I handled it all very well."

Adam stood silent for a moment, waiting.

"Sherry's dad's in town looking for her. He stopped by my place last night, mad as a bull, accusing me of keeping her against her will."

"Did you?"

"Hell, no. She left days ago. I haven't got a clue where she is. Probably took the old man's money, then ran off with that homeboy of hers."

"So?"

"So her old man is all over me. What do I do?"

Adam shook his head. For once, he had absolutely no compulsion to step in. "That, my dear boy, is for you to figure out."

He patted Rusty on the shoulder, and headed for the backyard to check on his crew's progress.

LAUREN WHIPPED into her parking spot at the agency. Humiliation burned through her. She slammed the gearshift into park, then sat drawing deep breaths. How could he? How could Adam have let her throw herself at him that way? Why hadn't he said anything?

She got out of the car, slamming the door behind her. And poor Mark. Closing her eyes, she tried to shut out the memory of the hurt look in his eyes. She'd done her best to let him down gently, but she'd been so stunned. She could hardly remember what she'd said.

All this time, she'd thought Adam was behind those romantic gifts. She'd ruined their friendship over a stupid misunderstanding. What a fool she'd been.

She stormed into the agency, nearly knocking over Elliot as she stomped to her office. He stared at her wide-eyed. "What's got your panties in a tangle?"

"I'm an idiot."

"I could call you lots of things, but never an idiot." He

set a mug of steaming coffee before her. "Here. It's decaf. You look like you could use it more than me."

"Thanks." She took a long sip, choking on the unexpected bite of alcohol in the drink. "What's in this?"

"Just a splash of whiskey. I'm celebrating all our recent success."

Frowning, she took a second sip. It slipped easier down her throat. Elliot patted her on the back. "So, what is it, doll? Business is great. We're rock solid with Bennett in hand and all this new business on the books. Must be Adam."

Lauren groaned and handed him the mug. "Why couldn't I have left well enough alone?"

Elliott tossed down a swallow, then handed the spiked coffee back to her. "I don't get what the problem is."

"I seduced my best friend because I let everyone convince me he was my secret admirer." She stopped for another sip. "Now I've screwed up our friendship for nothing and I don't know if I can ever make it right again."

"Adam's not your secret admirer?"

She clenched her fists in exasperation. Why did the fact that Adam hadn't sent those gifts have to hurt so much? "No."

Elliot's eyebrows arched. "Then who is?"

"This really sweet guy who helps out at the women's center."

"Oh."

"I set him straight that nothing was going to happen between us." She shrugged. "It would just never work."

"Because you're in love with Adam."

Anguish poured through her. "Why did he let me believe he sent those gifts?"

"Did he know you thought he was your secret admirer?"

She paused. Hadn't he? "I think so. I'm not sure. Maybe not at first."

"Then he was just responding to your initial seduction. You can't fault him for that."

"But we talked about it. I told him I was glad he'd taken my advice on wooing the woman he chose. He knew then. Why didn't he say something?"

"Well, you need to ask him, but I'd say he realized your mistake and knew you'd be upset, so he kept quiet. Does it really matter?"

"Of course it matters. None of this would have happened if I didn't think he was interested."

"But he never would have responded if he wasn't interested. So what if he wasn't your secret admirer?"

She took another swallow, then passed the mug back to Elliot. "I can't think about this now. I have work to do, then I have to see my mother. Rusty's in some kind of trouble. Then there's Norma's lingerie party. I don't have time to have a breakdown."

"Um, a word of warning about this lingerie party."

"What?" The too-familiar pounding started again in her temples.

"I know this is a girls' night out and you'll have a great time. Norma can be a hoot. I won't be surprised if she signs after this, but do be careful. She can sometimes be… well…she can…"

"Elliot, just say whatever you're trying to say and get it over with."

"I'm sure it'll be fine. Just make sure she isn't drinking tequila."

"Norma?"

"She gets a little wild on that stuff. She's well aware of it though, so I'm sure it won't be a problem."

"She's promoting her business. We'll be at the mall. I can't imagine things will get out of hand."

"No. Of course not. She'll probably have a few models showing off her lingerie. You can schmooze and drink champagne. You'll have a great time."

"You bet. Even though my love life is in shambles. I'm going to show that woman I know how to have the best of times."

Elliot raised the mug in a toast. "You go get 'em, girl."

14

NORTHPOINT MALL HAD all the familiar sights and sounds of any mall. The scent of coffee hung heavy in the air as Lauren passed a Starbucks on the lower level. The combined murmur of countless conversations diffused the soft music drifting from a nearby store. Early darkness glittered through a span of glass far above in the domed ceiling.

With a knot of worry planted firmly in her belly, Lauren turned into the upbeat kids' clothing store where her mother worked. Miniature outfits in bright jewel tones adorned a rack by the door. A young girl fingered the soft fabric, then turned pleading eyes to the woman beside her.

Lauren kept her gaze ahead, scanning for her mother. A fluff of blond hair peeked up from behind a table toward the back. Winding between fixtures bulging with the latest offerings for America's youths, she made her way toward the table, then stopped.

Her mother knelt beside a little boy, his eyes wide with indecision as he turned his foot from side to side, studying the dress shoes that matched a pair displayed on the table.

He turned to a woman sitting patiently in a nearby chair. "What do you think, Mama?"

The woman smiled, then gestured with her hand. "Get up and walk in them, see how they feel."

The boy sprang up, then raced away down the aisle.

"I said walk, Andrew!" With a shake of her head, the

woman hurried after him, muttering, "That boy has two speeds—stop and go, go, go."

Lauren couldn't help but smile as her mother turned to her. "Hi, sweetie! Let me see if I can get one of these youngsters to look after things and we'll go get a cup of coffee."

"That sounds good."

She followed Delores over to the front counter, where she spoke quietly to a young man who was just finishing ringing up a customer. Delores turned back to her with a small smile. "Come, we need to figure out what to do with this brother of yours."

They found an empty table in the food court and settled themselves with a couple of cups of java. Lauren sighed. "Lay it on me. What's up with Rusty?"

Delores scooted her chair closer. "Well, I got a strange call last night from a Jack Pickard. He was Rusty's foreman on the oil rig. He had my number from Rusty's employment papers.

"Now, I haven't been able to get a hold of Rusty to confirm any of this, but this man insists Rusty coerced his teenage daughter into going out with him when he was in Texas. Then he accused Rusty of seducing her into following him here. He says the girl called, ready to come home, but then she no showed on the flight she was supposed to arrive on. The man is here to bring her home himself. He insists Rusty's keeping her against her will."

Lauren blinked, stunned for a moment when her mother finished. "What?"

"This man—"

"I got it. I just don't believe it. Rusty would never do anything like that."

"No, of course not."

"It's obviously a case of a father overreacting."

"Obviously." The worry lines appeared around Delores's yes. "What do we do?"

"Kill Rusty?"

"No. We can't do that."

"I'll talk to him." Lauren patted her mother's hand. The not in her stomach tightened. "Don't you worry. I'm sure 's nothing. I'll take care of it." She paused a moment, then hanged the subject, "How is Claire? Did she find a job?"

"She did just like you suggested and found something emporary. She really likes the position and it looks like it ould turn into something permanent."

"Wonderful."

"Thank you, dear. What would I do without you?"

Warmth filled Lauren's chest. "You'd get along just ine."

"I don't know. I wonder sometimes."

"Delores?" A sandy-haired man, somewhere in his late-orties, dressed in khakis and a denim shirt, stopped by their able. His gaze ran appreciatively over Lauren's mother.

Delores straightened, blinking rapidly. "Phillip, hello. I hought you'd left for the day."

"I, uh, forgot my briefcase."

Lauren frowned as pink blossomed in her mother's heeks. Was she imagining it, or was there a sexual current unning between the two?

"Yes, I noticed it on your desk." Delores fidgeted with er coffee cup. "Oh, would you like to join us? This is my aughter, Lauren."

"Ah, the advertising executive." He leaned over to shake auren's hand. His grip was firm, confident. "I've heard so nuch about you."

Before Lauren could respond, his gaze returned to De-ores, who seemed to fluff up before their eyes. He said, "I don't want to intrude. I'll just head on to the store...and get my briefcase.''

"I'll be along in a minute." Delores gave him a shy smile.

Lauren made a show of checking her watch. "Oh, right. Look at the time. I've got a thing to get to."

"I'll see you back at the store, then?"

"Yes." Delores laced her fingers around her cup.

As he disappeared into the crowd surrounding the food court, Lauren turned wide eyes to her mother. "Let me guess. *That* was your new D.M.?"

"Frustrating man. He probably came back just to check up on me and here I am taking a coffee break."

"Oh, he was checking you out all right."

Delores's eyebrows arched. "I don't know what you mean."

"Mom, you two have the hots for each other."

"Don't be ridiculous, Lauren."

"You do."

"Enough of that. What is this thing you have to get to?"

"I'm going to see a client."

"You work too hard, dear. I really worry about you."

"I'm fine."

"Really?"

"Yeah. So, you and, what was his name, Phillip?"

"Hush."

"He seemed nice. Not the ogre I was expecting. Not bad looking, either."

"I suppose he has a certain appeal. For the right woman that is. Not that *I'm* interested. He's my boss, for goodness sake."

"You know, Mom, you should loosen up. Give old Phillip a shot. You never know what you might be missing."

Delores frowned as she stood. "You talk to that brothe

of yours. Tell him he's to return any unauthorized young women immediately.''

"You're changing the subject.''

"You have a nice thing, dear. I'd better get back to work." Her frown deepened. "You don't think we need to call a lawyer, do you? For Rusty, I mean.''

"Oh, God, I hope not.''

Lauren rose to give her mother a quick hug. "We'll work it out. I'm sure this girl just has an innocent crush on him. I'll get to the bottom of it. One thing I know for certain, though, whatever Rusty's done, he never meant any harm. I'm sure it sounds worse than it is.''

"Well, let me know.''

"Sure.'' She cocked her head, smiling. "Now, go get him.''

With a quick glare, Delores turned, then headed toward her store.

"LAUREN! I'm so glad you could make it.'' Norma hugged her, planting a kiss firmly in the air above her cheek. "Come in. Get comfortable.''

Turning in a concoction of flowing chiffon that hinted at the teddy beneath, Norma pulled down the gate that cut them off from the rest of the mall. They were cocooned in a place of soft music and flickering candlelight. Dark fabric draped the entire front of the store, further adding to the feeling of intimacy.

"My, this is cozy." Lauren's stomach churned. She probably shouldn't have had that cappuccino on top of the spiked coffee she'd shared with Elliot. And she had completely forgotten about dinner, but the thought of food at that moment made her queasy.

Worrying about Rusty wasn't helping, either. She hadn't reached him at his home number, but had left a message for him to call her right away. She patted her purse with its cell phone, reassuring herself it was handy.

Norma ushered her past cartons of merchandise stacked along one wall and an assortment of half-filled fixtures and tables. "When this place opened up, Charles and I jumped all over it, even though it's early yet for our launch date. This way we can take our time getting moved in and the stock ready."

And your advertising needs squared away. "It's a great spot."

"It has good energy, doesn't it?"

"Uh, yeah."

They stopped near the dressing rooms. Half a dozen women lounged in overstuffed chairs arranged in a semicircle around a mirrored area set off as a makeshift stage. A long coffee table had been placed in front of the chairs. A silver serving tray with glasses and an ice bucket chilling a bottle of champagne graced one end, while an assortment of lotions and creams cluttered the other. A velvet-covered box rested on the floor near one of the center chairs Norma indicated for Lauren.

"You can sit by me, dear. You're going to love the models I hired to show off my new line. I'm so excited." Norma took a moment to introduce Lauren to the rest of the ladies while she poured her a glass of champagne.

"Thank you." Lauren accepted the drink, then took a cautious sip. To her relief, her stomach didn't rebel.

A slim woman dressed in a black teddy with a matching lace cover-up padded in on bare feet and deposited a tray of cheese and fruit in the center of the table. She popped a grape into her mouth, her eyes closing with pleasure. "Oh, Norma, these are the sweetest grapes."

"I want one, Francine." A brunette near the dressing rooms leaned forward and Francine dropped a grape into er mouth. "Mmm, those *are* sweet." The second woman moaned in satisfaction as she ate the fruit.

Some of the calm the champagne had instilled dissipated, but Lauren checked herself. She was placing too much sexual emphasis on food since her encounters with Adam. These women were probably all close friends of Norma's. No doubt they enjoyed a good party. Where was the harm in that?

"Feel free to try anything on." Norma gestured as another woman stepped out of one of the dressing rooms. Several of the other women lounging in the chairs wore lingerie in provocative shades and styles.

The woman strutted before the mirrors, turning to see all angles of the white leather bra and panty set she wore with garter and hose. "Oh, Norma, you're going to let us buy some of this tonight, aren't you?"

"You want that? Take it, dear. Won't that cute hubby of yours go crazy for it?" Norma rose. With a practiced hand, she tugged the bra lower. "Now, fluff up your breasts. That's it," she said as the woman reached inside the cups to shift her breasts higher. "See the difference?"

A buxom redhead beside Lauren reached over and squeezed her arm. "Oh my God, look at *him*."

Lauren followed her gaze to where a man had emerged from one of the dressing rooms. He wore a short silk robe that enhanced, rather than hid, his solid body beneath. "I hadn't realized she'd be using male models," she said to the redhead, whose name she couldn't remember.

"I think there's just the one. She has a few items for men. I wish my boyfriend looked that good in a robe. I'd buy him one in every color."

Lauren nodded, imagining the soft silk skimming over Adam's broad chest. Her blood warmed. "Maybe I'll pick

one up for my…'' She let the sentence trail off, not quite
sure how to classify him at this point.

The music picked up to a livelier tempo. Norma clapped
her hands. ''I think that's our cue that they're ready to
start.'' She hurried over to her seat beside Lauren.

The lights above them dimmed. An Amazon of a woman
dressed in heels and a red lace robe, strode to the center of
the mirrored area. ''Good evening, ladies. I'm Loretta Dun-
can, I have my own agency here in Atlanta. I've brought
three of my models with me tonight. We've never done a
lingerie party before, but when Norma explained what she
wanted, I knew we could give her a real show. So we're
going to kind of go with the flow. My models aren't at all
shy and we hope you won't be, either. We love having the
opportunity to get close and intimate with you. Norma also
has a number of accessories…'' She gestured to the assorted
bottles and tubes.

''So if any of you have questions, just yell them out.
Nothing's too personal in the world of lingerie. And if
you're all good—'' her eyes shone ''—she'll show us what
she brought in the box.''

Lauren's gaze fell to the box by her feet. Curiosity filled
her. Would the shop be selling sex toys?

''Let me first show you what I have on.'' Loretta dropped
her robe. A murmur of admiration rose from the party
guests. ''This is a bustier and thong combination.'' She rotated to reveal the thong back disappearing between her firm
buttocks. ''Wonderful combined with matching garter and
silk stockings.'' She bent slightly, running her hand down
the long curve of her hip.

Lauren swallowed, remembering the crotchless merry
widow from Norma's line. Would they model the racier outfits? She drank deeply of the champagne and made an effort
to relax. It wasn't as though she was a prude or anything.

but somehow she'd thought of this as more of a business function.

"Here's Darren and Amanda." Loretta gestured to the male model and another lanky woman in a matching black robe.

The couple glided out, arm in arm, then turned gracefully and dropped their robes. Loretta moved off center. "You see the thong holds a vital place in this collection, so I hope you're all working those glutes, ladies."

One of the women on the end toward the dressing rooms moaned loudly. "Oh, honey. I want to work *him.*"

Darren, now dressed in the barest leopard-print thong, flashed her a dazzling smile, while Amanda brushed against him in her merry widow of black leather accented across the breasts with the leopard print.

"You see, not only is the thong an attractive feature, it's highly practical when you and your partner get caught up in that moment of passion." Loretta gestured to the couple.

Darren turned Amanda. He bent her forward, then simulated thrusting into her from behind. Lauren shifted uncomfortably in her seat, while several of the women catcalled and cheered.

Norma nudged her. "I've ordered that set for Charles and myself."

Lauren murmured something unintelligible into her champagne glass, trying desperately to blot from her mind the image Norma's comment painted.

Everyone applauded as Darren and Amanda glided back toward one of the dressing rooms and a new model cut her way across the carpeted floor.

"Ah, here's Darlene, ladies. Isn't she gorgeous?" Loretta's voice drifted over them.

Darlene strutted her stuff in black leather and lace reminiscent of Lauren's merry widow, but hers was another bust-

ier and thong combination. She smiled sweetly at them a
she turned, then shook her firm backside to the beat of th
music.

"Damn, Norma," Francine called from her seat. "I knev
you'd show us a good time. But this is getting me all hc
and bothered. Time for the quencher."

Several women hooted their approval as Francine leane
over to search in her oversize purse. To Lauren's dismay
she brought out a bottle of tequila and a number of shc
glasses.

Lauren stole a cautious glance at Norma, Elliot's warnin
ringing clear in her mind. "My, she seems to be enjoyin
the party."

Norma chuckled softly. "That Francine thinks she *is* th
party." She shrugged. "Actually, give her a couple shot
and she *is*."

Francine lined up a dozen or so glasses and started pour
ing shots as Lauren's stomach tightened and Loretta ex
plained in smooth tones, "This outfit has a nice feature, a
Darlene will demonstrate. Imagine you and your lover ar
kissing. It's long and wet and wild. His tongue strokes yo
into a passionate heat. His hands glide over you. At first
you like him touching you through the sexy leather an
lace."

Darlene ran her hands over her body, caressing herself a
Loretta continued, "But soon it isn't enough. You're burn
ing for the feel of his hands on your skin, on your breasts."

With the flick of her wrists and the rasp of Velcro, Dar
lene tore the cups from her bra. Candlelight flickered acros
her firm breasts. Closing her eyes, she rolled her nipple
between her fingers as the women watching tossed bacl
shots and gasped their approval.

"Don't you love it?" Norma squeezed Lauren's arm. "
told the designer what I wanted and he aimed to please."

"It seems pleasure was definitely on his mind." Lauren
verted her gaze from the model, amazed at how warm the
oom had become.

The redhead handed her a shot glass filled with tequila.
Here you go, hon."

"Oh, no thank you. I think I've had too much champagne
s it is."

"Go ahead," the redhead urged.

"I'd rather not." Lauren pushed the offering away.

"Here, don't force it on her," Norma cut in. "I'll drink
."

"Oh, no. That's okay, Norma. I'll take it." Lauren
raightened as Norma took the glass. What had she done?

Norma waved her hand aside. "I need a little something
take the edge off, since I sent Charles to Savannah this
veekend. What was I thinking? I knew I'd get all hot and
othered here." She tossed back the drink in one swallow.

She fluffed her hair as Darlene retired and Darren and
manda returned. "Now, there's nothing wrong with look-
g, is there?"

Lauren followed her gaze back to the front. Loretta
nned herself, apparently getting a little hot, too. "For
ose of you of a more daring nature, we offer this sexy
umber Amanda's wearing."

Darren, adorned in black silk boxers, lifted off Amanda's
auzy cover-up. The music kicked into a jazzy number as
manda gyrated against him, in her cupless, crotchless
erry widow. He glided his hands over her, turning her,
ending her to reveal each special feature as Loretta crooned
nd gestured to the couple.

Norma slammed back another shot. Francine moaned. To
auren's amazement, she massaged her own breast and fed
nother grape to the woman she'd accommodated earlier.
he woman sucked Francine's fingers into her mouth along

with the grape and Lauren gasped, suddenly finding it ha
to breathe.

She glanced at Norma. Perhaps their hostess would ca
a halt before things got out of hand, but Norma's ey
had glazed over. Her own breasts heaved as she burrowe
her hand down the front of her teddy.

Lauren clamped her eyes shut as an excited cry fro
Amanda hinted that Darren had moved beyond the simula
tion stage. Good God, they were on the verge of some wei
orgy.

Anxiety raced through Lauren as the nausea in her stom
ach built. She needed air. Would Norma notice if sl
slipped away? She gathered her purse, averting her gaze a
the redhead beside her moaned and threw her leg over th
arm of her chair.

"Ah, work it," Loretta purred.

In one horrid moment, Lauren realized she didn't hav
her car. An excited grunt from Norma's direction preclude
asking after the limo. Lauren kept her gaze riveted to th
floor as a rhythmic thumping sounded from the mirrore
area and Darren let out with a husky, "Oh, yeah, bab
Where's that box?"

Lauren yanked her feet away from the velvet box. Sl
had to get out of there. She blinked at a sudden ringing i
her ears. Was that her cell phone?

She dug furiously in her purse as the phone shrilled agai
She cupped the phone to her mouth, hoping to blot out th
sounds of sexual pleasure surrounding her. "Hello?"

"Lauren?" Adam's voice had never sounded so sweet.

"Adam." She breathed a sigh of relief. The redhead b
side her let out a loud moan as her chair rocked wildly.

"What's going on? Where are you?"

"Never mind. Just come get me. I'm at Northpoint Mal
Meet me at the main entrance."

"You okay?"

Someone slid the velvet box away from her feet.

"Yeah, just hurry."

"I'm on my way."

She disconnected, then quietly made her way back to the front of the store. Her heart raced in anticipation. She could forgive him for just about anything in that moment. Adam was coming to her rescue.

15

ADAM PEERED through his windshield as he pulled to th
curb in front of the mall. The unease that had gripped hir
since his call to Lauren intensified. She had sounded almos
panicked. She rose from a nearby bench, her arms wrappe
tightly around her middle. What had happened to her?

"Hi." She slipped into the passenger's seat. "Thanks fc
coming to get me."

"No problem. You okay?"

She shivered, then a smile broke across her face. To hi
surprise, she started laughing. She laughed until tears rolle
down her cheeks. "Oh God, I'm sorry."

Relief that she was all right mixed with the frustratio
over worrying for nothing. "What's going on? You sounde
so upset on the phone. And what were all those strang
noises in the background?"

Reining in her laughter, she swiped at her eyes. "Yo
won't believe it. I was just at a lingerie party that got a littl
out of control."

"What?"

"One minute they were modeling lingerie, then the nex
they were throwing back shots of tequila and getting it on."

"Getting it on?"

"I'll spare you the details."

He grinned. "I don't know. Sounds like something I'
like to hear."

She gave him a stern look. "Maybe later. Anyway, you

iming was perfect. I don't even think anyone noticed when I left. Though I may have lost our biggest potential client yet, I don't even care. I just needed to get out of there.''

With a nod, he pulled away from the curb. "Your place?"

"Yes, please."

They drove a short distance in silence. He glanced her way. Her earlier mirth had settled and she seemed pensive as she stared out the window. He squared his jaw. Somehow, he had to tell her he wasn't her secret admirer.

"When we get to your place I'd like to come in for a little bit, so we can talk, if that's okay," he said.

"Um, all right." She turned to face him. "You didn't happen to see Rusty today?"

"We caught a beer after work."

She folded her arms across her chest. "Did he happen to mention a certain Jack Pickard?"

Adam frowned. "I don't recognize the name."

"He's got a teenage daughter he says Rusty is hiding somewhere?"

"Oh." His gut tightened.

"Oh?" Leaning closer, she narrowed her eyes. "What does that mean? What do you know?"

"Look, Lauren, sunshine…it's nothing to get upset about. Rusty handled it. They found the girl."

"Back up. He handled what?"

"This girl, Sherry, followed him from Texas, without his knowledge. He didn't invite her. She showed up on his doorstep, bags in hand—"

"Was she a runaway?" She stared at him, eyes wide.

"Sort of. She's eighteen. I think she was living with her father at the time, though, and neglected to tell him she was leaving."

"That's just great."

"But I talked her into going home and we thought—"

"*You* talked her into going home? How and when an why were you involved in this?"

"Rusty asked for my help." He shrugged. "Well, at firs he did, but then he kind of changed his mind."

"You were meddling. Trying to fix everything for hin without breathing one word to *me*."

"You already had so much to worry about—"

"So you decided I didn't need to know what was goin on with my own brother? That man could have called th police. There could have been charges—"

"I don't think that would have happened."

"But you don't know that. The point is it *could* have When were you going to tell me? When they arrested him Thank God she wasn't a minor." She shook her head. "Yo can't possibly think you were helping me by keeping me i the dark."

He stopped at a light and turned to her. "I care abou you. What is wrong with sharing some of your burden?"

"Sharing? That wasn't sharing. That was you keeping th truth from me. That was you being the big man and takin, care of everything. Only it was never your place to do so!"

She cocked her head. "This wasn't the first time, was it How much else have you not told me about?"

Frustration welled up inside him. "Look, if it makes yo any happier, I think I've learned that lesson. That's wh, when Rusty came to me with Pickard on his tail, I told hin to handle the situation himself."

"Great. And it still didn't occur to you at that point t give me a call? Let me know Rusty was in trouble?"

He reached for her. "Lauren—"

She jerked away from him. "Don't."

He drove on in silence until they pulled into her driveway "I'd still like to come in."

"I don't see what else we have to talk about. Is this ho\

you'd act if *we* had kids? Because, this definitely doesn't work for me. Raising kids should be a joint venture.''

''I agree.''

''I don't think so. On the one hand you're insisting you need a stay-at-home wife to take care of your kids, but on the other, it looks like you want to take on all the problems by yourself. That's so unrealistic.''

''You're right—''

''Besides, I'm really upset with you. You've completely humiliated me.''

A feeling of impending doom crept over him. She knew. He should have told her sooner. ''Lauren, I'm so sorry.''

''You should be. I can't believe you let me throw myself at you that way. How could you, Adam? Why didn't you just tell me you weren't my secret admirer?''

He threw out his arms in defeat. ''I'm not sure. I knew you'd be upset.''

''I *am* upset.''

''I didn't want you to think this—'' he gestured between them ''—was a mistake.''

Silence hung over them, then she shifted away from him. ''I don't know what to think.'' Her voice sounded small and strained and hurt and he wanted to kick himself for making her feel that way.

''I just…'' She got out of the car, and peered through the open window. ''Don't…call…me.''

Without looking back, she climbed the steps to her town house.

LAUREN WOKE to a relentless pounding on her front door. She opened bleary eyes and peered at the digital clock on the nightstand. She blinked, focused again. Had she really slept past noon?

Grumbling, she stumbled from her bed, then pulled on

her robe. Her aggravation building, she yanked open the door, then straightened. Her mother stood on the doorstep. Her eyes gleamed with purpose.

"Mom? What's wrong? What are you doing here?"

"What's wrong?" Delores pushed her way inside. "I'll tell you what's wrong." Her intense look softened. "Look at you, all puffy-eyed. Have you been crying?"

Lauren stiffened. She shut the door, feeling raw and empty inside. All the upset from her conversation with Adam last night crowded in on her. Just as her father hadn't trusted them to handle his illness, Adam hadn't trusted her to handle Rusty's transgressions.

Her throat tightened and her eyes misted. The truth was, she'd cried herself to sleep last night. But long years of holding in her feelings prevented her from admitting that.

She drew a deep breath and blinked the moisture from her eyes. "Must be allergies."

"Right." With an unprecedented take-charge attitude, Delores propelled her into the kitchen. "Let's make you some coffee.

"Sit." Her mother directed her toward one of the chairs around the drop-leaf table.

"What are you doing?"

Delores paused as she rummaged for coffee filters. "I'm being your mother."

"What?"

"That phone call from Mr. Pickard really got me thinking." She turned and cast a narrow gaze Lauren's way. "It occurred to me that you've been sheltering me. I know your brother has a mischievous streak. Always has. I can't imagine he's scraped his way this far without more trouble than what I've caught wind of. I think what's different about this time is that I found out about it."

"Mom—"

"Wait. Hear me out." She pulled a container of coffee from the refrigerator. "I know I was a basket case when your father died—"

"Mom, don't—"

"And I fell to pieces on you. I figured you turned out so strong and independent, maybe it was a good thing."

"Mom—"

"But being too strong and too independent isn't always so good. You should never have had to take the lead, sweetheart." Delores stopped, coffeepot in hand. "And I never should have let you."

Lauren squeezed her eyes shut. She felt like a dam was bursting inside her.

Delores continued, "So, I've decided it's way past time for me to step back in as the head of this family. And my first job is to talk some sense into you."

"Me? You mean Rusty."

"No. I've already been to see him this morning. I think we've gotten your brother all straightened out. For the time being, anyway. We also had quite a lengthy discussion about you, though. I believe I've put two and two together on why you've been looking so run-down and strained lately."

Lauren shrugged. "I've been working a lot."

"I know the signs of lovesickness, dear. All has not been well between you and Adam, has it?"

One fat tear escaped and rolled down Lauren's cheek. A second quickly followed. "No."

"You blame him for almost losing a key account?"

"I did at first."

"And I'll bet now you're upset with him for not telling you what was going on with Rusty."

She nodded.

Delores set the coffeepot on the counter, and came to sit beside her. "For years I couldn't forgive your father. He

could have told us about his illness, helped us prepare
Maybe I would have handled his passing better if I'd known
it was coming. Half the problem was the shock of it. I never
understood why he didn't tell us, why he chose to suffer on
his own."

The pain in Lauren's throat grew almost unbearable
She'd been angry, too. "He was trying to be noble, to pro
tect us."

Delores nodded, her eyes glittering with unshed tears. "I
think he and Adam were maybe cut from the same cloth."

Lauren drew a deep breath. "How did you manage to
forgive Dad?"

"It took me a long time to get past the anger, but once
did, all I had left was love. I think when you love someone
that much, forgiveness is kind of built in."

"But it isn't just that. Adam wants a stay-at-home wife
and…children."

"Well, you can always compromise on working, but there
really isn't a compromise when it comes to having children
Either you have them, or you don't. And only you can de
cide that."

"I know."

"Whatever you decide, I'm here for you now. I'm so
sorry I haven't been in the past, but from now on I promise
you can count on me." She shrugged. "I'm counting on
you."

Warmth bloomed in Lauren's chest. "I'm always here for
you, Mom."

"Good." Pink tinged Delores's cheeks. "I'm going to
need all your advice. Phillip asked me to dinner last night
and I said yes."

"That's great!" Lauren smiled. If her mother could find
happiness, maybe there was hope for her yet.

"I'm sorry." Delores rose and picked up the coffeepot. "I never made the coffee."

"That's okay, Mom. I think I'm going to get dressed, then go for a drive. I have a lot of thinking to do."

"You do that, sweetie."

She opened her arms and Lauren walked into her embrace, letting herself be mothered for the first time in all these years.

SUNLIGHT DAPPLED the windshield as Lauren drove along a tree-lined lane. Her gaze traveled over the spreading branches of an old apple tree, its fruit golden in the shafts of light permeating the thick foliage. The distinctive curve of one limb struck a note of familiarity. She leaned forward, recognition flooding her.

"That's old man Sheedy's tree." She glanced around, amazed. She'd been in such a haze, she hadn't paid attention to where she was driving, and had unwittingly arrived in her old neighborhood. It had been forever since she'd traveled this way.

As children, she and Adam had spent many an afternoon in that tree. Its sturdy branches had provided the ideal structure for their climbing feats. Mr. Sheedy had let them pick and eat as much of the lush fruit as they'd wanted.

Her gaze fell on the row of neat brick homes shaded by aging trees. A corner house displayed a front border of azalea bushes. Her mother had always set a vase of the bright blossoms on their dining-room table when they were in bloom. They'd been her father's favorite.

Lauren continued down the quiet street. The old Wilson house remained the same, with its rock garden and pristine yard, while the ranch-style house where Adam had lived shone beneath a coat of fresh paint. A bicycle and wagon sat forgotten on the front walk, and the driveway sported a basketball hoop that hadn't been present in their day.

She pulled to the curb before the house next door, the one she'd called home for nearly seventeen years. They'd been forced to sell the house and move to an apartment after her father's death. A For Sale sign presided over the front corner of the yard. Weeds had started to overrun the yard, mixing with tall grass and poking up between cracks in the sidewalk. The azalea bushes along the front that her father had always kept meticulously trimmed now climbed toward the wide picture window, which, like all the windows, had been stripped and left bare.

The house appeared to have been deserted for some time. Its emptiness echoed the hollow feeling in her gut. Her throat tightened as sadness filled her. A deep sigh rose in her chest.

"So much for 'Home Sweet Home.'"

Biting her lip, Lauren exited the car. As she glanced again over the property, a memory of her father, hammer in hand and a look of pride brightening his face, swept over her.

"Hey, Pop, think the tree house is still out back?" She glanced around, but no one moved on the quiet street. Irresistibly drawn to the memories the house evoked, she stepped onto the grass.

The sweet scent of honeysuckle filled the air as she rounded the garage. Anticipation crept up her spine. She turned the corner and the backyard stretched before her, much smaller than she remembered. The weeds had taken over, making it a virtual jungle.

Picking her way through the tangle, she moved to the shaded area beneath the tree. Insects buzzed, seeking refuge from the afternoon heat. Somewhere in the distance a wind chime tinkled, the sound echoing like silver laughter. A slight breeze tugged at the frayed rope her father had hung decades ago from the ancient oak. Above it, the tree house sat nestled deep in the branches, peering out at her like an old friend.

She pulled aside some vines to reveal the old ladder running up the trunk. With her heart thudding, she ascended, one rung at a time. Ducking her head, she cleared the low doorjamb, then stopped just inside the threshold. The roof sloped down from a center point, clearing her head by an inch.

Adam wouldn't have been able to stand.

A cricket chirped from some hidden spot. The interior smelled of dust and oak and turpentine. She drew the old scent into her lungs as her gaze fell on the small table shoved into a far corner.

She smiled at the memory of Adam building that table. Even at seven, he'd been fairly skilled with hammer and saw, thanks to her father's help. He hadn't cared that the legs were uneven, or that she'd covered it with an old pillowcase to protect them from the splintery edges. In his estimation, the table had made their fort a home.

The pillowcase was long gone, as were the curtains she'd hand sewn with uneven stitches then tacked above the windows, but something about the place brought a warmth to her heart. She moved to the window that looked out over the yard and back of the house. Laughter from her past drifted to her.

Where's my princess? Her father's voice boomed from the backyard.

A seven-year-old Adam jumped up from his place at the table. "Your dad's back. Let's show him the radio we made."

Lauren peered out the window. Her father waved at her as he tucked her mother against his side. She rubbed one hand over her distended belly.

"Lauren, come on!" Adam started down the ladder, the lopsided radio in one hand.

"But it doesn't work," she grumbled as she hurried after him.

"That doesn't matter." Adam tugged on her braid, then tore off toward her parents.

"What have you got there?" Her father's face lit with interest as Adam halted, breathless before him.

"It's a radio." Adam pointed to the front. "I put the box together and Lauren added this speaker from her broken tape recorder. We both made the dials."

Disappointment tugged at Lauren's mouth as she stopped by her mother. "It doesn't work. It isn't real."

"Let's see." Her mother turned one of the makeshift knobs.

"Listen." Her father cocked his head. "Is that…'Moon River'?" He began to sing the words and her mother crooned along.

Her parents fell into each other's arms, singing and dancing to the imaginary tune.

Lauren giggled. Adam took her hand. "Let's dance, too."

He swept her awkwardly across the grass and she laughed harder. "I think we need a better station."

Adam leaned closer and whispered, "We'll change it after they go."

She smiled at the happiness on her parents' faces. Their joy seemed to reach out and infect her. "Naw, we can leave it."

Lauren turned from the window, her heart full and warm. They'd been happy here. Both she and Adam owed her parents a huge debt for supplying them a carefree, stable childhood. No wonder he wanted the same for his children.

Lauren's throat tightened as she thought of the warmth in her father's eyes each time he looked at her mother. Longing welled up inside her. What would it be like to have the simple, unwavering love of a man? Adam hadn't spoken of love, not even during their time at the lake. Could he ever love her the way her father had loved her mother?

He'd been a rock when Rusty was born, sticking beside her mother through it all, then falling to pieces once Rusty came wailing into the world.

Lauren blinked moisture from her eyes. Her hand went to her belly. *A baby.* What would it be like to bear new life? She rose, then headed back down the ladder, saying a silent goodbye to the tree house.

She'd been wrong to measure her success only in terms of what she did in the business world. No matter how many accounts she acquired, or how many hours of commercials she logged, she'd never find what she'd had as a child. Not if she kept putting her personal life second.

Unless she changed her priorities and changed them fast, she'd never have a loving home life. She pulled out the keys and headed for her car. If she didn't act quickly, she'd lose her shot at happiness. She'd lose Adam.

ADAM BREATHED IN the scent of the earth as he pushed the tiller through the hard Georgia clay. Squeezing his eyes shut against the image of Lauren walking away from him, he gripped the tiller tighter. He couldn't think about last night. He focused on the buzz of the motor and the vibration of the machinery, desperately trying to distract himself with the drudgery of the task.

He'd have to add some topsoil, but this spot received plenty of sunlight for a small garden. The afternoon sun beat down on him. September could be unpredictably hot in the South.

He made one more pass with the tiller, then stopped as

Lauren's car pulled into the driveway. His heart skipped a beat as she emerged from the vehicle.

She made her way toward him. "Hi."

Somehow he managed to speak past the lump of apprehension in his throat. "Hi."

"What are you planting?"

"Probably alfalfa for now, but more flowers in the spring." He shrugged. "You know I have a soft spot for roses."

Her eyebrows arched. "They've made you a successful man."

"Can I get you something to drink? Some juice? A soda?"

"Sure."

His heart thudding, he led her into the coolness of the kitchen. She perched on one of the stools by the breakfast bar as he washed the dirt from his hands and squelched the memory of their first night together as lovers.

He turned. Her gaze skittered off the long table and pink tinged her cheeks. Had she been remembering that night, too?

Blowing out a breath, he yanked open the refrigerator, and pulled out a can of soda. "What'll it be?"

"I'll have whatever you're having."

He handed her a second drink, then settled beside her as she drew a long sip from the can. She'd pulled her hair up into a loose knot. Stray tendrils brushed against her cheeks and the nape of her neck. He closed his eyes against a wave of desire.

"Lauren, look, about last night—"

"No. Me first." She set down the can, clasped her hands and laughed nervously. "I'm not sure where to start. I guess first I should apologize."

"Sunshine, you don't have to apologize—"

"Yes I do. I never should have blamed you for nearly losing that account. It was my decision to play hooky with you that day. Besides…"

He waited patiently while her gaze dropped and she fidgeted with the strap of her purse. Her cell phone rang from somewhere in its recesses. She fished it out, then to his surprise, instead of answering the call she turned the phone off.

"I've come to realize that due to certain events in my life, I may have lost sight of my priorities for a while," she said.

"You mean you're giving up your workaholic ways?"

She nodded. "*Not* that I'm giving up work, but I'm trusting now that the world won't come crashing down if I let up a little to concentrate on other areas of my life."

A shiver of hope shot through him. "Such as?"

"Hearth and home." She smiled shyly and he wanted nothing more than to drag her into his arms at that moment, but he held back.

"I should have told you about Rusty."

"It's okay. You meant well."

"And the whole secret-admirer thing. I should have come clean the minute I realized what you were thinking."

"Actually, it all worked out. I thought Mark was interested in Kamira, so I convinced her he'd be a good catch. She called before I headed over here to say they were on their first date."

"That's great."

She nodded.

"I remembered about your dad last night, and how he kept his illness from you. I wanted to kick myself. I don't know how you're ever going to trust us males again."

"I think I can find a way."

"There's something else I've been keeping from yc
That brother of yours pointed it out."

Her eyebrows arched. "What?"

"I love you. In the deepest, most romantic way a m.
can love a woman. I know I don't have the class or foresig
to send you fancy gifts, but the feeling's here." He press
his hand to his chest.

Her throat worked and her eyes glistened. "I love yo
too."

Relief and joy burst through him. "Really?"

"Yes, but if this is going to work, you have to be willi
to compromise."

"What kind of compromise?"

"Well, in a compromise we each adapt a little to me
somewhere in the middle, right?"

He nodded.

She reached into her purse and pulled out a small car
which she handed to him. "I joined your tennis club toda
Here's my membership card, proof that I'm ready to wo
smart, not hard."

Warmth filled him. "Sunshine—"

"Wait. Let me finish. So you know I'm not blowi
smoke, I got a call a little earlier. We got that big linger
account."

"That's wonderful."

"I've turned the entire thing over to Elliot. Budget a
all. It's his baby."

He was speechless for a moment as the enormity of h
statement sank in.

"Oh, and there's one more thing." She pulled a drawi
from her purse. "It's a wolf. I've decided you won't be t
only one in this relationship with a tattoo on your ass."

His throat tightened as he stared at the picture. His go
dess had truly quit running.

She folded her arms across her fine bosom. "I won't be stay-at-home mom, though, Adam. At least, not after the rst month or so."

"You mean you're thinking you might *want* to be some nd of mom someday?"

Her eyes misted. "As long as we do it together, I think m up for the challenge. Not anytime soon, but sometime the not-so-distant future."

"If you can do all that, then I can wait as long as you eed, and I can handle you working, as long as you keep asonable hours."

She nodded. "I will. From now on."

He swept her up and kissed her then, delving into the chness of her sweet mouth. Her tongue stroked his as she in her hands along his back. When at last she pulled away, ey both gasped for air. He feasted his eyes on her flushed eeks and bright eyes.

"I know you're not ready to have kids right away," he aid, "but that's such a big step, I think we should lead up it. Get in as much practice time as we can so we'll be ally set for when the time's right to impregnate you."

"That sounds like a good plan. And this time I'm ready make all your fantasies come true." She reached into her urse again, and pulled out the silk scarf she'd tied around is wrists that night by the fire. "I brought an extra." She eld up a second scarf. "In case you want to tie me to the ed."

His heart beat fast and his groin tightened uncomfortably. Sunshine, are you sure?"

Lauren nodded. She'd never been more sure about any-ing. She loved and trusted Adam. This day would see em off into a beautiful future together. "I've been thinking bout it all morning."

Desire raced through her as he lifted her from the stoo saying, "We're doing this in the bedroom, then."

He laid her gently on the bed, then slowly began unbu toning her blouse. She made a move to help him, but stopped her with the arch of his eyebrows.

Laughing, she spread her arms wide. "I'm yours. Do wi me as you will."

"I thought you'd never ask."

"I'm expecting you to get naked, too. Rules are rule after all."

"That's not a problem." He spread her blouse open, the pulled back to yank his own shirt off over his head.

She wriggled out of the blouse, but he caught her befo she unhooked her bra. "Let me savor this," he said.

He slipped his finger inside the lacy cup, then traced t swell of her breast, idling over her nipple. Her breath rushe out on a sigh. She reached for him, then stopped at h warning look.

"We should finish undressing you so I can tie you up.

"Guess you'd better. It's so hard for me to resist touchir you."

His gaze warmed. "Just indulge me this one fantasy, at I'll let you touch me as much as you want."

"Deal."

He unhooked her bra. Before she had a chance to chang her mind, she slipped off the bra, then presented her wris to him. "Tie me now."

His fingers threaded through the silk scarf. "Are yc sure? We can try it again without the scarf. Or we don have to tie you to the bed. We can tie you the way you tie me."

"I'm sure. But do it now. You're taking too long to ur dress me and my hands want to wander."

"Tell me if it's too tight." He knotted the scarves loosely round her wrists. "You can get out of this if you want."

"Now, to the bed." She leaned back, stretching her arms ward the two top bedposts.

"Let me know if you change your mind, or feel uncomfortable in any way," he said as he secured her, tugging the carves to give her plenty of slack.

She pulled on the silken cords and found she could rest er arms comfortably. Her breath caught as he moved round in front of her. The muscles across his chest rippled he drew a deep breath, his eyes shone with desire, and s erection strained the confines of his jeans. Confidence elled up inside her. She shook her hair, so it spilled across ie pillow, and arched her back, until her breasts jutted up welcome.

She smiled wantonly. "So, you just going to look?"

He swallowed. "No, ma'am. Not on your life."

He shed the rest of his clothes then. The bulge in his ans must have become almost painful. As soon as he was rough, he stripped her pants and panties from her in all aste, his long fingers gliding down her hips, then thighs.

"So, where to start?" He crawled up beside her, tracing s finger around her nipple.

"Anywhere you want. I won't make you stop this time."

"Sunshine." He brushed his mouth over hers, and dipped s tongue inside to stroke hers. She returned each thrust in ind, the hunger rising in her as she undulated against him.

"Okay…" He pulled back, his breath already heavy. This time, I really am going to kiss you all over."

As before, he started with her face, dropping kisses to her rehead, eyelids, then nose. He kissed around her cheek to er jaw, but stalled around her ear, tracing the delicate shell ith his tongue, before continuing down her neck.

When he reached her collarbone, he slipped his hand over

her breast, kneading her, sending spirals of desire trippi
through her. He had the perfect touch, not too light, not t
hard. He kissed a path along one full curve before centeri
on her taut nipple. He tasted her without mercy, drawi
small whimpers from her throat with the pointed tip of I
tongue. He favored her other breast in like fashion, th
suckled her until she sighed and bucked beneath him.

"Please, Adam, touch me. I'm so turned on."

Still tonguing her nipple, he slipped his hand low ov
her belly, through her patch of curls, to her swollen sex. F
fingers dipped into her warm wetness, slipping deep into h
heated passage. He caressed her as he left her breast to mo
down her body.

Lauren moaned softly. She should have known it wou
be like this. Why had it been so difficult for her to give
to this pleasure before? She shifted her legs to give him fi
access when he nestled between her thighs.

Her heart thrummed as she lay before him, vulnerable a
exposed and so turned on she nearly cried out in need. The
he touched her, put his mouth on her and the pleasu
washed over her, tilting her hips and drawing tiny gas
from her.

"Oh…Adam…Adam." His name was a litany on h
lips.

He took his time exploring her once again, pressing I
fingers deep inside her, while his tongue coaxed her into
heated frenzy. For long moments, she spun out in a sexu
haze, the tension inside now one of exquisite wanting. I
drew her closer and closer to the brink.

His tongue worked magic on her clit as his finge
stretched and caressed her passage. Her hips rocked. Sl
pulled against her silken restraints as her body convulse
His name tore from her lips one last time as the orgas
gripped her.

She drew deep breaths as he held her, stroking her back with his fingers. "That's my girl."

When she could bring herself to speak, she said, "I know it's your turn, but I'm a little spent."

"Ah, but who said I was finished with you?"

"There's more?"

"Much more. You game?"

She closed her eyes, trying to calm her pounding heart. "I feel a little limp."

"You don't have to do much. Just roll over."

"Roll over?"

"I did say I wanted to kiss you all over. We're only half through."

"Oh." She blinked. "I don't think I can."

He chuckled softly, then hurried to untie her. "I think we can cut you loose for this."

She arched her eyebrows. Being tied hadn't been so bad. In fact, it had been rather...erotic. "You sure you don't want to tie me?"

His eyes sparkled with laughter. "You'll still be somewhat limited on your stomach."

"I see." She rolled over. "Like this?"

He smoothed his hand down her length. "You don't have a bad angle on you."

"Thanks. I get to try this with you, right? I want to kiss your tattoo."

"I'm counting on it."

His fingers brushed the nape of her neck as he pulled aside her hair. "This is a good place to start."

She wiggled as he kissed her there. "That tickles."

"And here?" He brushed his lips over her shoulder blade.

"That's nice."

"Here?" His mouth touched the small of her back.

"Tickles again."

The next kiss came at the base of her spine, his breath warm and heavy against her skin. Erotic shivers passed through her. "I've never been kissed there before."

"How about here?" His tongue drew a lazy circle around her buttock.

"Oh, no. You're the first to claim that spot, too."

"Does it tickle?"

"Ah, not really. It feels...good."

He chuckled softly, then grew silent as he kissed her in earnest, traversing her derriere with an intimate joining of his mouth to her flesh.

Heat spiraled through her and to her surprise, a low moan escaped her. At his urging, she drew her knees beneath her and levered up on her elbows. He trailed his mouth under one curved cheek to that part of her that still pulsed from his earlier attentions. She arched her back, raising her bottom to better accommodate him.

With tongue and teeth, he explored every swollen inch of her, tracing down one side of her cleft, then up the other. He dipped his tongue inside her, laving the elixir of their loving with an enthusiastic growl. She moaned, bracing her forehead on her hand as she pressed back into him, new shivers of arousal racing over her. He spent long moments thrusting his tongue inside her, drinking of the liquid heat he evoked. Her arousal grew with each caress of his tongue.

When his mouth moved over her clitoris, the sensation was almost too much. "Adam, I need you inside me. Right now."

He hesitated so long, she feared he'd stopped, then she glanced over her shoulder as he rolled on a condom. Christ, she'd forgotten. Relief flowed over her as he pressed in behind her.

Entering her with one smooth stroke, he gripped her hips and pulled her onto him. Pleasure shot through her as he filled her, stretched her. They stayed locked that way for the briefest moment, then he glided back out, then thrust back in. She closed her eyes and gave in to the sensations.

The world seemed to contract around them until only the two of them remained in this timeless rhythm of coming together. She gripped the sheet and pressed back into him, meeting him thrust for thrust, while desire coiled through her.

"Faster," she urged and he accommodated, picking up the rhythm, until she moaned his name, again taking up the litany. He made her feel things she'd never known a woman could feel.

Sounds of satisfaction rumbled from deep in his chest, growing louder and more frequent as their loving peaked. He reached his hand around to her swollen nub and another orgasm hit her at his touch. She cried out, not even trying to hold back the sound.

And her Beast roared.

They collapsed in a heap, the room filled with the sound of their breathing. Long moments later, Adam finally stirred. He chuckled softly. "Well, we seem to have rid you of all your inhibitions."

She laughed. "Well, after all the food sex, how much more could there be?"

"Now that you mention it, I *have* worked up an appetite."

"Well, I still need to flip you over and try that with you. I've been wanting to get my hands on your backside and that tattoo forever."

"By all means, I'm yours to toy with as you see fit." His stomach growled.

"Good, but first I'd better feed you."

His eyebrows arched suggestively. "I could draw the blinds and we could cook in the buff. You game?"

"I think so, but I want to try something different this time."

An intrigued look crossed his face.

"Let's be naughty and have our dessert first."

He grinned as he ran an appreciative hand along her arm. "Sounds decadent. You, dear, know how to tempt a man."

She looped her arms around his neck. "And I plan to spend forever tempting you, dear Adam."

This is the family reunion you've been waiting for!

TRUEBLOOD
Christmas

JASMINE CRESSWELL
TARA TAYLOR QUINN
& KATE HOFFMANN

deliver three brand new Trueblood, Texas stories.

After many years, Major Brad Henderson is released from prison, exonerated after almost thirty years for a crime he didn't commit. His mission: to be reunited with his three daughters. How to find them? Contact Dylan Garrett of the Finders Keepers Detective Agency!

Look for it in November 2002.

HARLEQUIN®
Makes any time special ®

HARLEQUIN®

Duets™

C'mon back to Paxton, Texas!

The Hometown Heartthrobs have returned to delight their fans with a second double Duets volume from author Liz Jarrett!

Chase and Nathan got their stories in Duets #71 in March 2002...

Now it's brother-and-sister time, as Trent and Leigh finally find their own matches and true love not far behind, amidst the all-around wackiness of their neighbors and small-town life!

Look for this exciting volume, Duets #87, in November 2002, as we find out who's...
Meant for Trent and that *Leigh's for Me.*

Yahoo x 2!

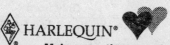

FALL IN LOVE
THIS WINTER
WITH
HARLEQUIN BOOKS!

In October 2002 look for these special volumes
led by *USA TODAY* bestselling authors,
and receive MOULIN ROUGE on video*!

*Retail value of $14.98 U.S. Mail-in offer. Two proofs of purchase required.
Limited time offer. Offer expires 3/31/03.

See inside these books for details.

Own MOULIN ROUGE on video!

*This exciting promotion
is available at your
favorite retail outlet.*

Only from

HARLEQUIN®
Makes any time special®